God in heaven, no! he thought.

The whip whistled again, this time opening a line of pink across the victim's dark hips. Again he groaned. The pink deepened to red as the blood oozed out.

The next cry was Peter's, as he snatched the shotgun and lurched forward. "No!" he yelled. "Stop it!" But he took only four steps before stumbling to a halt.

The green light had been waiting, it seemed, just as the mist had before. He felt as though he had lurched into an invisible web, soft enough to let him struggle but too thick to be bored through. It held him squirming like a trapped insect, while an unseen giant spider spun more strands to hold him fast. . . .

Then the room with its tableau of torture became merely a sea of green in which he knew he was drowning, and the voice of the man in the brown uniform said calmly, "So at last you have found us, have you, Mr. Sheldon? Welcome, friend, to the Devil's Pit."

Tor Books by Hugh B. Cave

Disciples of Dread
The Lower Deep
Lucifer's Eye

LUCIFER'S EYE

HUGH B. CAVE

A TOM DOHERTY ASSOCIATES BOOK
NEW YORK

LUCIFER'S EYE

A Tor Book
Published by Tom Doherty Associates, Inc.
49 West 24th Street
New York, N.Y. 10010

Cover art by Mark and Stephanie Gerber

ISBN: 0-812-51079-8

First edition: March 1991

Printed in the Unites States of America

0 9 8 7 6 5 4 3 2 1

December 1979

IT WAS DARK NOW, AND HE WAS LOST. HE KNEW HE
was lost. Earlier, he had thought he recognized some
of the misty peaks looming up around him—surely the
one called Blackrock, which was the second highest in
the whole island. But that was hours ago, when he first
became separated from his companions—when he'd
been calling out to them every few minutes, thinking it
was all a big joke that they would talk about for weeks
after they got back.

He wasn't calling out now. He no longer thought it a
joke. His voice was gone. His throat was raw and sore.
He was scared. Somewhere back there, just after he lost
contact with the other two, something had begun to
happen to his mind. Something he didn't understand at
all. As if he had sort of fallen asleep on his feet and
begun dreaming. Like when you had a nightmare in
which you couldn't do the simplest things, such as

opening a door or climbing a flight of ordinary stairs or bending over to pick something up.

As if he'd become a zombie and could only do what he was told to do. That was when he had stopped calling out to the others. And stopped thinking it was funny. When he had stopped even looking for the others.

And just stumbled on. And on. And on. As if he were being told where he must go, and had to obey.

Yes, he was lost now. Even before nightfall he had been lost because nothing around him looked the way it ought to look anymore. He and Danny and Wesley had studied maps and photos for days before embarking on this special wild-pig hunt, for God's sake. Had memorized every peak and ridge and gully. But the maps and photos had suddenly been all wrong. All at once nothing made any sense.

He was asleep and having a nightmare; that must be it. One of the really scary bad ones, like when you heard footsteps and a sound of heavy breathing behind you in the dark but couldn't turn around to confront what was there. . . .

For a while now he had been stumbling through a jungle of vine-draped trees—really stumbling as if drunk on St. Alban's wicked white rum. He ought to stop and rest; he knew that. He had lost his rifle—must have dropped it one of the half-dozen times he'd fallen, and been too dazed to pick it up before stumbling on again. Feeling a hundred years old instead of twenty-six, he was now close to falling again and being too exhausted even to get up. But he couldn't stop. Whatever had control of his mind would not let him.

All at once the jungle of hanging vines ended in a wall of stone. A cliff. He shouldn't have been able to see it in the dark, but he did—a black cliff, almost vertical, rising up before him with an opening at its base. A hole about a yard wide and four feet high.

A cave? There were many in St. Alban's Morgan Mountains. On more than one occasion he had taken time out from hunting wild pigs or wild pigeons to explore them, out of curiosity. Not this one, though. He hadn't known there was one this high up.

"Go on in," a voice was saying.

A voice? Here in this godforsaken wilderness, in the dark? So he really must be trapped in a nightmare, then. He had to be, because the voice wasn't reaching him from in front, or behind, or off to one side; it was inside his head.

"Go in!"

He would have gone in anyway—a little way, at least—in hope of finding some relief from the cold wind that had come up in the last hour or so. God, it got cold up here at night. You'd think on a West Indian island . . . But he had been climbing for hours and must be above seven thousand feet here, where it could fall close to freezing on a winter night such as this. He had been shivering since the wind came up.

He would need a light now. For some reason he'd been stumbling along without one all this time, but only a fool would venture into a wild cave without a light. He had one in his knapsack, he remembered. Sinking to one knee, he slid the strap from his shoulder and unbuckled the pack, and yes, thank God, he still had it. Clutching it in one hand, dragging the knapsack along with the other, he crawled on hands and knees into the opening.

Now the voice inside his head, sounding like something from far away that he was hearing on a bad telephone, was telling him to "Come on in." Not to *go* in, but *come* in. Was he losing his mind?

He was stupid to be doing this, some other part of his mind told him. Alone, at night—to be crawling into an unknown cave in the wildest part of St. Alban's in-

3

famous Morgan Mountains while exhausted? He was crazy. But he had to do it. He had to keep going. Then after a hundred feet or so the ceiling began to rise, and he could stop crawling and struggle to his feet.

"Don't stop there! Come to me!"

As he stumbled on down the tunnel, the wavering of his light beam showed him how unsteady he was on his feet. It showed him, too, an ongoing tunnel a couple of yards wide, with now a ten-foot-high ceiling that seemed to have no ending. "Jesus, man, stop this foolishness!" one part of his mind kept telling him. "Get out of this creepy place before you die in here!"

But—"Come to me!" the voice in that other part of his mind was booming now, like a roll of mountain thunder.

Sick with fear, he managed to stop and lean back against a wall of stone while his chest heaved with his struggle to breathe. "Who are you?" he whispered.

"Never mind that. Obey me!"

"What do you want with me? Why have you brought me here?" Because he knew now that he had not reached this place by accident. Since losing contact with Danny and Wesley, he had been told what to do, every step of the way. Maybe—yes, maybe the voice was even responsible for his being separated from them in the first place.

"All right, all right!" Was that his own voice, babbling in surrender? "All right . . . please . . . I'm coming."

"Put out your light. There is no need for childish things here."

He thumbed the switch and the voice was right; he didn't need the flashlight anymore. Here, this far in from the entrance, the tunnel was lit by an eerie, greenish glow, as though the walls and floor and ceiling were coated with some kind of chemical.

"Put your light away now," the voice instructed.

Leaning against the wall again, he opened his knapsack and dropped the flash into it, because you had to do what the voice commanded. He knew that now. Something terrible was bound to happen if you didn't.

"Now come, before I lose patience."

He stumbled on again and presently, not knowing why, turned off the main tunnel into a side one, and after a few more minutes entered a third. This cave was longer and more complex than any other he had been in. It must be one of the longest in the island, and might run on for miles. But he would not have to walk for miles, he soon discovered. After another series of turns, which he made because some remote control commanded him to, he found himself in a room that he knew instinctively was something special.

This chamber was almost a perfect circle in shape, with walls that rose twenty feet or so to a roof nearly as smooth as its floor. In it, the green glow was more persuasive than in the corridors he had traversed to get here. The walls appeared to exhale it as though they were alive and breathing, and it formed a kind of whirlpool that seemed to suck him in despite a warning from some small part of his mind—some diminishing fragment that still belonged to him—that he should turn and run for his life no matter what the cost.

The room was like a monstrous green eye that was watching him, but how could it be watching him when he was inside it?

He was not able to turn and run. Even the thought of doing so dribbled away, and his dragging feet carried him to the center of the whirlpool of light. There he stopped and waited fearfully for instructions, and after a seemingly endless silence the voice said matter-of-factly, "Take off your clothes."

He took them off and stood there naked, shivering.

"Now sit."

Terrified, clutching his shaking body with both hands, he sat. The stone floor was cold and clammy, as though the green mist or glow kept it forever damp.

"Do you know who I am?"

"No."

"Or where you are?"

"No."

"Let me enlighten you, then. All over this planet on which you live are places like this. I have had them for centuries. Points of contact, let us call them. Not all are in caves. I have one at present in a certain so-called holy place in the country you call Iran. Another is in a dark corner of the New York subway system. Still another is in the home of a prominent person in what you call Libya. Do you realize the significance of what I am telling you?"

He shook his head.

"Then consider this. In the recent past I have been most successful in Idi Amin's Uganda. In Hitler's Germany. In Stalin's Russia. And long before that in lands ruled by the Khans. At present it amuses me to be developing new points of influence. Now do you comprehend?"

"How can I? I don't know who you are! Or what this room is! Or why you have brought me here!"

"You are here for instruction."

"Instruction in what, for God's sake?"

"In time you will know—and it will not be for God's sake. At least, not the god you mean. Sit, now, and wait."

With the green mist slowly swirling around him, he waited. The cold of the room's floor crept up through his naked body and numbed his mind. After a time he became thirsty.

"I need some water. Please."

"Later."

His thirst increased and he became hungry as well. He had not eaten for hours. But his pleas for water and food went unanswered, and he was unable to get up off the floor. Hours passed, while the green mist swirled around him and the silence became pure torment. Then when he thought he would die if he had to sit there a moment longer, he lost consciousness.

When he came to, he had no idea how long he had been asleep. Nothing around him had changed. He was still alone in the circular chamber, with the green mist or fog slowly swirling around him. The silence was still that of a grave. But for some reason he was no longer thirsty or hungry and no longer felt he might die. Puzzled, he rose to his feet—and had no trouble doing that.

"Now do you understand?" the voice said.

"Yes."

"Get dressed and go, then. But remember—from now on I will be a part of you always. You will do my bidding at all times."

"I will do your bidding. Yes."

He put his clothes and boots back on. Took in a breath and felt ten feet tall and full of new strength, new power. With long strides he left the room he now knew was indeed an eye—an eye of his new master—and marched through the maze of corridors that had led him to it. Crawling out of the cave on hands and knees, the way he had entered it, he discovered he was no longer lost.

Knowing exactly where he was, and that he could come back at any time without faltering, he swung his pack to his shoulder and began the long hike home. Still a hunter, more than ever a hunter, but no longer a hunter of pigs or pigeons.

2

June 1987

THEY WERE CHURCH PEOPLE FROM THE STATES. MINisters, their wives and husbands, their children. On holiday. But many were concerned about the poverty in the slums of St. Alban's capital, too, and hoping they would be able to do something to help.

At the time it happened, they had been in St. Alban six days. Staying at an aged downtown hotel that was considered unacceptable by most tourists, they had walked about the city, visited its famous Royal Gardens, and shopped for the usual island-made handicrafts. Chartering a bus, they had spent one day visiting sugar and banana plantations on the island's coastal plain, another exploring old Great Houses built when St. Alban had been an English colony.

Now, on the same big yellow bus, with the same St. Alban driver, they were well up in the mountains en route to a plantation that grew some of the world's finest coffee. Ten men, the youngest twenty-one, the oldest sixty-three. Nine women in the same broad age bracket. Eight children ranging in years from six to fourteen.

Their destination was Armadale, whose young American manager had agreed to show them how the island's famous coffee was grown.

The bus was full of talk as it neared its destination.

"These mountains! I just can't believe them, they're so beautiful!"

"But, oh, this road. I'm going to be sick, I swear. Just look down there!"

"How far down is that stream, Calvin? Do you know?" Calvin was the driver, his questioner a girl of eight.

"About nine hundred feet, ma'am. And the stream is called White River."

As she again pressed her face to the window beside her, the child giggled—probably at being addressed as "ma'am." Gazing down into the steep-sided gorge along the brink of which the bus now crept, she shivered with delight as though in a roller-coaster car at the top of the first long drop. "Gosh!" she said. "It looks like a whole other world down there!"

A wave of nervous laughter ran through the bus.

"How much farther do we have to go, Calvin?" The leader of the group was tired this morning, and was one of several suffering from motion sickness. All day yesterday, in his hotel room, he had sought to prepare himself for a scheduled television interview in which he would try to explain just how his people hoped to help the desperate poor of the capital's slums. He was not a man to take such an opportunity lightly.

"About half an hour, sir. But the road is only this bad for another short while."

"Well, that's good to hear," said a woman at the rear. "Because some of us are getting carsick, as you can see. Or should I say bus sick? And besides, these people in the car behind us seem anxious to get by."

Calvin had been peering into his mirrors and knew about the motion sickness. Quite a few of his passengers' faces were whiter than they ought to be, and he hoped to have the worst of the road behind him before any asked to get out. As for the car, he had been aware of that, too, for a good while now. It was an English Cortina sedan with two men in it.

With a frown of annoyance Calvin said, "They would be foolish to try passing us here." Hacked out of the mountainside cliff, the road along this stretch was all curves. Between it and the nine-hundred-foot drop on the left was nothing except a yard-wide fringe of dusty weeds. St. Alban was too poor a country to afford safety railings on its unpaved rural roads.

Aware that the Cortina was edging even closer, Calvin took his lower lip between his teeth and wagged his head. Damn fool driver, he thought. But if the man wanted to pass, why did he not sound his horn?

Well, there was nothing anyone could do about it. With a shrug he fixed his gaze on the road and focused his thoughts on things more pleasant.

These people, for instance. He had been their chauffeur since their arrival in St. Alban and was truly fond of them. They genuinely cared about his island and its people. They asked sensible questions. They treated him like a friend, not just somebody being paid to drive them around.

Not all visitors to his island were that considerate. He drove a taxi at times, and he knew.

But why was the Cortina tailgating him like this on a road so dangerous? What was the matter with that idiot driver?

The church people, too, were all aware of the car's strange behavior now. The chatter had stopped and the bus was unnaturally quiet. Almost everyone was looking back through the rear window, no doubt wondering what was going on.

Was it the dust, maybe? You sometimes met drivers on these country roads who would take any kind of chance rather than eat the dust from a car ahead of them. But today wasn't all that dry, and anyway, there was a fair mountain breeze to quickly blow away what little dust the bus was churning up.

Stupid, that's what those fellows were. Just plain stupid. Maybe he should stop and tell them so. But if it turned into an argument, they would be two against his one. So just drive on; that was the thing to do. Get past this stretch, then pull over and let them pass. Yes.

In the car behind, the driver said to the man beside him, "You ready?"

"Ready." This one held in his right hand a black object similar to and about the size of a television remote-control transmitter. It had only one button, however. A red one. The man's thumb hovered over it as he watched the bus ahead. "Just tell me when."

"Wait for Dead Man's." It was a name the mountain people had given to an especially dangerous curve in this road.

"Okay. How many would you say are in that thing?"

"I make it twenty-eight with the driver."

"Me too. He will like that. Up to now, the best anyone has done is seven."

"Seven? I don't recall—"

"Last year, in the church fire at Harmon Bay. Six died in the fire and one later in the hospital. Before that, the best score was four. Never mind. Where did Winslow plant it? You know?"

"Under the driver's seat, he said."

"Good. No one will ever be sure what—"

The man at the wheel broke in with a hissed "Get

ready!'' Ahead, the yellow bus with its twenty-eight occupants had entered Dead Man's Curve.

The driver of the car tightened his grip on its wheel. The man at his side sat straighter and sucked in a breath.

"Now?"

"Now!"

In the bus, the floor under the driver's seat erupted with a roar. The seat shot upward in a tangle of metal and plastic. With his hands torn from the wheel by the force of the blast, Calvin had no time even to give his agony a voice before his head became a crimson smear on the vehicle's roof. Out of control at the worst possible moment, the bus failed to round the curve and went soaring into space.

With its driver dead and its cargo of screaming men, women, and children tossed about like figures of straw, the vehicle turned end over end as it fell the nine hundred feet to the stream below. There it crashed among stream-bed boulders with force enough to make it an instant coffin for its occupants. If any survived the impact by being lucky enough to have others cushion the shock for them, they perished in the flames that shot from the ruptured gas tank to engulf the wreckage.

On the road above, the two men in the Cortina gazed down at what they had accomplished, then smiled at each other and touched hands. "Our leader will be pleased," the driver said. "For a contribution such as this he may even take us to the Eye for communion with the master."

3

August 1990

He had arrived early, but not by much. All aglitter in the Caribbean sunlight, the plane he had come to meet was even now descending over the whitecapped waters of the harbor. Due in at 3:30, it was ten minutes ahead of schedule.

An omen, undoubtedly. Miss Edith Craig had even beaten the clock to confront him. He had better prepare for the worst.

At St. Alban's airport, the place to watch an incoming plane was the second-floor Waving Gallery. He had gone directly to it. Now he stepped to the railing.

Behind the approaching metal gull, the island's cloud-capped Morgan Mountains bulked ominously against an otherwise cloudless sky. Thinking of the scouts, he looked at them and asked the silent question again. Eight young boy scouts and their new scoutmaster had been missing among those wild peaks for eight days now, in a trailless wilderness that had swallowed careless explorers in the past. He, Peter Sheldon, had been the last to talk to them when they sought his permission to climb though Armadale's mountainside coffee fields to begin their grand adventure.

He could see them now, trudging happily up the main coffee track, turning to wave to him as he stood watching them from the old Great House veranda. "We'll bring you back a picture of the Devil's Pit if we can find it," one bright lad with a camera had promised. "That is, if old devil don't catch us and carry us down into it." A joke, of course. They weren't the type to believe that old mountain tale. But most of Armadale's workers believed it, and some had predicted disaster.

Eight days. The whole island now held its breath, waiting for news.

He watched the plane land and taxi to a stop. It was from Miami, but the woman he was to meet had begun her journey in England. Studying the passengers as they descended to the tarmac, he failed to spot anyone who fitted his mental picture of a daughter of Philip Craig.

Her letters had told him almost nothing—only that with the shockingly sudden death of her father in London, she was now the owner of Armadale and therefore his employer. "I'll fill you in on the rest when I arrive. And don't worry about my recognizing you at the airport, because I have several photos of you taken on the plantation by my father. I shall look for a man of about thirty years"—good guess, that—"six feet two or three, with rather untidy blond hair and an equally untidy mustache. It might help, though, if you were to wear something a touch out of the ordinary, such as—well, what? Shall we say a red handkerchief in your jacket pocket?"

On his way downstairs to the customs exit where he would first make contact with her, Peter touched the folded bit of red cloth in the pocket of his tan jacket.

It was not a handerkchief. Where could he have found a red handkerchief at Armadale? He'd snipped it from a bandu donated with a smile by his forty-year-old housekeeper. He had donned a red tie, too, though grimly aware that he wouldn't have worn either a tie or a pocket adornment—or, for that matter, even a jacket—had he been going to the airport on any ordinary errand.

Now as he stood outside customs in the sweltering August heat, peering through an unwashed window at passengers beginning to trickle through from immigration, he felt a tightening in his stomach.

Five years. For five years you performed to the absolute best of your ability a managerial job you dearly loved, rebuilding a ruinate coffee plantation into one of the finest on an island noted for the quality of its mountain coffee. For five years you labored harder and longer than anyone else on the payroll, yet loving the challenge. Now, with your mouth dry and your stomach in knots, you were waiting to greet a woman you had never seen who could wipe you out with a mere signing of some legal document.

Damn it, where was she? Failing again to pick out any woman who might conceivably be Philip Craig's daughter, he moved along to the door through which she would have to make her exit.

People began coming out, led by skycaps with piled-high luggage carts. Most were obviously island residents; the heat of August was not a tourist attraction. He paid almost no attention when a youngish white couple came through the doorway, glancing about as though in search of someone.

Abruptly halting, the woman peered at Peter and said to her companion, "Alton, hold on. I believe I've found him." The man obediently stopped and told their skycap to wait.

Wearing a beige dress of some lightweight, linenlike material, the woman stepped toward Peter. Her eyes and hair were the rich golden brown of a cacao pod. Her mouth formed a quizzical but most attractive smile.

"Peter? Peter Sheldon?"

It wasn't possible, he told himself. Philip Craig had been sixty-nine when he died, and she couldn't be more than twenty-five. He was almost afraid to accept her hand. "Are you Miss Craig?"

She smiled again. It seemed she smiled easily, and for that he was grateful, feeling the way he did about her being here at all. "Didn't Daddy ever tell you about me?"

"Yes, of course, but—"

"It doesn't matter." She turned her head. "Alton?"

Leaving the skycap and their luggage—four large leather bags that seemed to indicate a longish stay on the island—her companion came forward.

"Mr. Sheldon, this is Mr. Preble, my fiancé. There wasn't time to let you know he was coming. We didn't decide until the last minute."

About Peter's height, Alton Preble had a long face and was too thin. He shook hands without enthusiasm. "Is it always this hot here?"

"In summer, on the coast. We'll be out of it soon."

"The sooner the better, I don't mind telling you."

"Let's go, then." With a nod to the waiting skycap, Peter led them through the parking area to Armadale's pale blue station wagon. There he tipped the fellow, unlocked the back, and had the luggage neatly stowed before the two from England caught up with him.

When he swung wide the doors to let out some of the pent-up heat, Edith Craig slid onto the seat beside the driver's while her fiancé, frowning, squeezed in behind her. It was not a large car. The government had long since ruled that large cars were dangerous on the island's roads, many of which resembled roller-coaster tracks and were barely two lanes wide. The knees of Edith Craig's unhappy fiancé were close to his chin when at last he got himself settled.

Peter tossed his jacket onto the empty side of the backseat. His tie followed, and he unfastened the top two buttons of his shirt. His glance at Preble invited the Englishman to do the same, but the thin man merely gazed at him in silence. With a mental shrug Peter slid in behind the wheel.

The airport occupied the tip of a peninsula, and Miss Craig seemed genuinely interested in her surroundings as he drove out to the main road. For a time she gazed across the harbor at the city on their left; then she turned with apparent pleasure to the boisterous open sea on the right. "I had no idea St. Alban was such an attractive island, Mr. Sheldon," she said.

"I'm glad to you think so, Miss Craig."

"It's damned hot, Edith," her fiancé complained in a petulant growl.

Peter glanced into the rearview mirror. "Why not take your coat off, Mr. Preble? We've a way to go along the coast before we start climbing."

"Thanks. I can wait."

Edith Craig's laughter was soft and brief. "Alton is a London barrister, Mr. Sheldon."

"I see."

So the banker's daughter was to marry a lawyer, Peter thought. Armadale's future—and his own—looked bleak indeed. Why the hell couldn't she have chosen a farmer?

4

WHEN HE TURNED OFF THE COAST ROAD AT ELEVEN Mile to ascend the corkscrew spirals of Oxton Hill, Peter watched his passengers for their reaction. There were some breathtaking views from this crazy ladder of a road.

Presently, behind them, the sea was a jeweled blue carpet, and scraping the sky ahead were spectacular mountains creased with deep gorges. Then came the awesome, sheer face of Vengeance Cliff, the missing part of which had thundered down to bury an unknown number of settlers at the time when the Great Earthquake had sent the old capital to the bottom of the harbor.

Miss Craig was like a spectator at a tennis match as she tried to absorb it all. But when the station wagon climbed through the midmountain town of Ledge, where the road was crowded with country people going about their assorted tasks, she relaxed with a deep sigh of contentment.

"Oh, it's just what I had hoped it would be! Real people doing real things!" she said.

Peter waved to a young man striding barefoot along the roadside, an expert coffee-tree planter who turned up for work when in the mood but almost never when needed. Ah, sister Craig, if only you knew how complex the simple things sometimes are, he thought. The young man, a startling sight with his bare brown chest caked with the road's white limestone dust, grinned and returned the greeting. "Evenin', Mr. Peter!"

"I suppose you know everyone," Edith Craig said.

"I've been at Armadale five years, Miss Craig."

The road swung sharply right to cross what was probably the highest and least safe bridge on the island, causing Edith Craig and her barrister to hold their breath while gazing through its flimsy railing at the swirling stream below. Loose planks clattered under the car's tires like the bars of a xylophone.

"The White River," Peter supplied.

"It's an important stream?" Miss Craig asked.

"Very. And a branch of it starting just under Morgan Peak comes leaping down through the plantation."

"Leaping, Mr. Sheldon?"

"Up there it's a string of wild cascades, mostly inaccessible. It's the source of Armadale's water, however."

"How exciting!" Her enthusiasm was obviously genuine as she swung about to confront her fiancé. "Did you hear that, Alton? I own a river with waterfalls! Oh, I'm going to like Armadale!"

In the rearview mirror Peter saw the man on the backseat make a face. "It won't be your usual English country estate, you know," Preble warned.

"Who cares?"

"Even your father complained of its being at the absolute end of nowhere, and sometimes wondered why he bought it."

"He bought it because he loved it, Alton. We both know that."

The barrister did not answer.

The bridge behind them, the road clawed its way upward now with a vengeance, and for some time there was no comment from the backseat. Curious, Peter glanced into the mirror again. Alton Preble's long face had become nearly as ashen as the dust pluming out behind the car's wheels.

Recognizing familiar symptoms, Peter braked the machine to a stop. "Is something wrong, Mr. Preble?" Something was, of course. But would such a man admit it?

"This ghastly road is making me ill," the man groaned.

"You're carsick?"

"Yes! Oh Lord, yes!"

"It happens to some people. We'd better just sit until it passes. Then maybe you ought to ride in front."

Edith Craig, turning her head, frowned with concern. "I didn't know you suffered from motion sickness, Alton."

"I didn't either, God help me." Fumbling the door open, Preble staggered from the car to a dusty tangle of brush and grass at the road's edge, and began to heave.

Edith opened her door and ran to him. But when she put an arm around him to steady him, he thrust her away.

She stood there watching him for a moment, then slowly returned to the car and took her place beside Peter again. "Does this happen often, Mr. Sheldon?"

"No, but it happens."

"Alton is embarrassed."

"Being carsick is nothing to be ashamed of, Miss Craig. And this road has done more than make people woozy at times. Three years ago a tour bus missed one of these curves and landed down there in White River, killing twenty-eight people."

"My God," Edith Craig breathed.

"It was bringing them to Armadale, where I had promised to show them how your coffee is grown."

Her face almost as ashen as Preble's, Edith Craig closed her eyes for a few seconds, then turned to gaze at her fiancé. She was shaking her head in sympathy when an alien sound infiltrated the mountain silence, causing her to look up. Peter leaned out the car window on his side and did the same.

Appearing suddenly through a gap between high crags, a dark speck sped toward them through the cloudless sky.

"Is that a helicopter?"

"Yes, Miss Craig. The army has a few here. They're searching for some boy scouts who are lost in the mountains."

She frowned at the blue-black peaks ahead, close enough now to be impressively wild and overpowering. "Lost? Up there?"

"Long overdue, at any rate. Eight of them set out with their leader eight days ago from our place—your place—to climb to Morgan Peak, then go along the ridge by way of Albert Gap to Blackrock and—" He suddenly realized she could have no idea of what he was talking about. "Anyway, they've disappeared."

She watched the copter grow smaller in the distance. "Is it possible for a person to disappear on an island this size? St. Alban is only a hundred and fifty miles long, isn't it?"

"Miss Craig, the whole Morgan Range above Armadale is as inhospitable as anything in the Caribbean. When escaped slaves took refuge there back in the old days, even English soldiers couldn't get them out.''

''I'm afraid I haven't done my homework,'' she said.

Following the river upstream, the copter vanished behind a distant peak above Armadale. Its mutter lingered briefly in the mountain air, then the silence returned. Miss Craig's fiancé trudged unsteadily back to the car, his expensive leather shoes creating explosions of dust.

''Better?'' Peter asked.

''I hope so.''

''Want to ride in front now, do you?''

''No, no. Let's just get this over with.'' Preble stubbornly sat in back again. ''How much farther have we to go?''

''It's thirty miles from the airport to the plantation. We're more than halfway.'' Peter carefully refrained from adding that the road at times seemed sixty miles long instead of thirty. On pitch-black moonless nights, for instance, or when a tropical deluge triggered a string of mud slides that forced a car to creep along the edge of space.

But after they had passed the dangerous bend known as Dead Man's Curve, where the tourist bus had gone over the brink, the road was no longer difficult, and Preble's face in the mirror showed no increased distress. As the car moved more or less horizontally through scenic Pipers Vale, the Englishman's countenance even took on a look of relief, while Philip Craig's daughter became brightly eager again. She voiced little sounds of delight when children at play in peasant yards waved greetings. Her eyes shone with pleasure as she waved back.

Maybe, just maybe, she would not be selling Armadale, after all.

"These trees along here are coffee, Miss Craig," Peter volunteered.

"Oh? With the green berries?"

"You'll see many more at the plantation, of course. This is small-farmer coffee."

"I thought coffee berries were red."

"When they're ripe. And we call them 'cherries' here."

"I see."

When they had crept across the small bridge at the head of the vale and were climbing again, he turned his head. "Everything all right now, Mr. Preble?"

"Just keep going, please."

"We don't have to—"

"Please."

"As you say."

Peter had to stop, though, when a woman he knew, coming along a side road from the village of Look Up, called out to him and frantically flapped an arm to catch his attention. Hurrying around the front of the station wagon, she clutched at the driver's door.

"Mr. Peter, did them hear anything from the boys yet?"

"Not that I know of, Bronzie." About thirty-five, she was handsome and straight, with remarkably wide-spaced eyes and gleaming teeth. The nickname referred to the color of her skin, which was the same golden brown as Edith Craig's hair. Her real name was Jessie Dakin. One of Armadale's best workers, at harvest time she was able to pick a bushel and a half of ripe cherries a day, and you could depend on her doing it.

"Mr. Peter—if you hear anything, you will let me know? For sure?"

"Of course, Bronzie. Is Gerald any better?"

"No, squire." Only a few of the workers called him

that. The older ones, mostly. "He still talks peculiar. I do wish you could come to see him."

"I'll come as soon as I can. I promise." Peter briefly laid a hand on one of those gripping the door. "And if I hear anything at all about the scouts, I'll of course come at once." When she stepped back from the car, he solemnly returned her nod and drove on.

"Who was that interesting woman?" Edith Craig asked.

"She and her two sons work for you, Miss Craig. Her husband did, too, until he was killed last year."

"Killed?"

"Shot—by accident—when he was visiting a brother in the capital one day. He was one of two innocent bystanders who got caught in a gunfight between the police and some of our nasties."

"For such a small island, St. Alban seems to have more than its share of violence," Alton Preble observed from the backseat. "And I don't suppose all of it makes the English papers, either."

"Isn't the whole world becoming more violent, Alton?" Edith Craig said.

"Touché. But we're not personally interested in the whole world."

"Anyway," Peter said, "I should warn you that the woman you've just met speaks better English than you can expect from some of the others. She finished grammar school and does the Bible reading in her church."

"She seems to have a problem," Edith said.

"One of her sons, Georgie, is with the missing scouts. The other, Gerald, has been behaving strangely for the past few days."

"Strangely? How do you mean?"

"Well, yesterday I put him to bushing out a stretch of track. When I went to check his work at three o'clock, he was sitting on the ground staring into space, talking to himself, and nothing at all had been done. I walked him home.''

Miss Craig turned her head to do some staring of her own—at him. ''You must feel quite close to these people. You spoke to that woman with true compassion.''

Peter settled for a shrug and drove on to the little mountain village of Cedar Ridge, where Armadale received its mail. At this time of day the shops and post office veranda were all but deserted. To the man on the rear seat he said, ''Just a mile or so more, Mr. Preble.''

''Thank God,'' the barrister said.

Much rougher now, the road climbed between yards filled with coffee trees. The sun blazed on the zinc roofs of farmers' houses as though determined to set them ablaze. ''This is called Grove Path,'' Peter said as they passed a dilapidated shop where a woman waved to him from behind the counter. ''And this,'' as the car splashed through a shallow stream a few moments later, ''is the Armadale boundary, Miss Craig. Everything from here on is yours.''

He glanced at her as he said it, and saw her eyes dance with excitement as she leaned forward to peer through the windshield. Then as the car turned in through Armadale's open gate and she caught her first glimpse of the old Great House on its hillside half a mile ahead, her soft, full lips trembled apart to utter a cry of delight.

5

Armadale's Great House had been built by a Scottish pioneer in 1793, the year Captain William Bligh, surviving the *Bounty* mutiny, had arrived at another of England's West Indian colonies, Jamaica, with the first breadfruit trees from Tahiti.

Built into a steep hillside, the house had its kitchen and servants' quarters downstairs, the latter unused now because Peter's housekeeper went home at night, and all the other rooms on the level above. Its double front doors opened onto a long, high veranda reached by climbing a flight of steps.

When Peter showed Edith Craig the front bedroom made ready for her by his housekeeper, she voiced murmurs of pleasure. Apparently she was fond of old houses and old furniture, even of juniper floors so buckled with age that walking on them demanded a certain spirit of adventure. After admiring the huge four-poster, she went to one of the four windows, choosing one that afforded a view of terraced gardens and, farther down, a wooded slope descending steeply to the roofs of the village of Look Up. Many of Armadale's workers lived there.

"Not disappointed, Miss Craig?"

"Oh, no, Mr. Sheldon!"

Her fiancé was less impressed. His bedroom, hastily made ready while he waited in the drawing room, had much the same view, but only the bed interested him at the moment. Without removing even his shoes, he lowered himself onto it with a groan.

"What about dinner, Mr. Preble?" Peter asked.

A clock on the chest of drawers said 6:30. "What time is dinner, please?"

"Seven, usually. But if you'd rather—"

"No, no, don't alter the routine on my account. I'm not hungry."

"We can easily—"

"Just let me lie here." The barrister closed his eyes. "I suppose I'll recover eventually."

"Car sickness is no joke, Mr. Preble."

"Look in on me later, will you? See if I'm still breathing?"

"Of course."

So, Peter thought . . . he and Edith Craig were to dine alone.

"How, Mr. Sheldon, did you happen to come here? I've never really been told. All I know is that you're American."

All through the meal Peter had waited for the expected inquisition while the two of them exchanged small talk. Now, after pumpkin soup to melt a stranger's heart, and chicken that must have been marinated for hours in herbs and spices, and vegetables from Armadale's own gardens, and a sweet-potato pudding that was his housekeeper's specialty, they were sipping some of the plantation's own prizewinning coffee. And his job, he realized, might depend on how he answered Edith Craig's questions.

"I came here from Florida to visit friends who had a winter home on the north coast, Miss Craig. They introduced me to your father."

"When was this?"

"A little over five years ago. Your father had bought Armadale the year before and was trying to run it from the capital, with a local farmer as headman."

"Did you know about growing coffee?"

"I'd studied tropical agriculture in college. But I don't think that's why he offered me the job of running this place. It may have been a factor, but what sold him on me was my enthusiasm. I loved everything about Armadale the minute I laid eyes on it: this old house, the challenge, the possibilities, even the mountains. Only a Floridian would be that insane about mountains. We don't have any, you know. Not even an honest hill."

"So he offered you—what, really?"

"He asked me if I'd consider running the plantation for him. Replanting it. Restoring it. Building it back up to what it was when its coffee won world awards. He had bought it because he, too, fell in love with it, but he couldn't tackle such a project himself. He was managing a bank in town, as you know."

"And?"

"I applied for work papers and have been here ever since. Then last year, of course, he was recalled by his bank to London and I became solely responsible for what happened here."

"And then he died," she said quietly. "We hadn't a clue that his heart was bad, you know. It came like a bolt from the blue."

"He left you everything?"

She nodded.

"You're much younger than I expected, Miss Craig."

"Would you mind calling me Edith, Mr. Sheldon?"

"I'd like to. We all use first names here."

"And may I call you Peter?"

"Please."

"Yes, I suppose I am younger than you expected. Mother was quite a bit younger than Daddy, you see. She died of pneumonia when I was only twelve."

A movement in the doorway had caught Peter's eye. His housekeeper, Coraline Walker, stood there—a forty-year-old Look Up woman who from the beginning had treated him like a son. In a state of agitation now, she apparently was awaiting a chance to interrupt.

"Yes, Coraline?"

"Mr. Peter, you must turn on your radio! The searchers did find two of the boys-them! Someone is talking about it this very minute!" She must have been listening to her small radio in the kitchen.

Peter rose swiftly and hurried into the drawing room where a battery set of good quality stood on one of the many casual tables. As he switched it on, he noticed that the windows were turning dark and heard the first slow throbbing of the diesel power plant that supplied the house with light. Coraline must have pressed a remote-control button.

As the radio voice filled the room, the lamps began to glow. Slowly the power plant attained its running speed and the glow brightened. Edith Craig had followed him in from the dining room and now stood at his side, intently listening with him.

The man talking was apparently doing so over a telephone. ". . . and were found wandering in a dazed condition near the small mountain village of Durham, in the parish of Chester. A farmer working in his field discovered them, and someone with a jeep brought them here to Port Anthony. They are now at the hospital here

29

for observation. As I have said, they appear to be exhausted, hungry, and badly frightened.''

"You were able to speak to them personally, Lieutenant?''

"For a few minutes.''

"Could they tell you what happened? How they became lost?''

"Only that when all the scouts were together, approaching Blackrock Peak at dusk and looking for a place to bed down for the night, they seemed to become confused. 'Sort of crazy or light-headed, not knowing what they were supposed to be doing,' was the way Derek Crosdale put it. He said he didn't remember wandering away from the others but found himself alone hours later when he came to his senses. Day was just breaking. For another two or three hours he just wandered around, calling out and praying someone would hear him. When he finally got an answer, it was from Calvin Vernet, and after a while they were able to reach each other.''

"Had Calvin, too, been wandering about in confusion all through the night?''

"Yes, he had. He didn't remember leaving the group but found himself alone when he recovered. He heard Derek calling and answered him. Then the two of them spent hours searching for the others but couldn't find them, so decided to try to reach the north coast by themselves. They got lost repeatedly but managed to keep going on wild fruits and berries.''

"Is the search for the others now being concentrated in that area near Blackrock, Lieutenant?''

"You would know more about that than I would, with the search being directed from the capital. But yes, I'm sure the Blackrock area will be getting most of the attention now.''

"Thank you, Lieutenant. That was Lieutenant Foster of the Port Anthony police, talking to us by telephone about the finding of two of the missing scouts. Radio St. Alban will keep you up to date on further developments in this baffling mystery as they are brought to our attention. We return you now to—"

Peter shut the radio off and turned to the woman beside him. "Miss Craig, I know I shouldn't be leaving you at this time, but—"

"But you promised to tell that woman if you heard anything, didn't you? And you must. Where does she live, Peter?"

"In Look Up." Noting the expression on her face, he added, "That's a village. We have some odd village names here."

"Is it far?"

"You were looking down on its roofs from the windows of your room."

"Let me go with you, then."

He was only mildly surprised. True, she had just completed a long and tiring journey from England, culminating in a two-hour climb from the airport over a road that had sent her barrister to bed. But she was no ordinary woman.

"I'd better let Mr. Preble know," he said, "and tell Coraline to stay here with him until we return."

"Yes, that might be wise."

He hurried along the hall to her fiancé's room but found the man asleep and saw no need to wake him. In the kitchen his housekeeper was listening to her radio, and he explained the situation to her.

She would stay, she said. No problem. "Bronzie Dakin have a radio," she added, "but perhaps her won't be using it just now with Gerald behaving so peculiar."

"Perhaps she won't."

"You go along, Mr. Peter. Her will be glad to know two of the boys-them was found, at least. It will give her some hope."

6

THE YARD WAS DARK WHEN HE LED EDITH CRAIG
out the massive front door of the Great House and down
the veranda steps. He had picked up a pair of flashlights
and now handed her one. "It's possible to drive to Look
Up," he explained, "but we'd have to go back to where
we met Bronzie this afternoon, and the side road to the
village is pretty bad. The shortcut the workers use is
faster."

"I like to walk," she said.

She had to stay behind him as they went down through
the terraced flower gardens. The path was not wide
enough for them to walk side by side. It continued the
same way down through the vegetable gardens, where
their two flashlights transformed shoulder-high gungo
pea bushes into distorted night creatures that seemed to
crowd forward, threatening their intrusion. At the bottom a barbed-wire fence designed to keep out peasant

livestock contained a small gate that was never locked. Then the road.

It had been a driving road once, he explained as they circled boulders and mounds of rubble in a cautious descent. "Used to run from Armadale to Look Up. I drove it once in the jeep to see if I could convince the parish it ought to be restored. They weren't having any."

"It does look used, though."

"The way we're using it, though most of those who do are barefoot. Trouble is, we have rains here that cause slides. You bulldoze a track like this, and after the next six-inch downpour you have to do it again. Anyway, here's the village."

He meant the start of the village. Though small, Look Up was one of those communities that seemed to sprawl along almost endlessly: a house here, another a hundred yards farther along, with coffee or banana walks in between. Now that night had fallen the yards were empty, though there would be people on the road for a while yet. Men, mostly, unsteadily making their way home from some shop where hard-earned wages, mostly from Armadale, would have been slapped on a soiled wooden counter for a drink of rum or a bottle of St. Alban beer. Edith and he met no one, however, before reaching their destination.

Slightly larger than some they had passed, the house stood alone behind a rail fence of bamboo poles he had allowed Bronzie Dakin to cut on the Armadale property in return for her loyal service. Its two front-room windows, lit from within by lamplight, had the baleful look of spectral eyes floating disembodied in darkness.

Saying "Here we are" to his companion, Peter stooped for a stone in the road and rapped on the gate with it. "Bronzie," he called, "are you at home?" She would be, of course. With a sick son to look after, she would not be out after dark. But one didn't barge un-invited into a peasant yard after dark, either. Many of these good people believed in ghosties, duppies, and other feared night prowlers.

The door opened, creating still another rectangle of lamplight, this one framing Bronzie's figure. "Who is it?" her voice demanded.

"Peter Sheldon, Bronzie, with a friend. We've news for you about the boys."

She rushed to the gate and clutched at him as he stepped through. "What news, Mr. Peter? Oh, dear God, tell me them all right!"

He put a hand on her shoulder. "Now, Bronzie, it's not too bad, and we've come to tell you all we know about it. Bronzie, this is Miss Craig, who owns Armadale now." He waited for the expected curtsy, then gently took her by the arm and steered her back to the house, with Edith trailing.

When they were inside and seated, he quietly repeated what Edith and he had heard over the radio, while Bronzie looked at him wide-eyed. In the light of the one oil lamp that was burning in the room, her handsome face with its wide-spaced eyes seemed to have been lifted from a bright copper coin.

"It happened near to Blackrock Peak?" she whispered when he had finished.

"Yes, Bronzie."

"Where the Devil's Pit is supposed to be?"

"Now, Bronzie, you don't believe that old mountain tale. You're too levelheaded."

"I only know my Georgie is missing!" she wailed. "And now something terrible is happening to Gerald, too. What is going on, squire?"

"There can't be any connection between Blackrock and Gerald," Peter said. "It makes no sense. May I see the boy, Bronzie?"

"Yes, yes, I want you to!" Clutching his arm, she pulled him across the plank floor into a bedroom.

A lamp burned in that room, too, though dimly, and by its glow Peter saw Gerald Dakin on a bed. It was a wide bed of the ornate, highly varnished kind favored by country people who could afford better furniture than that made by themselves or a village carpenter. Probably, since there was but one other bedroom, the lad normally shared it with his brother.

Wearing pajama bottoms but no top, the sixteen-year-old lay not in the bed but on it. His eyes, wide apart like his mother's, gazed up at Peter without blinking. Bronzie stepped forward to place a hand on his moist forehead.

"Gerald, you see who come to call on you? Is Mr. Peter. And Miss Craig, who own the Armadale property now. They come here to tell us that two of the boys your brother Georgie went off with has been found." She waited for a response and, getting none, said in the same patient voice, "You hear me, Gerald?"

Seemingly without understanding, he shifted his gaze from her to Peter, then to Edith. Bronzie repeated what she had said, and a frown formed on his face. "What them say happen?" he asked.

Peter answered the question, speaking slowly and distinctly. "They had some kind of trouble up near Blackrock Peak, Gerald. All of them became confused up there for some reason and didn't know what they were doing. The two who have been found, Crosdale and Vernet, wandered off separately, it seems, then discovered each other by accident and made their way together down to a village in the parish of Chester."

"Not Georgie?"

"No, not Georgie. But we have every reason now to hope he and the others will soon be found. Doesn't that make you feel better?"

"My head hurt me," Gerald mumbled.

"You mean you have a headache?"

"Not a headache. Worse."

Peter turned to the boy's mother. "Has he been complaining of headaches, Bronzie?"

"No, squire. All the time he say he feel cold and wet."

"What do you mean by wet, Gerald?"

"Me don't like this place!"

"But you're in your own room, in your own home. It isn't cold or wet here. Is it, Bronzie?"

"No, squire."

"Miss Craig," Peter said, "do you feel uncomfortable here?"

"Not at all," Edith responded quickly. "It's a very pleasant room, in fact."

"Me can't get to move," the boy moaned. "Something holding me. And it all green in here, so me frightened the whole time! Do, suh, let me out of here!" Suddenly tears trickled down his face and an outburst of whimpering cause his mouth to tremble.

Gazing at Peter, his mother said with a heavy sigh, "All day long so him talk, squire. Over and over again, same thing. He cold, he wet, he feel like he in some strange green place, and he can't move to get away. What must I do?"

Peter touched the boy's forehead and decided the perspiration there was abnormal, even for so warm an evening. The medic in charge of the little government clinic in Cedar Ridge was on leave, he knew. To find another would not be easy.

"We could drive him to the hospital," he said. That would be the Princess Margaret in the coastal town of Wilton Bay, twenty miles distant.

"But I don't think him truly sick, squire," Bronzie protested. "All of this is in the head."

"I agree. But still—"

"Better I go for Mother Jarrett."

Peter had never met the woman they called Mother Jarrett. She was said to possess certain powers, including an ability to heal the sick when doctors could not. "Where does she live?"

"In Pipers, squire."

"The vale or the gap?" The climb from one to the other on foot was a major undertaking. In a car it was probably impossible at this time because recent hard rains would have all but destroyed the road.

"The vale, squire. A little way up the gap road, but not far."

He hesitated. If he volunteered to drive her, they would have to walk back up to the Great House to get a vehicle, leaving the boy alone here. If she went to Pipers on foot, leaving Edith and him here to watch over the boy, it would take her more than an hour. As he looked at Edith, his indecision must have shown on his face.

"Why don't you take her, Peter?" the woman from England calmly suggested. "I can stay here with Gerald until you return."

"Would you?" He was astonished.

"Of course. Besides, I'm a nurse." She touched his hand. "Do run along if you think this Mother Jarrett may be able to help."

"When are you going to stop surprising me?" Peter said.

"But I really am a nurse. I thought you knew."

"I didn't mean that."

"Run along," she urged. "We're wasting time."

7

As he walked Bronzie Dakin up to the Great
House they did not talk much. The climb left little
breath for conversation. Then the need to concentrate
on his driving kept him silent over the rough stretch of
road to Cedar Ridge. Expecting they would be bringing
Mother Jarrett back with them, he had taken the car,
not the plantation jeep.

Once Cedar Ridge was behind them, however, and
the road widened, he asked his passenger what she
thought of her son's strange remarks about feeling cold,
wet, and unable to move.

"That was not Gerald talking, squire," she said with
conviction. "It was his brother Georgie."

"I don't follow you."

"The two of them are more than just brothers, squire.
All their lives they been so close they could tell what
each other was thinking."

Peter pondered that in silence for a time. From a

small shop on the left, a sound of male talk and domino slapping disturbed the stillness. Then the car's lights picked out a barefoot girl-child, no older than six, whose eyes resembled table-tennis balls as, with a bucket of water balanced on her head, she stepped off the road to be sure the car would not run her down.

"You think Gerald is getting these thoughts from his brother, Bronzie?"

"Yes, squire. It happen before."

"I can't believe it."

"Mr. Peter, Gerald is not in no cold, wet place where he can't move. He is home in bed."

How to answer her? Silence took over again while they descended to the vale. In the dark, the old stone church there loomed like a fortress.

"She lives on the gap road, Bronzie?"

"Yes, squire."

He passed the church and turned left, shifting to low gear at once for the climb. Even under normal conditions, this was a road few drivers ever challenged at night. But he had battled its deep ruts and holes for only a few minutes when the woman beside him said, "You can stop here, please, squire."

He did so, and she got out. "Wait, please," she said. "Or turn around if you can. I will soon come."

He watched her disappear along a footpath, behind the glow of a flashlight she carried. To turn the car around he had to climb another hundred yards before the road widened enough to make the maneuver possible.

Back at the path he dimmed the lights and waited, trying to recall what he knew of the woman they called Mother Jarrett.

It wasn't much. A native of St. Alban, she had spent part of her life as a missionary in some rather remote parts of the world, including Africa and India. Now she was known as a healer and a mystic.

She was no obeah woman; of that he was certain. He knew the obeah practitioners in the district, and was also aware that a sizable portion of Armadale's wages eventually ended up in their greedy hands. Mother Jarrett did not charge for her services.

Because the evening was so hot, he opened the car door to let in more air. The ceiling light cast a lane of illumination up the path Bronzie Dakin had taken. Into the light strode a stranger.

What a remarkable woman!

She was easily seventy, yet taller than he and straight as a eucalyptus tree. All in white, even to a white headcloth, she looked as though she ought to be striding down some hospital corridor on an urgent errand. When she reached the car, he found himself looking up into eyes that glittered like black opals set in as dark a face as he had ever seen. Not brown as were most of those in the Armadale area. Not even dark brown. This face was as black as though carved out of coal, and by an artist with a message.

"Good evening, Mr. Sheldon." Her vibrant voice was a series of dark, low tones played on a viola.

Answering her, he stepped out of the car to offer his hand. She used both of hers to accept it, yet calmly, quietly, not with exuberance. Coming up behind her at that moment, Bronzie Dakin introduced them. "This is the man who runs Armadale, Mother."

"I know. Our people love him."

Startled, Peter could reply only by holding the rear door open while she bent herself onto the backseat. Bronzie followed, leaving him to occupy the front seat alone. As he headed back to the house where he had left Edith Craig, the woman with the deep voice said,

"Bronzie tells me the new owner of Armadale is here from England, Mr. Sheldon."

"Yes. You'll be meeting her."

"I hope she has not come to sell the property."

"I hope so, too."

"If she decides to keep it, will you continue to be in charge?"

"I don't know, Mother."

"I must talk to her."

As he turned along the side road to the village of Look Up where Edith Craig awaited them, the tall woman spoke to Bronzie. "This thing that happened to the boys took place at Blackrock Peak, you say?"

"Yes, Mother. Or as they came near there."

"I have heard stories about strange things happening at that place. Have you?"

"Yes, Mother."

"What have you heard?"

"That Lucifer lives there in some terrible place called the Devil's Pit. That people have been carried into it and never heard from again."

"Yes. There is said to be a place like that in Haiti, too—a cave called Trou Forban. There may be others in various places. Do you believe in such things, yourself?"

"Mother . . . I don't know."

"Very well, we can speak of it later, after I have talked with Gerald." Silence took over as the car followed its wildly bouncing headlight beams down the precipitous road to Look Up. Then: "Mr. Sheldon, may I ask if you have ever heard of our Devil's Pit?"

"A time or two, Mother."

"And you think?"

"It's just another duppie tale, I suppose. But there are folks who believe it. Gerald could be one of them."

"Yes." And she fell silent again, obviously not one who talked merely to keep a conversation going.

In the village a lantern glowed above a shop counter and three persons standing there turned to watch as the car passed. They knew whose car it was, of course. They knew, too, that it had to be going to one of the village houses, for the road ended here. After a brief stretch of ruts, Peter stopped at Bronzie Dakin's gate.

Following the two women into the house, he was relieved to find Edith Craig still there. She rose from a chair in the sitting room and was introduced by Bronzie to the tall woman with the shining eyes. In reply to Bronzie's question she said the boy in the bedroom was sleeping.

"He fell asleep just after you left and hasn't made a sound since, except to moan a few times. I've looked in every few minutes."

"And now," Peter said, "you and I had better get back to the Great House and check on Alton, don't you think?"

"Won't you want to take Mother Jarrett home?"

He hesitated. The tall woman answered the question for him by saying quietly, "Oh, no. I will be staying. You have done enough, Mr. Sheldon. We thank you for your kindness."

"God bless you, squire," Bronzie added.

Edith and he said good night and departed.

"Tell me something," the Englishwoman said as he drove homeward. "Are Gerald and his missing brother twins?"

He shifted his gaze from the dark road just long enough to direct a frown at her. "Why, yes. Didn't I tell you?"

"Not exactly, but it makes me wonder. He talks of being cold and wet and—well, confused somehow. And obviously he's afraid. Could he be unconsciously echoing Georgie's thoughts, do you suppose?"

"Some kind of ESP, you mean?"

"In a way, but it goes beyond that at times, I believe. How much do you know about twins, Peter?"

"Not much, I'm afraid."

"We had a curious case in England, in a midlands hospital I worked at once. So curious that I later read everything I could get my hands on about identical twins. Gerald and Georgie are identical, aren't they?"

He nodded.

"A man about thirty—his name was Alfred Jones, I remember—was brought to the hospital in great pain, with what the doctors diagnosed as a burst appendix. They operated at once to save his life, then were dumbfounded to find nothing wrong inside the man. He recovered and was discharged. And can you guess what happened afterward? A few weeks later he returned to tell us that his brother, Andrew Jones, an identical twin who was a ship's engineer, had died of a burst appendix that same day, that same hour, on a freighter in the Indian Ocean."

"I've read of such things," Peter said.

"Do you suppose Gerald's brother Georgie and those other missing scouts may be trapped in some place that is cold and wet? Mightn't it be wise for you to get in touch with the people searching for them?"

Peter was turning the car into the Great House driveway. "Would they pay any attention to me, do you think?"

"I'm sure I would if I were searching."

Having parked the machine in the old stone carriage house that now served as a garage, Peter walked with her the rest of the way in silence. On the veranda his housekeeper, Coraline Walker, was waiting for them.

Alton Preble was asleep, she said. "Should I make some coffee before I go home, Mr. Peter?"

He looked at Edith.

"Are you very tired, Peter?" she asked.

"Not at all."

"Then let's. Because we ought to talk a little about the future of this place, don't you think?"

"Without Alton?"

"He doesn't own Armadale, Peter. I do."

8

In the morning Edith Craig had still another surprise in store. Peter found her on the Great House veranda, gazing down at the roofs of Look Up. A sultry, dark red sun had just climbed clear of the mountains.

"Do you always get up this early?" he asked as she turned to the sound of his footsteps.

She smiled. "I'm sure I would if I lived here."

"Sleep well, did you?"

"Like a child."

She looked rather like a child this morning, he noted. Perhaps it was the ultra-simple white cotton dress she wore.

Looking past her, he saw his housekeeper trudging up the path and said, "Here comes Miss Coraline. She's early, too—probably in your honor."

They had breakfast alone together, her barrister still in bed. Over eggs, bacon, and more of the plantation's own coffee, he said, "Yesterday you thought I should tell the people searching for those scouts about Gerald—what he's been saying about being cold and wet and confined in some way. Do you still feel that way?"

"Yes, Peter, I do."

"If I suggest he may somehow be in contact with his brother, they're likely to wonder about me, you know."

"But if he is in contact with Georgie and you don't tell them . . ." She looked across the table at him and waited.

Peter nodded. "All right. I'll run down to the police station and they can contact the capital. We've never had a phone here, as you know; the line ends in Cedar Ridge." He finished his coffee and stood up. "While I'm gone, why don't you be thinking of what you'd like to do today?"

"I already know. I'd like to see something of the plantation."

"And Alton?"

"He'll probably want to start looking at the books," she said with a little smile. "That's the way his mind works."

Peter drove the Armadale jeep to Cedar Ridge and walked into the little police station there. The corporal in charge was a man he knew well. Dropping onto a chair in front of the desk, Peter told of his visit to Bronzie Dakin's house, being careful to repeat everything he could remember of what the boy on the bed had said. He then told the corporal Edith's story of the Englishman who had mistakenly been operated on for a burst appendix.

Young Corporal Clement MacQuarrie, slim as a ballet dancer from rigorous training at the St. Alban police school, frowned in disbelief and said, "You want me to pass this along to the army, Mr. Sheldon?"

"It may be a clue to the boys' whereabouts, don't you think? At least, it can't do any harm."

The corporal considered it and shrugged. "I'm not sure I—well, never mind. I won't have to call them, anyway. We're expecting some Defence Force men here this morning."

"Are you? What for?"

MacQuarrie shrugged. "All I've been told is that they're coming and I must find a place to put them up. Eleven of them. You don't suppose—" He hesitated, but only briefly. "You don't suppose they could bed down at your place, do you? I don't have room here and can't spread them around with local families. They'll want to be together."

Peter wondered what Edith Craig and her fiancé, especially her fiancé, would say if he gave permission for eleven army men to make the Great House their headquarters.

"I doubt they'll be sleeping there except for a night or two maybe," the corporal said. "They'll just want to stow their gear while they're off in the mountains."

"Well . . . I suppose I can okay it. The new owner is here, you know. I really ought to ask her permission."

"Her?" A scowl changed the shape of MacQuarrie's boyish face.

"Mr. Craig's daughter."

"What's she like?"

"Younger than you might expect, and she seems to like our island. Especially Armadale."

"She won't be selling the property, then?"

"I wish I knew. Anyway, I'll take a chance and let you send the soldiers up. I believe she'll want to do anything she can to help find those boys."

"Thanks." The corporal got to his feet. "And I'll tell the army lads what you said about Bronzie's boy, though I expect they'll think us a little crazy. If they do, you can talk to them yourself.''

Why, Peter wondered while driving back to the house, were the soldiers coming here? Armadale was not the nearest point of approach to Blackrock Peak, where the scouts had reportedly become confused and lost their way. The old Farm Hill estate and Whitfield Hall were both closer, and Whitfield, now a guest house, was certainly better equipped to handle them.

He shrugged it off. They probably had a good reason, and if so inclined would tell him. Meanwhile, he had better think about his forthcoming walkabout with Edith. Armadale with its nearly six hundred acres, much of it as wild as anything the scouts would have encountered higher up, was not a property you could explore in a few hours or even a few days.

He would take her, he decided, up the main track through the most important coffee fields, the way the scouts had gone. It might convince her that Armadale was too promising a property to be relinquished.

At the house he found Alton just finishing breakfast, and a casual conversation ensued.

''I hope you're feeling better.''

''Yes, thank God.''

''That road is rough on strangers sometimes.''

''On anyone who isn't a mountain goat, I should think. And I hope to God I see it only once more—on my way out.''

''Miss Craig has asked me to show her some of the plantation this morning,'' Peter said. ''Will you be coming along?''

''Thanks, no. I'll make a start on the books if you don't mind.''

''Want them now, do you?''

''If it's convenient.''

''A drop of rum, too, perhaps? Or whiskey?''

"That's an idea. Scotch, please, if I may."

Peter went to his office, formerly one of the many bedrooms, for the books he had kept since being made manager. On the way back he picked up a bottle of Scotch from the pantry and called down to Coraline, in the kitchen, to bring up a glass and some ice. Where, he asked the barrister, did Miss Craig happen to be?

"She spotted a corral with some mules and donkeys in it from a window here, and said she wanted to make their acquaintance," Preble said dryly. "I expect she'll be back soon."

It was half an hour, though, before Edith reappeared. "Do you know," she said, her eyes aglow, "I have never in my life touched a mule or a donkey before? Not even once! And they came right to the fence to be petted!"

"They're pretty friendly," Peter agreed. "Which is uncharacteristic of St. Alban mules. Most of them just want a chance to kick you."

"Oh, come now!"

"Fact. Are you ready for our walkabout, Miss Craig?"

"I'd better change first, don't you think?"

"Well, if you have slacks . . ."

"I'll soon come," she said, and laughed. "That's how your people say it, no?"

"Almost. Some would say 'Me soon come.' "

"You see how quickly I'm picking things up!"

Peter grinned. Alton Preble, already at work on the books, looked up with a frown of censure. To Peter he said, "Tell me something, Mr. Sheldon. When you pay your workers, don't you ever have them sign? Page after page here just lists a string of names with the amount paid out for weeding, fertilizing, and so on, but never a signature to prove they were actually paid."

"We pay on Fridays, starting at four o'clock, Mr.

Preble. In the beginning I tried for signatures and found myself still at it at eight.''

"Pardon?"

"Too many can't write their names but, out of pride, insist on trying. Have you ever seen a signature slowly and laboriously drawn—like a picture?''

"I see. But do your tax people accept this?''

"They understand the problem.''

With a shake of his head the barrister returned to his work—using, Peter noticed, a small, battery-powered calculator half-hidden behind the stack of account books. Edith had disappeared, apparently to change from her white cotton dress into something more suitable for mountain climbing. From outside came the growl of a heavy vehicle toiling up the plantation road to the Great House yard.

Peter walked out onto the veranda. In front of the old carriage house a covered gray-green truck had stopped, and men in khaki were jumping out of it as though executing some kind of military maneuver.

A short, husky fellow about thirty years old jumped down from the seat beside the driver and approached the veranda steps. Looking up at Peter, he briskly saluted. " 'Morning, sir. Mr. Sheldon, is it?''

"Good morning. Yes, I'm Sheldon.''

"Sergeant Wray, sir. The corporal in the village told me—''

"I know. Come on up, please.''

Sergeant Wray climbed the steps and they shook hands. "I'll show you the rooms we have available,'' Peter said, thinking, Good Lord, why didn't I tell Edith while I had the chance? But, of course, he hadn't expected the military invasion to take place so soon. MacQuarrie at the police station had said they were coming, not that they were already on the way.

He had another problem now. Unless he wished to

display a certain rudeness by walking his caller back down the veranda steps and around to a door at the rear, he would have to escort him through the room where Alton Preble was working at the table. He chose the interior route, and the Englishman looked up.

Peter stopped. "Mr. Preble, this is Sergeant Wray of the island's Defence Force. He and his men are among those searching for the scouts. Sergeant, Mr. Preble, from England."

Remaining in his chair, the barrister acknowledged the introduction with a nod. The sergeant said, "Good morning, sir."

Peter led the way to bedrooms in the rear. "Will these do, Sergeant?"

"Certainly, sir. And it's very kind of you."

"No trouble at all. I want to find those boys as much as you do. But I'm puzzled. If they ran into trouble near Blackrock, why are you working out of here? I should think Whitfield Hall—"

With a pair of solid-looking hands planted on his hips, the sergeant said, "Other men are working out of Whitfield, sir. But we aren't sure just where those two became separated from the rest. They said it was near Blackrock, but when they were closely questioned, they didn't seem to know where it was."

"Changed their stories, you mean?"

"Not so much that. They just seemed to be confused and couldn't remember things with any certainty. The way I heard it, they were trying very hard to help us but couldn't seem to get their minds in order. As if they were not quite right in the head, sir."

"So you're planning to begin here where they did and go the whole route," Peter guessed.

"That's it, sir. And we'll be leaving at once."

"Now?"

"Every minute may be precious. The lads left here

nine days ago, and that's a long time to be up there in those mountains with only three or four days' food.'' The sergeant hesitated. ''Let me ask you something, sir, if I may. Do you happen to know if any of those fellows had ever done this kind of thing before?''

''Their leader said he had. At least, he'd been up there somewhere, and they were counting on him to keep them from getting lost. I understand he was only recently made a scoutmaster, though.''

''Their leader. Linford Grant, you mean.''

''I believe that's his name.''

''That's it. Linford Grant. Sir, I'd like to ask a favor. Could you perhaps draw us a map of the route they planned to take?''

''I can draw you one of the way from Armadale to Morgan Peak,'' Peter said. ''I've been there several times. From there they planned to travel west along the ridge to Blackrock and descend into Chester Parish. Wait, though.'' It was his turn to hesitate. ''You mean you and your men have never been up there?''

''No, sir, we haven't.''

''You ought to have a guide, then. Perhaps I can find one for you.''

''That would be very kind of you.''

''Bring your men in and get them settled. I'll see what I can do.''

On returning to the dining room, Peter found Edith talking to her barrister, and told them what was going on. Edith seemed eager to cooperate. She was wearing khaki slacks now and a long-sleeved khaki shirt.

''Where will you go to find a guide?'' she asked.

''There are some men working in Field One, near the gate. I'll take the jeep down.''

''May I come, as part of my tour?''

''Of course.''

When he stopped the jeep by the gate, the men he

sought were scattered through the field, using machetes to chop out weeds and grass. At the beep of the horn they straightened from their backbreaking task and came to see what was wanted. He spoke first to the oldest one, a tough, wiry fellow of seventy. On his hikes to the Peak, Emmanuel Williams had always been not only willing but eager to be one of the group.

But when asked if he would guide the soldiers, Williams scarcely gave the request a thought. "No, squire. Me not going up there now after what happen to the boys-them."

"But, Manny, you've always—"

"No, suh. Me not doing it!"

"Don't tell me you're afraid."

"Yes, suh! Me frighten!"

"What about the rest of you?" Peter's gaze traveled from face to face, and all were good, strong faces. "There's money in it, you know. More than you can earn here."

"Mr. Peter," one said, "no money can pay us to seek out the devil in him den. The soldiers-them don't know what we know. Them is playing with hellfire."

He knew better than to argue. They would do almost anything for him, as a rule. After a big rain, for instance, when leaves in the river cut off the plantation's water supply by choking the intake at the river, these same men would fight their way up through the waterfalls to clear the screen without even being asked. But this involved fear of the unknown.

"I'll have to try down in Grove Path," he said to Edith.

But the little community down the road also rejected his plea for help, and Look Up, he guessed, would be the same. The truth was, if Manny Williams could not be persuaded to go, the quest for a guide was certain to fail. Manny had spent half a lifetime hunting wild pigs in those high-up places and must be listened to.

Reluctantly Peter drove back to the Great House and reported his failure to Sergeant Wray.

"I would be glad, then, if you would draw me the map I mentioned," Wray said.

From a filing cabinet in his office Peter took a surveyor's map of Armadale—an old one drawn long before Philip Craig's acquisition of the property. While he used it as the basis for a sketch of the route to the Peak, the sergeant stood beside him and studied it in fascination, reading aloud such notations as "Great Broken Ground," "Inaccessible Precipices," "Tremendous Deep Hole," and "Great Overhanging Rock."

"Lord, sir," Wray said in awe, "it don't sound very nice up there!"

"I believe it's even worse along the ridge. I can only tell you what I told the scouts. Be very careful."

Wray carefully folded the sketch map and tucked it into his shirt pocket. "Thank you, sir. We'll be leaving now."

"When shall I expect you back?"

"When you see us."

They shook hands. "By the way," Peter said, "did the corporal at the police station tell you about the Dakin boy in Look Up? The one who insists he is cold and wet and somehow imprisoned?"

"Yes, sir, he did."

"And do you think it may be a clue?"

"I'm bound to say I'm doubtful. I can only say if we come across any place that seems to fit the lad's description, we'll be sure to look at it."

From the Great House veranda, with Edith Craig at his side, Peter watched them go. Alton Preble had even abandoned the books long enough to come and watch with them. It was an impressive sight: ten men in spic-

and-span khaki briskly striding up the main coffee track behind their chunky, short-legged leader. Each of them wore a knapsack and had a rifle slung from a shoulder.

They would be a lot less brisk and natty by the time they reached the Peak, Peter thought. And probably not so eager. Glancing at his watch, he turned to the woman standing beside him at the veranda's old wooden railing. "It's quarter to ten, Miss Craig." He simply could not call her Edith in front of Preble. "Would you like to do some hiking, too?"

"Indeed I would."

"Sure you won't come, Mr. Preble?"

"Another time, perhaps. If we're here long enough, that is. Which I doubt."

Edith said, "Do you suppose we could take along some sandwiches, Peter? Then we won't feel obliged to hurry back for lunch."

"I'll ask Coraline to make some."

He hurried away, noting that barrister Preble did not look exactly happy.

9

ALTON PREBLE WAS NOT HAPPY. NOT HAPPY AT ALL. Left alone in the Great House except for the housekeeper, who was downstairs in the kitchen, he did his best to concentrate on the plantation books for the next half hour, then gave up and walked back out to the veranda. There, stiffly motionless in one of the wide-armed cedar chairs, he gazed unseeing into sunlit space and sought to analyze his feelings.

He could understand why Edith liked Armadale. Of course. The serenity of the place after the hurly-burly of London. The spectacular beauty of these tropical mountains. The charming ignorance or unworldliness of the peasants, with their amusingly primitive patois. Yes, yes, he could understand.

And, after all, St. Alban had been a colony of England until a few years ago, and was still more English than anything else.

But there was another face on the coin about which Edith was almost totally ignorant.

Not he. Even before her father's death, knowing Edith would sooner or later become Mrs. Alton Preble, he had made a point of learning as much about St. Alban as he could. Because it would be hers eventually, and the prospect of owning a coffee estate on a West Indian island had both intrigued and frightened him.

She would want to go there, naturally. Not to stay—that would be out of the question when she was his wife—but perhaps to spend a certain amount of time there each year. In which case he would of course face the prospect of having to go with her or remaining in London without her. So . . .

There were ways of finding out things when you put your talents to work. At the library he discovered a St. Alban daily newspaper called the *Island Post* and promptly arranged to have it sent to him regularly by mail. It wasn't the *Times*, of course, but it did cover happenings in the island. It was also blessed with a perceptive and obviously courageous columnist—one who called himself William Bold—who could actually write.

One thing about St. Alban had become apparent almost at once. As he had remarked to Edith only a few hours ago, while on the way here to Armadale, for an island of its size it seemed to be far too violent a place. The *Post*'s front-page stories had brought this home to him from the very beginning and continued to shock him at least once a week.

He hadn't told Edith he was subscribing to the island's newspaper. That was his own little secret. His ace in a hole, a gambling person might say, there to be played if she forced him to use it.

Thinking about it now, with his long face ridged in frown lines, Preble rose suddenly from his veranda chair and went striding back into the house. Although slightly worried that the people in customs might question his reason for having such stories in his luggage, he had taken the risk of bringing some *Post* clippings with him to St. Alban. The chap in customs had spent most of his time beaming at Edith, and the clippings were now in his room.

Preble returned with them to his veranda chair and sat again. It was important, he felt, to prepare himself for the possibility—God forbid it should become a reality!—that Edith might decide she wanted to keep the plantation and retain the American chap to continue running it for her. With a barrister's trained eye he went through the clippings to refresh his memory of what they contained.

The stories he had saved were grim. Here was one about a family of four being slain and dismembered in their home by one or more intruders who had left no clue to their identities. The young parents slaughtered in their bed, the two very young children, a boy and a girl, in theirs. Machetes had been the weapons, apparently. According to the newspaper, the house had resembled an abattoir.

An equally grim story had appeared only a month later. There had been so many robberies, it seemed, that many residents of the capital's most affluent suburb, called Langley, had had bars installed at their windows. But in this case the bars had not afforded the expected protection.

Appearing at a living-room window while the elderly man of the house and his equally elderly wife were watching television, the unknown assailant in this case had thrust the barrel of an automatic rifle—an automatic rifle in little St. Alban, for God's sake—through the glass and ordered the husband to go to the front door and unlock it, "or I shoot your wife." When the poor fellow opened the door, two accomplices of the gunmen were waiting there to step in and attack him with knives.

All three of them, then, had pursued the wife, who fled upstairs and locked herself in a bathroom. They broke the bathroom door down and attacked her as well.

Hearing the screaming, neighbors next door had telephoned the police. But the police arrived too late. The intruders were gone. The husband was dead, the wife dying, though she was still able to tell what had happened. Money the pair had withdrawn from a bank that day for a visit to their married daughter in England was missing. So was the wife's jewelry and everything else of value that was small enough to be carried off.

The frown lines on Alton Preble's face deepened as he went through the rest of his clippings. So much violence, he thought. Why?

There was violence in the island's history, of course. The slaughter of the gentle Arawak Indians by Spanish explorers. The struggle that had brought about a change of ownership from Spanish to English. The buccaneers with their bloody plundering. But why now? Why today? This was not the Middle East.

The question was echoed in a column by William Bold.

"What is happening to our once-civilized little island?" Bold had written,

True, it was never the paradise depicted in the travel folders. Such paradises exist nowhere. But we were reasonably peaceful here except when certain conscienceless politicians stirred up the more ignorant among us for the sake of obtaining votes. We were not more violent than the people of other Caribbean countries.

Now look carefully at what has been happening

here over the past ten years, if you will. Crimes of violence have increased in St. Alban nearly 900 percent, according to police and Defence Force figures. And what violence! These merciless slayings have not been the work of amateur thieves caught in the act of committing routine robberies. They have not been ordinary crimes of passion. Only a few have been political.

No. What we are seeing more and more are the senseless, totally ruthless acts of men who appear to revel in violence for its own sake. You don't just break into a house and rob it; you hack or club its residents to death. You don't simply command a victim on some dark street to hand you his wallet; you rip him open with a knife even after he has obeyed you. You don't simply rape a woman; when you have satisfied your lust, you disembowel her.

Something is going on here. Something hideous and terrifying. We seem to be breeding a kind of criminal who has sold his soul to the devil and actually enjoys committing the most shockingly evil crimes for the sheer joy of doing so.

I weep for my beloved island. Weep with me.

Alton Preble stopped reading and simply sat there on the Armadale veranda, gazing into space again. Should he show these clippings to Edith?

Wait, he decided. She was a good, sensible woman. In a very short time the island and the plantation were bound to lose their attraction for her, and she would be only too glad to return to England.

He was glad he had brought the clippings, though. There was a side of Edith that disturbed him at times, even occasionally made him somewhat apprehensive. It would be good to have an ace in the hole, just in case.

10

EDITH AND PETER WERE HIGH ABOVE THE OLD GREAT House when they stopped to eat the lunch Coraline Walker had prepared for them.

As they toiled up the main track, which had recently been cleaned so the new owner might be suitably impressed, Peter had shown his employer some of the best of her coffee fields. In them the trees were eight feet tall, with leaves that seemed to have been dipped in dark green enamel that hadn't dried yet. He thought she was pleased. At least, as they continued the climb she asked question after question.

"I'm sure I should have read some books on the growing of coffee before I came here," she said apologetically. "But there never seemed to be time. I had so much else to do after Daddy died. You must forgive my ignorance."

He not only forgave it; he welcomed the chance to acquaint her with some of the many problems. How, for instance, the serpentine soil here was so light that he had chosen to use chicken manure instead of commercial fertilizer, though it meant trucking the manure from a poultry farm miles away. How, because forest rats were fond of coffee and always selected the plumpest red cherries, his workers had to lace the fields with warfarin blocks each year before the coffee ripened.

Now as they sat side by side on the trunk of a fallen silk oak, enjoying lunch and a welcome respite, she startled him by saying with surprising candor, "I notice you call me 'Miss Craig' in front of Alton, Peter. May I ask why?"

He hesitated. "I get the feeling he's not a first-name kind of man."

"He is, you know," she corrected with a smile. "I mean to say he'd like to be. It's a little hard for him sometimes, I expect."

"Because of his legal training?"

"And his strict upbringing. But if you were to ask him to call you Peter, I'm sure he'd be pleased and would want you to respond in kind."

"Fine. I'll do it."

"Thank you. I don't believe he's very happy here, and I wish he could be."

So do I, Peter fervently told himself. Or else you'll both be leaving.

Lunch finished, he walked her another half mile up the track. The coffee at this height was not the best. For years the mountain rains had eroded the soil, and in his eagerness he had foolishly planted slopes where the humus was less than adequate. He explained this to her as they climbed. His destination, he also explained, was a place from which the view of the surrounding countryside was spectacular.

The spot was a cliff top some ten yards to the left of the track—the "Great Overhanging Rock" noted on the surveyor's map that had so intrigued the Defence Force sergeant. The inch or so of soil on its almost level surface supported a few coarse weeds, some scraggly knee-high brush, and surprisingly, a solitary, twisted juniper of great age.

Peter had reason to remember the juniper. Growing at the very edge of the precipice, with its roots penetrating deep into the rock, it leaned out over empty space like a bent flagpole on a high building. On one occasion he had been forced to lean with it.

Well, not forced, exactly. But he had been climbing to Morgan Peak that day with some of the plantation workers, including the old pig hunter Manny Williams, and the party had stopped here for a rest. And it seemed there was a ritual expected.

They hadn't climbed the tree, exactly. Even they were not macho enough to risk falling three hundred feet into the river. But each of them had walked to the leaning trunk and gingerly laid his body against it, encircling it with his arms. Then, with the angle of the tree bringing their eyes to a point some three or four feet out in space, they had looked down as a demonstration of their courage.

Each of them had dared to do it. So, of course, their boss must find the courage for it, too.

He still remembered his cold chill of fear as he looked down. Could still see the three hundred feet of nothingness beneath his gaze, culminating in the broken white thread of the plantation's river leaping and twisting through the black depths of its gorge. He could still taste his ghastly certainty that the roots of the already leaning tree would let go if he even took a deep breath, while a hundred feet below him a John Crow serenely glided through the gorge like a black phantom that quite properly belonged there.

Now as he stopped Edith twenty feet from the brink,

wanting to go no closer, he told her that his workers called the place the John Crow's Nest. "John Crows are the big turkey buzzards you see riding the air currents here so often, just floating around high in the sky with their wings outspread. They always nest in the scariest places. Now look closely down there to your right and you'll see a cluster of roofs. That's Look Up, where we were last night. Below that is Sherwood—the long rectangular building is a school. Over to the left are the buildings of the Grove Walk coffee works, once a colonial plantation like yours, now a co-op that buys most of the small-farmer coffee in this area. And the houses below that are in Grove Walk itself, where we were this morning."

While talking, he watched her face and was somehow not surprised to see in it the same excitement he himself had felt on standing here the first time. Was Armadale doing to her what it had done to him?

"Can we go a little closer?" she asked.

"Better not. It's spooky there near the brink."

"Yes, I suppose it is. And I'm not that comfortable with heights." Silent again, she studied the panorama below them so intently that he felt she must be searching for something. Guessing what it was, he said with a smile, "No, you can't."

"I can't what?"

"See the Great House. That big bump there"—he pointed—"is in the way."

With a mock frown she swung about to confront him. "How did you know I was looking for the house?"

"Well, for one thing, you own it."

"So I do, don't I? You know, I haven't gotten used to that yet."

"And if you're anything like me," he said, "the house owns you. At least, a good part of you."

Her frown was a real one now. "I think I know what

you mean, and I'm not sure I want that to happen, Peter. I'm a nurse, remember. I'm not sure I want to make a drastic change at this time.''

Her mood had changed, he saw. It was as though she had unwittingly ventured too close to a personal precipice of her own and suddenly realized her peril. Sympathetic, he said quietly, ''Shall we go back down?'' and she nodded quickly to indicate her willingness. Apparently the magic of the John Crow's Nest with its incredible view had fled.

But as he walked with her back to the coffee track, she suddenly halted. ''Now what's this?'' she said, stooping to reach for a scrap of brown paper half-hidden in a clump of brush. ''Why look, Peter. It's a map of some sort.''

It was indeed, he saw as he studied it with her. And the paper on which it was drawn with a pencil had apparently been wrapped around a sandwich. At least, there were grease marks on it.

''It's a sketch map of the route to the Peak,'' he said. ''Must have been drawn by one of—'' Peering at the ground, he voiced a sharp ''Yes, of course!'' and bent to snatch up a second piece of brown paper, this one unmarked, and a brightly colored chewing-gum wrapper. ''They must have stopped here for lunch that day. This wrapper isn't faded enough to have been here long. Maybe their leader drew the map to show the boys where they were going.'' He felt a scowl twisting his face. ''But there's something strange—''

She must have sensed he was troubled. Gazing not at the map but at him, she said anxiously, ''What is it, Peter?''

Something was wrong, and not only with the map. What was strange about the map was easy: the route sketched on it went quite properly up through the Armadale property to Morgan Peak and then westward

65

along the ridge, but before reaching Blackrock, it stopped.

Nothing on the paper indicated how the scouts—if, indeed, the sketch had been drawn for them—were to complete their journey from Blackrock down the north side of the range into the parish of Chester.

But something more personal was wrong, too, Peter realized. Something with his own eyes—or was it his mind? As he stood there scowling at the marks on the paper, he felt his vision blurring and turning red at the edges, as though he had foolishly raised his head and looked straight at the sun.

He felt his body swaying as though it were being pulled first in one direction, then another, by some invisible, external force that had power over it. An instant headache, as severe as any he had ever experienced, was filling his skull with pain. His mouth had lost all moisture and burned with a bittersweet chemical taste he did not recognize. He was having trouble drawing air into his lungs.

The seizure, if that was the word for it, became even more frightening as it continued. He knew that he still clutched the paper, but it was larger now. Much larger. It was a brown blur as large as a sheet of newspaper, and the lines penciled on it were weirdly in motion, as though alive and crawling like snakes intent on escaping from the page. Suddenly he felt a hot sweat oozing from his pores, soaking him under his clothes.

What in God's name was happening to him?

He looked about wildly for an answer but could not remember now where he was supposed to be. A greenish fog or mist swirled about him, furiously in motion, concealing any familiar objects—if there were any—he might clutch at to pull himself back to reality.

What was real here? Was he actually hearing distant rumbles of thunder as he seemed to be? And the crackle of unseen electricity in the air? And a voice or voices whispering what sounded like commands in an alien tongue he did not understand? Or were these things only products of a sick imagination?

He was cold now, icy cold, and shivering so violently he could hear his teeth chattering. His heart was an air hammer. He could not remember a time when it had beat so hard or so fast. His whole chest hurt from the pounding. Yet his body was ramrod straight and rigid.

Cold. Wet. Unable to move. That was what Bronzie Dakin's boy had said, wasn't it? "Cold . . . wet . . . Let me out of here!" Sensing that the paper had some part in what was being done to him, he fought silently to break free of his invisible bonds and get rid of it.

Partly he succeeded. His hands did move. But like sticky flypaper the map clung to his fingertips and refused to fall.

Worse, it has hot now and burning him!

Incredulous, he watched a curl of black smoke rise from the center of it, and felt the smoke sting his arms where it made contact. No ordinary smoke, it burned like a splash of acid. Suddenly, like the darting tongue of a snake, a shaft of bright orange flame leaped up to lick at his face.

With a yell of pain and terror he flung his arms wide, his hands feeling as though they had been thrust into the jet from a blowtorch. Torn raggedly in half, the paper became two separate gouts of flame that seared even his wrists before turning black and fluttering to the ground. Still trembling from head to foot, still bathed in sweat but icy cold, he stumbled backward and saw that Edith was reaching for him. Though obviously puzzled by what was happening—badly frightened, too, if the look on her face meant what it seemed to mean— she was nevertheless trying to help him.

Then suddenly she, too, was in desperate trouble.

With her it was not the map. Through the mist that swirled over the promontory he saw her turn and start walking away from him, toward the brink of the precipice. Only a few steps in that direction would take her to the base of the leaning tree. Her stride was that of a sleepwalker.

Something in what she was doing and the hypnotic way she was doing it, in the explosive realization that she was committing herself to a hideous death, wrenched him out of his own mesmeric state and goaded him into action.

"Edith!" As he flung himself toward her, his yell was a thunderclap in the mountain stillness.

As anyone might on being screamed at, she hesitated. But only for a second, and without turning to face him. Then she resumed her death walk.

He raced to catch her. At the last possible second, in desperation, he left his feet in a horizontal dive with his arms outflung. His face met the hard black rock and plowed along it, blinding him with pain. Like hawk feet clutching a vertical sapling, his burned hands closed around one slim leg, sending lightning bolts up his arms. Down Edith went in a forward lunge that would carry her past the cliff's edge into space.

But the juniper was there and she crashed into it. And though the impact sent a shudder to the old tree's topmost branch, its roots retained their grip. The blow jarred Edith out of her trance. Though stunned, she was able to curl her arms around the leaning trunk and cling for her life.

Groping to his knees, Peter grasped both of her legs now just above the ankles. Coaching her in a low voice to lessen the chance of panic, he carefully drew her back to safety. When she was clear of the brink and able to risk rising to her feet, he put an arm about her waist and held her. Held her a long time, until she stopped sobbing and trembling. Then with words of re-assurance he walked her back to where they had looked at the map.

There was no map now—only charred remnants that the first light breeze would scatter. He looked at his hands. They were as red and raw as though he had thrust them into a fire. Even his wrists were discolored. The pain made his head swim.

But what had caused the paper to catch fire? The sun on one of those grease spots?

"What happened to us?" he asked the woman at his side. "Do you have any idea?"

She was looking at his hands now, shaking her head over them. "The paper did this, Peter? When it caught fire while you were looking at it?"

He nodded.

"My dear, we have to go back and take care of you!" Then suddenly she seemed to remember more, and, letting his hands go, turned to look at the leaning tree. "Did I—Peter, did I try to walk off the cliff?" Fear held her voice to a whisper.

"I think that's what you meant to do."

"But why? Why?"

"Why did I have hallucinations that scared me half to death? Why did the map catch fire and burn me?" Plucking a smooth green leaf from a nearby shrub, he dropped to his knees by the charred paper and carefully scooped as much of the ash as he could into a hand-kerchief, then folded the handkerchief with care and tucked it into his shirt pocket. Edith watched in silence.

"Will that tell us anything, do you think?" she asked when he rose to his feet.

"I don't know."

"I'm frightened, Peter. Nothing like this has ever happened to me before."

"Nor to me. Come on, let's get out of here." Automatically, he reached for her hand, but caught himself. Already he had used his own ravaged hands more than he should have. "Come," he said again, and let her follow him back to the coffee track.

On the long walk down the mountain he would have discussed what had happened, or what he thought had happened, but Edith would not permit it. They must get to the house as quickly as possible, she insisted, so she could look after him. But she could not stifle his thoughts.

What the hell was going on? he asked himself. First the missing scouts. Then the Dakin boy saying all those things that made no sense. Now this.

If Edith elected to heed her fiancé and return at once to England, he could hardly blame her: But at the moment his hands and face hurt so fiercely—his hands from the fiery map and his face from its bruising contact with the rock—that he was willing enough to let tomorrow's problems wait for tomorrow.

11

"**D**ID IT REALLY HAPPEN, PETER, OR DID WE IMAGINE most of it?" Edith Craig asked later.

Peter looked at her. It was 11:00 P.M. and they were alone together for the first time since their return to the Great House. They sat on the long front veranda. A wave of hot, humid air had rolled up the valley earlier to wrap the house in a suffocating shroud of damp heat, sending Alton Preble to his bedroom.

"It happened," Peter replied. "Something did, anyway. The first thing Mother Jarrett noticed was my face, then my hands."

That had occurred a couple of hours ago, when he had walked down to Bronzie Dakin's house in Look Up to inquire about her son Gerald. He had not exactly planned on doing that this evening, but after dinner Edith and her barrister had gone for a stroll in the gardens, and after watching them awhile from the veranda, seeing Preble's arm around her and then the two of them

71

holding hands, he had suddenly felt a desire to be elsewhere. It didn't matter that at dinner, remembering his promise, he had asked the man to stop calling him "Mr. Sheldon," and as Edith had predicted, Alton had seemed pleased and replied in kind.

Look Up, then. After waiting for the lovers to stroll into a part of the garden where he would not have to pass close to them, he had left the veranda and gone briskly down the path. They saw him, of course, but he had only to wave and call out, "Going to see Gerald! Soon be back!" Ten minutes later he was at Bronzie's door.

It was not Bronzie who opened to his knock but that remarkable black woman with the piercing eyes. Still wearing her white headcloth and robelike dress, and seemingly glad to see him, Mother Jarrett stepped aside to let him enter, then frowned at him and said, "What have you done to your face, Mr. Sheldon? And your hands!"

He had anticipated the question and decided how to answer it, for though Edith and he had been candid with Alton Preble, he did not want anything close to the truth circulating among Armadale's workers. "I fell in that nasty Great House kitchen, Mother. Grabbed the stove to save myself, but went down anyway. If you've been there, you know how rough that stone floor is."

"Sit, please," she said, and bent over him. "Bronzie went to the shop, but will soon return." She studied his face. "I think I can help you. May I try?"

"I'd be grateful."

What she did then puzzled him. Going behind him and reaching around his head, she placed her palms against his cheeks and, surprisingly, it did not hurt. He himself had not been able to touch the abrasions without wincing. Even Edith's application of a said-to-be healing salve had brought tears to his eyes.

But Mother Jarrett's hands were cool and whisper soft. And in a moment, though they did nothing but remain motionless against his face, the soreness that had been deep enough to make even his bones ache seemed to melt away.

She lifted his hands then and studied them. "This will take longer, but let me try."

He felt a trifle silly with this tall woman kneeling in front of him, stroking his burned hands with the tips of her long, thin fingers. When he realized she meant to keep it up for some time, he tried to relieve his embarrassment by saying, "How is Gerald, Mother? That's what I came for, really—not to have you look after me."

"He is better now."

"Then why—" He caught himself, realizing the question might be considered impolite.

"Why am I still here?" she supplied, smiling.

He was astonished. Could this remarkable woman also read minds? "Well, I—"

"Because I am still afraid for him, Mr. Sheldon. Twice we have thought he was free from what is troubling him, only to have him fall under its spell again. When your hands are better, we can go and talk to him."

At this point Bronzie Dakin came in, carrying a woven basket filled with items from one of the village shops. Greeting Peter, she placed the basket on a table, then stood there in the lamplight silently watching Mother Jarrett's ministrations. What handsome women they both were, Peter thought.

And what a remarkable power the hands of Mother Jarrett possessed! Because his own hands, his wrists, even his forearms up which the pain of his burns had crept, were hurting less already, and he could see the burned areas returning to normal. At the Great House Edith had done what she could with the medications on hand, and that had helped. But this incredible woman was actually restoring his hands simply by gently massaging them.

Had she, too, used some kind of oil or lotion? She hadn't when touching his face—he was sure of that—but perhaps before easing herself onto her knees before him . . .

No, no. The magic was in her bare hands, not from any tube or bottle. Nor could she have used leaves or roots, as certain practitioners of obeah were said to do at times. And his hands, his face, his arms, all were as good as new again.

"Better?" She looked up at him.

"Thank you, yes. Much better."

"Please come and see Gerald, then." Rising, she turned to the brown woman with the far-apart eyes. "He fell asleep again just after you left, Bronzie. Perhaps when we wake him this time, he will be himself."

Peter followed them into the bedroom. On the bed, wearing the same pajama bottoms, Bronzie's son lay on his back with his eyes closed, the lamplight yellowing his face and chest. Relaxed and breathing gently, he seemed to be at peace now. Mother Jarrett leaned over him and touched him on the forehead.

His eyes opened—large, dark brown eyes that seemed to have trouble focusing on the face above him. His lips parted and he licked them. "Please," he said in a pleading voice. "Oh, do, sir, let me go!"

"Gerald," the tall woman said quietly, "where are you?"

"It dark but green down here. It cold . . ."

"Where are you?" Mother Jarrett asked again.

"Me don't know. It under the ground and them won't let me out. It cold and wet, like Riversink . . ."

The tall woman looked at Bronzie. "Riversink?"

"He must mean Riversink Cave near Waldon, where

my sister lives," Bronzie said. "The boys went into it once when we were visiting her. They were young then, and it frightened them."

"You're in a cave, Gerald?"

Sobbing now, the boy only repeated, "It cold, and them won't let me out."

"Who won't let you out?"

"Me don't know who them is. Them come in the green dark and talk. Them want me must do something."

"Why don't you do it, then, and get out of there?"

"No, no!" His voice was almost a scream. "Me can't do it! It not right!" His arms came up, flailing, and he seemed to be trying to drive something or someone away from him. "Leff me alone!" he shouted. "Leff me alone! Me won't do it!"

Peter stepped forward to Mother Jarrett's side. Was the boy still asleep, he wondered, even though his eyes were wide open? Was he talking in his sleep, not knowing what he was saying? If so, the dream must be terrifyingly real. There were tears in his eyes now and his whole body was violently jerking.

With a questioning glance at the two women, Peter laid a hand on the lad's bare chest. It was cold and damp, though the room was hot. The taut skin was rough with goose pimples.

Experimentally, Peter said sharply, "Gerald! Do you know who I am?"

The eyes focused on him. "Mr. Peter?"

"Now look around this room. Tell me where you are."

Gerald struggled to a sitting position and gave the room a thorough scrutiny. "It—my own room, suh?"

"It is. So what's all this about your being in a place that's cold and wet, like Riversink Cave?"

"Huh?"

"Don't you remember what you said to us just now?"

The boy's face had gone blank. He looked at his mother, at the tall woman in the white robe and head-cloth, then back at Peter. He shook his head. "Did me say something wrong, suh?"

Peter stepped back. "Bronzie, do you suppose he actually is hungry? Could that explain some of it?"

"No, squire. He ate a whole dish of stew peas less than an hour ago. He can't be hungry after that."

"Gerald, are you hungry? Do you want some food?"

"No, suh. Me don't want nothing."

"Wherever he was," Mother Jarrett said quietly, "he is not there now, it seems. This is the way it has been, Mr. Sheldon, all through last night and today."

"The hallucinations come and go?"

She nodded. "And I think I will ask you a favor, if I may."

Impressed again by the forcefulness of her black-opal eyes, Peter returned her gaze and waited.

"I think he should not remain in this room where these fantasies can steal in upon him, Mr. Sheldon. Do you suppose you could let him return to work tomorrow? And put him with others, so he will have someone to talk to?"

Peter thought about it while the three of them watched him. Not trying to hide his uncertainty about the wisdom of it, he said at last, "Well, there are some men weeding Field One, by the gate. I suppose if anything went wrong there, they could get word to me fairly fast."

"Thank you, squire!" Bronzie Dakin said with feeling.

But if anything does go wrong, Peter thought, I may lose some of my best workers. Those are the men who refused to go with the soldiers.

He was committed now, though. Turning to the boy

on the bed, he said, "You hear, Gerald? You can join the others in Field One at the usual time tomorrow." That would be eight o'clock.

"Yes, Mr. Peter."

"See that you behave yourself, now. I don't want any trouble."

"Yes, suh."

"Above all, don't discuss with the others what you've been telling us here. You understand?"

The boy nodded, his far-apart eyes unblinking as his gaze remained fixed on Peter's face. Peter turned away, and the two women followed him into the front room. There he said to Bronzie, "I'll try to keep an eye on him," and to the tall one in white, "How long will you be staying here, Mother?"

"As long as I am needed, Mr. Sheldon."

"Praise the Lord," murmured Bronzie.

Peter solemnly shook hands with them and departed. But on the steep uphill walk back to the Great House, through a warm darkness rich with the smells of earth and growing things, he wondered again whether he had been wise in agreeing to let the twin of missing Georgie Dakin return to work in the morning.

12

"**I** WONDER IF CORALINE COULD HAVE PUT SOME-thing in those sandwiches."

Peter said this to Edith Craig on the Great House veranda after his return from Bronzie Dakin's. The power plant filled the night with its usual low humming, but the windows of Alton Preble's room were dark now.

"Yes," he continued, "I can't help wondering if Coraline . . . I don't mean intentionally, of course. But food is sometimes a problem here, with the nearest real stores eighteen miles away in Wilton Bay. It's just possible the ham in those sandwiches had been around too long."

"Are you serious, Peter?"

No, not really, he thought. But he had to suggest some sort of explanation for what had happened at the John Crow's Nest, or she might be frightened into leaving. Turning on his chair, he looked at her. "Why shouldn't

I be serious? I've been thinking about this since it happened, as I'm sure you have. There must be some logical answer, Edith.''

"Why didn't you say this at dinner, when we were trying to tell Alton what happened?''

"Because at that time I couldn't think of anything a lawyer might accept as reasonable. Anyway, he didn't seem too concerned.''

"He was, though. When we were walking in the gardens, it was all he talked about.''

"At dinner he was more interested in what he'd discovered in the books.''

That, at least, was true. The one thing on Preble's mind at dinner had been, apparently, the fact that Armadale was earning no money. "You have all this coffee planted, but the returns don't begin to pay expenses,'' he'd said. "I find this disturbing.''

"We began to plant coffee here only five years ago.''

"Meaning?''

"At this altitude, over three thousand feet, a coffee tree can take four years or more to come into bearing in our kind of soil. The only trees that have produced any cherries so far are those we planted the first year. Naturally the return hasn't been enough to offset the cost of caring for the whole place.''

Alton Preble did not like to be told to think again, it seemed. His long face registered displeasure before, with a shrug, he said, "Are you saying Armadale won't show a profit until everything you've planted comes into bearing?''

"Not that. By the time the second year's trees are producing—with next year's crop, that is—we should be in the black.''

" 'Should be'?''

"Nothing in farming is certain. Especially in the tropics.''

With a shake of his head Preble had looked across the table at Edith. "For the life of me, Edith, I can't understand why your father thought this a wise investment."

"I don't believe he thought of it as an investment at all," Peter said.

"How in the world did he think of it, then?"

"He was a man with a streak of adventure who had spent most of his life in the humdrum business of banking. When he was given a chance to buy Armadale and restore it, his imagination took over."

To Edith the barrister said dourly, "Do you agree with that, my dear?"

"Yes, Alton, I think I do."

"I must say I never knew that side of your father. If there was such a side."

"Did you ever look at the books in his study, Alton?"

"Books?"

"Conrad, Stevenson, Maugham . . . He was fond of fantasy, too. Long before Tolkien won wide recognition, Daddy was telling people about *The Lord of the Rings*. No, I'm not at all surprised that he bought this property. I'm only sorry he didn't live to see what might be done with it."

"By you?" Preble's long face drooped with displeasure.

She shrugged. "By someone, I'm sure. After the start Peter has made here, it would be criminal not to carry on, don't you think?"

"So long as I'm not the one to do it," the barrister grumbled. "I've a law practice to look after."

That had been the end of the conversation about Armadale. The end of dinner also. The talk had not returned to the strange happenings at the John Crow's

Nest, and soon afterward Peter had departed for Bronzie Dakin's house in Look Up.

He said now, "Should we have a go at the kitchen, do you think? See if there's any of that ham left in the fridge?"

Edith nodded, and they went inside together. Flipping on light switches as they proceeded through the house—because Coraline had turned them off when she departed, despite his telling her he would let the power plant run all night with Edith and Preble here—he led the way downstairs to the kitchen. There, a switched-on light revealed a room some twenty feet square with stone walls, a stone floor, and long wooden counters as scrubbed as the deck of an old-time sailing ship.

Stepping past the stove, which functioned on propane gas that had to be trucked up from the Bay, Peter halted before an English fridge that also ran on gas. He opened its door and stooped to peer in.

There were eggs from a man in Cedar Ridge who raised chickens. There were some unrecognizable cuts of pork from an open-air market in Darleyville where goats, pigs, and even cows were dissected with machetes on the weekly market day. The butter came from New Zealand by way of a Chinese-owned supermarket in the Bay. Mustard greens, Swiss chard, turnips, and Chinese cabbage were from Armadale's own vegetable plots. Among these and other items was part of a island-cured ham, wrapped in plastic, on a plate.

He carried the ham to one of the scrubbed counters and unwrapped it. After sniffing it, he silently held it under the nose of his companion. She tested its aroma, too, and shook her head.

"It seems all right to me, Peter."

"To me, too. Still . . ." Sliding open a drawer, he took out a kitchen knife. But when he would have used it, Edith thrust out a hand to stop him.

"Should you?"

"I don't know any other way to find out."

"But—"

"Just enough to taste. Not the amount we ate in the sandwiches. If I try to do anything irrational, you'll be here to stop me."

She watched anxiously as he cut a thin sliver and lifted it to his mouth. He was nervous, himself, as he chewed and swallowed it.

"Does it taste all right?"

"Seems to. I'm suspicious enough at this point not to be certain."

After washing the knife under a tap, he dried it on a dish towel and returned it to the drawer. Then after rewrapping the ham and replacing it in the fridge, he turned to Edith and shrugged.

"I don't feel anything. How about going back upstairs and having a nightcap?"

She nodded. "And then I should go to bed."

Taking some ice from the fridge, he filled two glasses and handed her one. "The liquor's upstairs in the pantry. An awkward arrangement I ought to change but never seem to get around to. Fact is, when you live alone, you don't feel inclined to drink much. At least I don't."

In the pantry he added Scotch to her glass—that was her drink, she said—and St. Alban rum to his own. Scotch, he remembered, was her fiancé's drink, too. On the veranda they sat in the dark with the glasses on the broad, flat arms of their chairs, and looked at the stars, waiting to find out whether the ham he had eaten would have any effect on him.

By the time the drinks were finished he was sure it was not going to.

Edith stood up. "Well, it's been quite a day, hasn't it?"

"I hope it hasn't turned you off. About Armadale, I mean."

"No, I don't believe it has done that. It leaves a lot of questions, though." She could still smile, thank God. "Well, Peter, I'll say good night. Will you show me more of the plantation tomorrow?"

"Of course."

"The river you've talked about? The waterfalls, close up?"

"I'll be glad to."

"Good night, then. And I do hope the ham—"

"I'm fine," he assured her. "Don't give it a thought." And after watching her go along the veranda to the outside door of her bedroom, he headed for bed himself.

13

HIS ROOM WAS AT THE REAR OF THE HOUSE, NOT THE front. Nor was it one of the larger ones. Philip Craig, when living and working in the capital, had frequently come out for weekends, and the best room—the one now occupied by his daughter—had of course been reserved for him. Others, including the one now used by Alton Preble, had been set aside for friends he might bring with him. Still, Peter's room was adequate.

As he undressed in it now he felt comfortably at home, as always. On the walls were framed photographs of his father and mother, and of the Highlands County cattle ranch in Florida where he had grown up. The frames had held faded prints from a Scottish calendar when he arrived at Armadale. His parents had sent the photographs later, at his request.

Another thing that made him feel at home here was a stack of letters, many of them read over and over, in the top drawer of an old cedar chest of drawers. Some were from home, some from college friends both male and female, and some were from a girl named Jennifer who might now be Mrs. Peter Sheldon had he not fallen in love with Armadale. A week's visit had persuaded Jennifer she did not care to live even for a short time at the end of a dirt road in St. Alban's Morgan Mountains. Not even in a handsome old Great House.

Ah, well, his folks approved of what he was doing. Especially his father.

His father. It was odd, but when troubled, he could almost always conjure up a vivid picture of Dad—tall, lean, supple, with his ruggedly handsome face shaded by a cattleman's hat that concealed a shock of reddish hair. The man in the mental picture was usually on the back of a horse, as he was in the photo on the wall.

Mother was somehow less vivid, perhaps from having lived so long in the big man's shadow. But her letters were always full of warmth.

So, too, were the letters from his only sister, Laura. Opening a drawer now, he took out her latest, carrying it to the bed so he could reread it before going to sleep.

"Dear Petey," he read, and laughed at her still calling him that. And then stopped reading, aware that something strange was happening at the windows.

Up to now, the only alien things in his room had been the faint chugging of the power plant and an oversweet smell of night-blooming jasmine from the garden. Now the room was being invaded by tendrils of mist or fog, though there was no breeze to propel them.

He sat up as the mist shut out his view of the walls and closed in on him. What was happening here? A repeat of what had occurred up at the John Crow's Nest? Had the ham been tainted, after all?

Or poisoned?

He could not believe it. His visit to the kitchen with Edith, his dramatically tasting the ham, had been no more than a charade to persuade her to believe that the events of the afternoon had a logical explanation: if not the ham, then something else. Not for a moment had he believed the sandwiches were really the cause of it. But now . . .

The room was full of this swirling, pale green mist, and he was remembering there was something he had to do. Still clutching his sister's letter, he swung his feet to the floor and reached under the bed for his slippers.

Through the whirlpool of fog he groped to the door, which opened onto a central corridor. Still groping, because the fog flowed out with him when the door swung wide, he turned left and made his way to the top of the stairs leading down to the kitchen. His right hand clung to the old wooden railing as he made his way down to that room with the stone floor and scrubbed counters.

Though most of the house lights were still on, he had turned off the one in the kitchen when Edith and he left. After all, neither she nor her fiancé would be going down there at night. Now, feeling as though the walls were crowding in on him, he fumbled for the switch and the sudden brightness caused the walls to recede and let him breathe again. The mist still swirled about him, though, filling the room and half concealing its contents.

What had he come here for? Ah, yes—the fridge. Groping toward it with his hands outstretched, he touched it and found it cold. Should it be this cold on the outside, when the night had been so warm until a few minutes ago? But he himself was so cold he was shivering. Not quite sure what he was doing, but knowing he must do it, he felt his way around to the back of the box.

There, on his knees, he sought the flexible plastic tube, six feet long, that carried the gas to the fridge from a much longer length of copper tubing that came into the kitchen through a hole in the wall. The plastic fitted over the copper and was secured with a metal clamp held tight by a screw.

The letter from Laura was still in his left hand. He dropped it now and scowled at the screw for a moment, then rose to his feet and strode through the small court-yard off the kitchen to a room on the opposite side. This was a storeroom where paint, pipe fittings, and assorted small tools were kept.

Snatching a screwdriver from a wall rack, he returned to the kitchen with it. There, kneeling again, he loosened the clamp behind the fridge and dropped the screwdriver. With one hand on the copper tube and one on the plastic, he tugged the two apart. As he let them go and groped erect this time, the kitchen filled with a faint hissing sound, as though he had awakened a sleeping snake.

All right. It was done now and he could forget it. Satisfied, he made his way back to his bedroom and shut the door behind him.

Strangely tired—exhausted, in fact—he stumbled to the bed and collapsed on it.

The mist had followed him up from the kitchen, but now was dissolving. Presently it was gone altogether and he could see the stars through the windows. And by the light of the lamp he could again see the familiar, comforting pictures on the walls. His father. His mother. The home he had grown up in.

After a while he fell asleep.

14

THE ALARM CLOCK ON THE TABLE NEXT TO HIS BED read ten past six when he awoke. It was just visible in the room's grayness. His head throbbed as he sat up and rubbed his eyes.

He had promised to put Gerald Dakin to work today, he remembered. After breakfast he must go down to Field One and see if the lad had turned up, and whether he was actually in condition to do any work.

Something else had happened last night. What was it? Ah, yes, the mist, the fog, his trip to the kitchen. But, of course, none of that had really taken place. He had only dreamed it.

Leaving his room, he went down the hall to his bathroom and showered, using cold water in the hope it would dispel the heaviness in his head. It did seem to help a little. Back in his room, he had almost finished dressing when someone knocked on his closed door.

"Yes?"

"Mr. Peter!" The voice belonged to his house-keeper, but was so shrill he scarcely recognized it. "Can you come downstairs? Something is wrong in the kitchen!"

He opened the door and saw that she was indeed upset. The eyes that stared at him were overly large and bright with alarm. "All right," he said quietly. "Just let me get my other shoe on."

As he trailed her downstairs, she wailed back at him that the fridge was not working—that the kitchen smelled of gas. And so it did. On entering it, he at once recognized the sweetish reek of propane.

A glance told him the plastic tube behind the fridge had come loose from the copper one that brought the propane in from the cylinder in the yard. On the floor lay a screwdriver.

He stooped to sniff the end of the copper tube and smelled no gas emerging from it now, nor could he hear any. Striding out to the yard, he rocked the tall, hundred-pound cylinder back and forth and could tell by its lightness it was empty.

"It's finished," he said to Coraline, who had fol-lowed him out.

"But it was a new tank only last week, Mr. Peter!"

"The tubes must have come apart during the night and let the gas escape. Probably the clamp let go, and the pressure caused a separation."

His housekeeper had never been one to deal in non-sense. Hands on hips, she said, "Someone did unscrew that clamp, Mr. Peter! The screwdriver they did use is right there on the floor!"

"No, no. I must have left that there when I checked the clamp last."

"Mr. Peter, the kitchen floor was washed the day before yesterday by me. The whole entirely kitchen floor! And no screwdriver was there then!"

Unable to think of a reply that might quiet her, he went back into the kitchen. She followed in silence. Turning to the counter next to the stove, she lifted something white from it and swung around to confront him again.

"And this was under the pipe with the screwdriver," she said, watching his eyes.

He took it from her and glanced at it. Feeling as though his body were encased in ice, he turned slowly to look at the stove.

When he walked over to examine the pilot light, he found it not burning. "What's wrong with the flame here?" he said in a voice that came out like something from a record played too slowly.

"The pilot? Me did decide long time ago to use matches instead. Gas cost a wicked amount of money these days."

"It was out last night?"

"It been out for two months or more."

He stared at the fridge again. In his mind he saw gas hissing from the copper tubing behind it to fill the kitchen. He saw the swelling cloud reaching the pilot light on the stove and exploding with a cannon blast to tear the kitchen apart. The walls and floor of this basement dungeon were of stone, true, but the many cupboards and the ceiling were of wood, and the ceiling had probably absorbed enough grease through the years to fuel a raging fire.

Above that kitchen ceiling was the floor of his bedroom.

Stunned, he looked again at the sheet of paper Coraline had handed him. It was the letter he had been reading in bed before the start of his nightmare. The one from his sister Laura, with the "Dear Petey" salutation.

* * *

At breakfast Peter said nothing of his nocturnal visit to the kitchen. After reconnecting the tubes and putting a fresh cylinder of gas on the line, he had warned Coraline to be silent, too. "I don't know what's going on here," he told her grimly, "but if it frightens Miss Craig into leaving, you and I may find ourselves out of work."

"What you think going on here?" she had demanded, facing him with a look of fear on her face. "Me would truly like to know, suh!"

"I haven't a clue. So keep your eyes and ears open, please. And if you learn anything, come at once and tell me."

Now, finishing breakfast, he asked Edith and her fiancé how they had slept.

"Except for the heat, rather well," the barrister replied.

Edith said, "Yes, so did I."

So much for that, Peter thought.

After breakfast he drove the jeep down to Field One. The weather had changed. The air was crisp and cool this morning. The humidity that seemed to play such havoc with Alton Preble had been put to flight by a sea breeze flowing up the valley. As he left the vehicle and walked into the field, he looked about him with pride, and for a few moments stopped struggling to make sense of what had happened during the night.

This field was the first he had planted. Five years old, the handsome trees had already produced a fine first crop and were now so laden with green cherries that almost every branch drooped to touch the ground. He should take a color photo, he thought, and send a print to Philip Craig in England.

But Philip Craig was dead. His daughter was even now at the Great House deciding whether to keep the property or sell it. And but for a peasant housekeeper's frugality in shutting off a pilot light, there might not even be a Great House this morning. Thinking of that, he could only shake his head in frustration.

What in God's name had made him do it? What had made Edith behave so insanely at the John Crow's Nest? Why was Gerald Dakin babbling about being cold, wet, hungry, and a prisoner in some fanciful ''green dark'' underground?

Was there a connection? Were the missing scouts somehow involved in what was happening here at Armadale?

The weeding in Field One was nearly finished, he saw. A first-rate job, as always when that marvelous old pig hunter, Manny Williams, was in charge. He had to walk almost to the track that separated One and Two before finding the workers.

They stopped work to greet him, and he saw that young Gerald Dakin was one of them. Good. The lad was not still imprisoned in his imaginary cave, then. ''Carry on,'' he told them, and was content for a while to stand and watch them work. Especially to watch Manny.

Few men even here in St. Alban's mountains used a machete—or cutlass, as some of them called it—as skillfully as did Manny Williams. Most of them simply chopped the weeds, pausing every few minutes to take a small file from a hip pocket and rub the tool's edge with it. Manny, holding his gleaming blade almost flat, all but shaved the earth with each fluid stroke, and the strokes followed one another as rhythmically as a reggae beat. That broad back and those corded arms were all muscle. Yet this same man could plant a coffee seedling so gently that it grew, Peter was convinced, just to show its gratitude.

When Peter stepped forward to his side, the pig hunter stopped work with obvious reluctance. No man was supposed to interrupt that rhythm.

"Manny, may I have a word with you?"

The old man turned his head to glance at young Gerald Dakin. "Of course, suh."

"Let's have a look at what's to be done in Field Two, shall we?"

"All right, suh."

They walked across the track into the adjoining field, and when there was no longer any danger of their being overheard, Peter halted. "I just want to ask you how Gerald is doing, Manny."

"Seem like him all right now, squire."

"Has he been talking a lot?"

"Well, nobody been doing much talking. We looking to finish the field by midday and get started on this one."

Peter felt a touch of relief. The fields were given out as task work, usually to one man who hired any helpers he needed. In this case the job had been given to Manny, and sending Gerald Dakin here could have incurred his displeasure. "Thanks for letting him work with you, Manny. I had a feeling you'd understand the situation."

"Miz Bronzie a fine woman," Manny Williams said. "But"—frowning now—"what really happen to Gerald, squire?"

"I'm not sure. I believe, though, he's afraid for his brother. You know how close they are, almost like one person."

Manny nodded.

"Let's hope the scouts are soon found. Listen, Manny. If I'm needed for anything and you don't find me at the house, look for me at the river. I'm taking Miss Craig to the intake." Then, satisfied that all was well, Peter returned to the jeep.

At the house Edith had again put on her khaki hiking apparel and was waiting for him. He was surprised to find Preble, too, dressed in clothes suitable for a walk through rough country.

"If you don't mind, I'll come along," the barrister said. "Rivers are a hobby of mine, sort of."

"Alton goes salmon fishing in Scotland," Edith supplied.

Peter's smile of pleasure was genuine. "I'm afraid you won't find any fish in our stream, though. Except crayfish here and there—the people call them 'jangga'— under rocks in some of the pools. When the big rains come in April and September, the river is a killer. No fish could survive in it."

The trail began at the back of the Great House yard and, climbing, curled around the shoulder of a mountain. It was only a footpath, in most places so narrow that the three of them had to proceed in single file. Peter led the way; Preble brought up the rear. Almost before the Great House was out of sight behind them, a sweet scent of wild ground orchids brought an exclamation of delight from Edith. "Where are they?" she demanded.

Peter pointed out clusters of white and purple blooms under the forest trees, and delicate pink ones on slender bare stems higher up on the mountainside.

"Can we take some home?"

"If you like. The scent is pretty strong indoors, though. You may change your mind about wanting them after you've lived with it awhile."

She laughed and clapped her hands, turning to share her enthusiasm with her fiancé. She was like a child, Peter thought. Was it because this Caribbean island was so unlike her England, or was she just fond of the outdoors? Whatever, he hoped it would last. But as their walk to the river continued and the forest stillness deepened about them, his thought fastened again on what had happened at the John Crow's Nest and last night in the Great House, and he began to feel apprehensive.

The forest seemed too quiet. Almost always on this half mile of trail he encountered wild pigeons that burst from cover with a loud flapping of wings, and the big doves called mountain witches that raced clumsily along the path just ahead of him before crashing off into the bush. Gray kingbirds, too—called pecheeries here because of their shrill cry—defended their territory by swooping down like tiny attack planes, sometimes so violently an intended victim had to fling up his arms to protect his face.

But this morning there was nothing. Was it just the change in the weather, the sudden cessation of heat? Or was the sender of that damnable mist planning some new assault on their minds?

"Is that the river I'm hearing?" Preble asked.

"Yes."

"It sounds formidable."

"It does," Peter agreed, puzzled by the loudness of it. This was not the rainy season; the stream's voice should be muted. But the clouds had been threateningly heavy over the upper reaches of the property yesterday. Had there been a rain up there?

"Must we cross it?" Edith asked.

"If you want to see the cascades—"

"Of course!" she said with mock indignation, and then as they rounded the last turn of track, she saw the stream and gasped.

Peter nearly supplied an echo. There had been a heavy rain near the Peak, obviously. As he looked down on the white water swirling through its rocky gorge some twenty feet below them, he thought of Sergeant Wray and the men of the Defence Force, and wondered whether they had encountered it. The stream was a good four feet above normal, creating a rumbling thunder as it hurled small boulders against one another and sent them crashing into the canyon's walls.

Edith and her barrister stood there in silence, obviously apprehensive. "How do we get down there?" Preble said at last.

"Follow me."

There were steps in the cliff wall. Peter and some of his workers had hacked them out of the porous black rock with mattocks, to replace an old wooden ladder that had been the means of descent when Edith's father bought the property. To reduce the risk even further, they had drilled holes and driven in some lengths of one-inch pipe to support a handrail of sturdy rope. Turning at the top now, he went down backward to show his companions how it was done, then at the bottom looked up to watch them.

Somehow it did not surprise him to see Edith descend almost as boldly as he himself had done. It did when Alton Preble came down just as casually.

He turned to the river. The established way of crossing it was over a felled cedar tree, a giant, that extended from one bank to the other some eight feet above the normal level of the water. At times, after the worst downpours of the rainy season, it was actually underwater, and crossing the stream became impossible. Stripped of its bark because old bark could break and cause an accident, the tree had been notched with a machete at intervals to make it less slippery.

He looked at Edith. "Are you sure you want to do this today? It's a bit scary when the water is this high."

"I don't think you should, love," Alton Preble advised.

She hesitated long enough to convince Peter she was about to agree, but then stepped out onto the tree, took a few experimental steps, and said, "I can manage. I'll be all right."

"Better let me go first," Peter said. On the other bank lay some bamboo poles, one of which he could extend for her to grasp if she became nervous when halfway over. They were kept there for that purpose and had been used on more than one occasion.

Starting across, he was fully aware that the rush of the swollen stream against its banks was making the tree bridge tremble like a thing alive. What a place this would be for that hellish mist to reappear, he thought, almost expecting it to come swirling around him. And once more the obvious questions nagged at him. What was the mist? Where did it come from? Who or what was sending it?

Edith cautiously crossed the bridge after him, not needing a bamboo pole after all. Her fiancé followed without hesitation.

If this keeps up, Peter thought, I'll find myself liking the fellow in spite of myself.

Now the track became a ladder, curving upward at an angle so steep that hands became as useful as feet in climbing it. Off to the right the river crashed down over a series of ledges, with an unbroken roar that made any kind of talk impossible. The Cascades, this stretch was called on the old map at which Sergeant Wray had marveled. Peter simply toiled on upward and let the two from England follow.

Once, though, on looking back, he discovered that Edith Craig had stopped to gaze at the wildly plunging stream as if lost in wonder. Her father had been fond of the Middle Earth fantasy world of J.R.R. Tolkien, he recalled. How that same writer would have loved this untamed fragment of earth called Armadale!

Ten minutes later, completing the climb, he stood at the pool from which the plantation drew its water.

15

Left alone in Field Two when Peter returned to the Great House, Manny Williams, deep in thought, walked slowly back to rejoin his workers. The machetes stopped flashing as he approached. Their owners gazed at Manny in silence, waiting for him to speak.

"Nothing is wrong," he said. "You can go back to work."

Seemingly unconvinced, they sent questioning glances in the direction of Bronzie Dakin's son Gerald. But after a moment, when the old pig hunter said no more, they obeyed him.

Manny walked off a little way, laid his machete carefully on the ground, and sat on a fallen silk-oak tree. With his hands limp between his knees, he thought about what was happening, or what seemed to be happening, on this coffee plantation where he considered himself a kind of assistant to the manager.

Mr. Peter Sheldon appeared to be in some puzzling

kind of trouble, no? Some trouble connected with the Devil's Pit.

Of course, there were people who jeered at the idea of a Devil's Pit and called it a peasant superstition. But he, Manny Williams, had been hunting wild pigs in these mountains since he was a boy—and was convinced there was such a place.

How long ago had he gone up there with not-bright Witford Cushie? Not quite two years ago. And look at Witford now. Hardly a soul in Cedar Ridge called him by his right name anymore.

Witford hadn't been crazy when he asked to be taken along that day. A little queer, sure—the boy was always a little queer because his mum was that way and nobody even knew who his daddy was. But he had seemed almost normal when he rapped on the gate that morning just at daybreak.

In the morning light he had looked almost handsome, too, standing there in clean pants and shirt, with boots on his feet and his hair combed. Anyone would have thought he was a lot older than fourteen.

"Manny, me hear you going pig hunting today. Can me come along, maybe, and carry you gun?"

"Why you want to do that, Witford?"

"Just to be with you, Manny. To learn how you does it."

At first Manny had thought, No, him will only be in the way. Then he thought, Well, look now, me don't have no dogs today to keep me company, so why not let the boy come along? He will be someone to talk to, anyway. So he took time to put some extra bammies in his lunch bag—those cassava cakes were easy to carry and could keep a man from being hungry—and he set out with Witford Cushie struggling to keep up with him. A man seventy-some years old; a boy fourteen.

He'd seen his first pig in an old run on Wakely Ridge,

but never got into position for a clean shot at it, and didn't fire off his rifle for fear of scaring away every other pig in hearing range. Then on the ridge above he did get a shot at one, but only hurt it.

That was a big boar for this part of the Morgan Mountains, running close to two hundred pounds, and there was no way he was going to lose such a prize. It bled enough to leave a trail. So even though it was soon out of sight and sound, he was able to follow it. Here was a chance, too, to give his companion a few lessons in woodsmanship.

They went on slowly, the two of them, because if that pig was hurt bad, it would eventually have to stop and rest, and if it wasn't hurt bad, they'd never catch up to it anyway. He took time to tell his companion what to look for.

"We must have to follow him sign, see? Now a hurt pig don't going to travel any regular pig run; him will just go crashing through the brush. So we must have to find broken branches and maybe footprints in wet places, and because him is wounded, we must have to watch out for blood on leaves and things. You understand?"

"Yes, Manny. Me understand."

But that was a big, strong pig. They never did catch up to it. And by the time Manny realized they were not going to, they were high up on the ridge between Morgan Peak and Blackrock—through Albert Gap, in fact, and close to Blackrock itself. He was astonished that young Witford had been able to keep up with him.

"You a good boy, Witford."

"Thank you, Manny."

"Plenty others you age would be only stumbling along now."

"Well . . . me got to admit me a little tired."

"All right. Why you don't sit here and rest you'self

awhile, sonny, whilst me have one last look around? It might be the pig, too, got tired about now, and me will find him resting.''

"Well . . ."

"You not afraid to be left alone, is you? If you is—"

"No, no, Manny! Me not afraid!"

"All right, then. Me won't gone long."

He was not gone very long, either. He hadn't worn a watch, but thinking back on that day now, he was still certain he had not been away from the boy for more than half an hour. Yet when he returned to that place, Witford Cushie was gone. The not-bright boy had foolishly wandered off somewhere.

And it was raining.

No chance to follow sign.

Lord, have mercy.

He called the boy's name. Over and over, every minute or so, he called it until he was hoarse from yelling. A yell would travel a long way up there, but not when rain was falling hard. Rain made such a racket in the forest, pounding down on the thick carpet of dead leaves, that a man's voice was next to nothing.

But he yelled and he searched. He searched for hours, not stopping to rest until he was so tired he just had to. Dear God, he never should have brought a boy like Witford up here, knowing a thing like this might happen.

Then, just at dark, he heard a sound of crying, and hurried toward it, and came upon Witford Cushie stumbling aimlessly through the forest twilight like a drunk trying to find his way home from a rum shop. Stumbling along, not knowing where he was going or what he was doing, and without even holding a hand out in front of him, the boy could have walked into a tree at any minute and knocked himself unconscious.

Manny had run to him and eased him to the ground,

then sat down beside him, with an arm around the boy's shoulders, and tried to talk to him. But you couldn't talk to him. He wouldn't stop crying and sobbing long enough to listen.

There were words mixed up in the crying and sobbing, though. When Manny realized that, he listened.

"Please, suh, let me go!" Witford Cushie babbled. "Me cold and frighten here. Please. Oh, please. This green light making me feel sicklike!"

"What you talking about, Witford?" Manny asked.

"Me don't supposed to be in places like this, suh," the boy whimpered. "The one near where me live—the one them call Bat Cave—me did go in there once and Mum did whup me for it. Please, oh please let me go!"

Manny leaned closer, with an ear all but touching the boy's lips. It was important to hear every word, he felt, and hard to do that because of the noise the rain was making. Who was Witford talking to, anyway? Where did he think he was?

"Wha', suh?" the boy babbled on. "Well, yessuh, me did go to school once, a long time ago, but them send me home. Me fourteen, suh. Please, oh please, this green light in here making me sick in me head, like when people yell at me and call me the name. Please let me go!"

The name, Manny thought. Witless. And it was true, when people called the boy that—Witless instead of Witford—it sometimes made him so crazy his eyes would go wild and his mouth would fill up with spit.

"Witford, come," he said then. "We goin' home now." In the rain, in the dark that would soon come down on them, getting there would be a problem, but he had to try. They couldn't sit here and shiver all night in the high mountain cold. Besides . . .

It was up here near Blackrock Peak somewhere that folks said the Devil's Pit was, and Witford Cushie's talk was making Manny uneasy. Lots of people believed there truly was a place of evil around here. They said nothing else could explain so many disappearances over the years. If the missing ones had only just got lost up here, their remains would have been found, no? Some of them, anyhow. Bones didn't rot for years, and animals didn't eat them.

It was important, Manny felt, to get himself and Witford away from here now, right now, before black night came down to make the going even more difficult. Because what else could the boy be babbling about if not some kind of Devil's Pit? And who in such a place would he be calling "suh" except . . . well, who?

"Sonny, come now. Get up."

"Manny, me cold and wet. And so tired. And so scared. That green light . . . those people . . ."

"You can tell me all about those things later. We going home now. Come!"

With Manny's help, the boy struggled to rise. "Manny, me not sure—"

"Yes, you can. Just put you mind to it now. We have a big way to go, and it getting dark."

Swaying on wide-apart feet, the boy leaned forward to peer into Manny's face, and his own face twisted into a frown of incomprehension. "Who you is? You not one of them did talk to me before."

"In the cave, you mean?"

"Me is not in the cave now? Them did let me go?"

"No, you is not in any cave now, Witford." Manny got an arm around him and forced him to start walking. "Them must did let you go like you ask, and you is safe again with me, Manny Williams, and we going home. So come!"

"But—"

"Witford, we not talking no more now. It time for we to get out of this place! You can tell me all about it some other time!'' With that, Manny simply stopped listening and made the boy walk.

Thanks to Manny's experience as a pig hunter, they reached his home without accident some four hours later, despite the rain and the dark. There, Manny made the boy drink some bush tea and eat some warmed-up porridge, then put him to bed. Manny, too, turned in, expecting to find out later just what had happened to the lad up there near Blackrock.

But on that score he was in for a surprise.

''Now, then, Witford, suppose you tell me where you did go when you did wander off up there.''

It was past noon, and Witford Cushie gazed at him uncomprehendingly over a bowl of goat stew. ''Huh?''

''Up there near Blackrock, when you did get into that cave. Or whatever it was.''

''Cave, Manny? Blackrock? What you saying?''

''When we was hunting pig up there, Witford.''

''When, Manny?''

''Yesterday, for heaven's sake, man! When you did beg to go along with me and we did shoot a pig and follow him sign to near Blackrock, and you did wander off by yourself and get lost! What the matter with you?''

The boy gazed at him with eyes full of questions. ''Manny, me don't understand what you telling me.''

Manny tried for an hour to find a word, a phrase, anything, that would bring it back. It wouldn't come. Apparently it just wasn't there anymore. Giving up, he took the lad home and talked to his mother. ''Miz Cushie, if him should remember and tell you anything, me beg you let me know.''

She grasped her son by his shoulders and shook him in anger. ''You hear what Manny saying? Put you mind together now and tell him!''

Witford Cushie began to cry.

''It all right, Miz Cushie,'' Manny said quickly.

"Leave him be. If he remember, me sure him will come and tell me."

The boy did not, though. And to this day he did not remember what had happened up there near Blackrock when he wandered off.

Unless, of course, he was lying.

But Manny did not think he was lying. His mind had simply emptied itself of something it didn't want to hold, that was all. Or it had been emptied for him.

From that time on, in fact, Witford Cushie had gradually become more and more a boy without any mind at all, until today he was unable to remember much of anything. All he did now was wander around like a zombie, failing even to recognize anyone. Ask him his name and he would roll his eyes and grin at you and say, "Me name Witless."

Not Witford. Witless. The name he had hated.

With a shake of his head Manny Williams emptied his mind of the memory. Machete in hand, he walked back to where he had been weeding the coffee. But before resuming work, he allowed his mind one more distracting thought.

What had happened that day to Witford Cushie was a lot like what Bronzie Dakin's boy was talking about now, no? And Gerald's twin brother was one of the scouts who were lost up there near Blackrock.

Something bad had happened to Witford that day, but he, Manny Williams, had never talked to anyone about it because he knew the boy would not or could not back him up. No man, by God, was going to be given reason to call proud old Manny Williams a fool!

But now something equally bad was happening again.

It was a time to be on guard.

16

"THIS IS THE PLANTATION INTAKE," PETER SAID AS
Edith and her fiancé reached him. "All our water comes
from here."

He stood at the edge of a circular pool, twenty feet
in diameter, into which, from an inaccessible niche
some sixty feet above, thundered the most spectacular
cascade they had yet encountered. It had always seemed
to him an eerie kind of place because so little sunlight
ever penetrated its noisy, deep green shadows. Most of
his workers felt the same, and shunned it except when
duty sent them here to clean the screen in the concrete
feeder trough.

Because the rain higher up had raised the water level
so swiftly, the screen was half-choked now with leaves
and forest trash. Deciding to clean it, Peter sat at the
pool's edge and removed his boots, then emptied his
pockets before sliding into the water. Waist-deep where
he entered it, it was cold enough to make him shiver.

After all, it came untouched from near the top of seven-thousand-foot Morgan Peak, nearly four thousand feet above the pool here.

As he used one hand to steady himself and the other to claw the matted leaves away from the mesh, he saw Alton Preble frowning down at him.

"This is the whole installation?" the barrister asked, seemingly finding that hard to believe.

"This is it. The trough directs the water into an eight-inch iron pipe. That feeds into a two-inch galvanized pipe farther down, which carries it half a mile or more to the plantation buildings. You may have noticed it crosses the river in a couple of places, suspended from overhead cables."

"You designed this?"

"Not altogether. I did replace an older pipeline, but I couldn't improve on the intake here." Peter discarded the last handful of trash and boosted himself up onto solid rock again. "As you see, all we have to do is clean this screen after a storm."

"There is no need for a pump?"

"No pump, Alton. You're much higher here than you may think. Much higher than the Great House. In fact"—Peter pointed to the waterfall confronting them—"just above that is the start of the long, deep gorge Edith and I were telling you about. The one we looked down on from the John Crow's Nest."

"Have you ever been in that gorge, Peter?" Edith asked.

"I tried once with Manny Williams, but we couldn't find a way to climb the cascade here. And there's no way to get down into it from above, as you know."

"It's unexplored, then?" Preble asked.

"So far as I've been able to find out. But that's not exactly unusual. A number of places on the property are considered inaccessible. I must show you . . ." Pe-

107

ter's voice ran down and was lost in the roar of the waterfall at which he was staring.

"Show us what?" Preble frowned at him.

"A map . . ." Peter had to grope for the word. "An old map I have . . ." Still gazing at the cascade, he squeezed his eyes shut and opened them again, hoping the mist he was seeing would disappear. It did not. It continued to flow down from the gorge above, not opaque enough to blot out the jagged rift through which the cascade arched into space, yet swirling down toward him like a thing alive.

He had the fantastic notion it was a giant green slug, nearly transparent, slithering down from some secret habitat in the gorge he had just been talking about.

He had to get out of here!

Willing himself not to look at the thing, and trying to keep the fear out of his voice, he said, "Well, there's nothing more to see here. Shall we go back?"

His companions looked at him in some surprise. "Are we in a hurry?" Preble asked.

"I think we should be, a little. The river is still rising, if you've noticed. And we've seen everything there is to see here."

It seemed to satisfy them, though if the stream was still rising, it was certainly not doing so with any speed. Without further protest they followed him down the track. Twice he turned to see if the mist was in pursuit. It was not, and presently he convinced himself it had been no more than a mental invention brought on by the movement of the waterfall.

Perhaps his gazing at the fall and envisioning that dark, never-explored gorge above it had triggered some fear-producing mechanism in his mind.

By the time they reached the tree bridge he was beginning to feel a little foolish, all but convinced his imagination had been playing games with him.

Then it happened again.

He had reached almost the precise center of the span, with Edith two or three steps behind him and, as before, the barrister from London bringing up the rear. Suddenly the greenish mist swirled around him, blinding him.

A misstep here would mean a possibly fatal plunge into the swollen stream. He stopped.

Edith, watching her feet, walked blindly into him and all but knocked him from his precarious perch.

She cried out in alarm as she lost her balance. For a few seconds she teetered like a performer on a tightrope, trying to save herself by using her outflung arms as a balancing pole. Then she went down, but in a last-second effort twisted her body and fell with her arms across the tree.

Her feet hit the water and the current pulled at them as she struggled for a grip. Just as the river seemed certain to drag her clear, the fingers of her right hand found one of the machete-cut grooves and she was given a second or two of grace.

It was enough for Alton Preble, behind her. In one bold leap he reached her and caught her by a wrist. Struggling to maintain his own balance, he lifted her by sheer strength and wrapped his arms around her, then held her suspended until her groping feet found the tree again. When he succeeded in steadying himself, Edith was safe in his embrace—gasping for breath, terrified by the closeness of her escape, but safe.

Peter had seen it all, first through the swirling green mist that distorted everything around him, then more clearly as the mist slowly faded.

Holding Edith steady, Preble glared at him in a rage. "My God, man, why did you stop like that?" he shouted. Then, controlling himself with a visible effort:

"All right, all right, never mind now. Go on, will you? Let's get off this damned thing!"

In a daze Peter finished the crossing and turned to await further condemnation. Numbly he watched Preble steer Edith to solid ground by walking behind her with his hands firmly gripping her waist. On the bank, with the river roaring past at their feet as though enraged at having been deprived of an expected victim, the barrister spoke again.

"Why?" was all he said this time, but his caustic voice spoke volumes more.

"Didn't you—see it?" Peter finally managed.

"See what?"

Peter looked at Edith. "You were right behind me. Didn't you see anything?"

"I don't know what you mean." She gazed at him wide-eyed. "I was watching my feet, Peter."

"That damned fog. The thing that blinded me up on the John Crow's Nest. My God, Edith, how could you not—" Then he remembered that she had not seen it there, either. In telling Preble about it afterward, she had made that point clear. The mist had affected only him. Up there on the cliff she had become confused, disoriented, and had tried to walk off into space, yes, but she had actually seen nothing.

"I don't know what happened," he finished in a low voice. "Something blinded me."

Alton Preble, still unforgiving, said acidly, "All right, Sheldon. Let's get back to the house, please, before some other idiot thing happens."

110

17

To Peter, that walk from the river back to the Great House was one of the longest of his life. Something was going on that no amount of thinking could explain away. At the pool it had not frightened him too much, but at the bridge it had terrified him. At least it did now, as he realized how close he had come to causing a tragedy.

What was happening to him? Until the arrival of the plantation's new owner and her fiancé, life at Armadale had been just a grand adventure. Even up there at the John Crow's Nest he had never encountered anything unusual before—not even the time when, to save face, he had leaned against the old juniper tree and dared to gaze down into the gorge.

And last night . . . that eerie business of his going down to the kitchen and disconnecting the gas line. Was he ill? Or could there be some connection between these moments of madness and what was affecting Bronzie

Dakin's boy Gerald? Some tie-in with the missing scouts.

Edith and her husband-to-be could not have come at a worse time. What must she be thinking? That Armadale was a haunted place to be disposed of at once before it destroyed her?

At sight of the house he was almost relieved to find it still standing. But his relief was short-lived. Even as he began the last descent to the yard, he saw the old pig hunter, Manny Williams, striding so fiercely up the road that his errand had to be an urgent one.

Manny saw him and stopped. Cupping both hands to his mouth, the old man yelled through them, "Squire! Come quick!" Then he stood there, wildly beckoning.

Pausing only long enough to look back at the two following him, Peter broke into a run that took him swiftly through the yard to where the pig hunter waited. Out of breath, he gasped, "What is it, Manny?"

"Gerald Dakin gone crazy, suh!"

Peter pulled him toward the carriage house. "Come on. We'll take the jeep."

As the vehicle rattled down the road, Manny tried to tell him what had happened. "All of us was in Field Two, suh, him working a little way off from me, when all on a sudden him straighten up and commence to yell, 'No, no, me won't do it!' It seem like him was having a fit, suh."

"He wouldn't do what?"

"Him never say. Him just stand there shaking all over and yelling him wouldn't do it. Then him come running to me and grab hold of my arms and beg me to help him. Me mustn't let him do it, him keep saying."

"You mustn't let him do what? How could you stop him if you didn't know what he was talking about?"

"That is just it," Manny said. "That is the very thing

me did tell him. But all him do is run to a next man and a next, begging them to help him.''

"Where is he now, Manny?"

"All at once him stop yelling and just stand there in the field, shaking all over. Then him sink down on him knees and cover him face with him hands and commence to cry. That's how him was when me come to get you.''

Peter stopped the jeep by the gate, as he had done the morning before when seeking a guide for Sergeant Wray. Where were Wray and his men now? he wondered as Manny and he hurried through newly cleaned Field One toward the field now being bushed. Unfamiliar with these mountains, they had probably spent the night in some Forestry Department hut short of their destination, then finished their climb to Blackrock this morning.

To Blackrock? Or only to the unnamed terminus marked on the sketch map Edith had picked up at the John Crow's Nest? The map that had burst into flames as he tried to decipher it.

"There them is, squire," Manny Williams said.

The men were not working now. In a part of the field already weeded they stood clustered about someone lying on the ground, and as Peter and Manny approached, the group parted to reveal Bronzie Dakin's Gerald. On his back, with his knees drawn up, he held his hands over his face and sobbed convulsively through his fingers, seeming to choke on each loudly sucked-in breath and shake all over as it exploded out of him.

With a nod to the silent onlookers, Peter knelt by the boy's side. Not without a struggle, he managed at last to draw Gerald's hands away from his face.

"Gerald, do you know me?" It had worked before, at Bronzie's house.

Their whites a dirty yellow streaked with scarlet, the

113

boy's eyes looked up at him and struggled to focus. The mouth quivered uncontrollably for a few seconds before forming words. "Mr. . . . Peter?"

"That's right. Now tell me what happened."

"No, no!" The words seemed to bubble up from some deep well of terror.

Peter reached for the boy's hands to keep him from covering his face again. "But, Gerald, if you don't tell me what happened, how can I help you?"

"I beg you take me to Mother Jarrett, suh," Gerald whimpered.

"Will you tell her what happened?"

"Y-yes, suh. Me will try."

"Is she still at your house?" Realizing the boy could not know that, Peter reworded the question. "Was she still there when you left this morning?" If not, he would have to drive to Pipers Vale, where she lived, and would be wasting precious time if he mistakenly drove to Bronzie's first.

"Yes, suh," Gerald replied. "Her did promise to stay till me come."

"All right. Now just forget what's troubling you and help us get you to the jeep." By glancing at the circle of workers Peter silently asked for assistance, and several of them stepped forward to help the stricken boy to his feet. They were surprisingly gentle. On the way to the jeep Gerald stumbled constantly, and the difficult journey ended with his being lifted into the vehicle.

Manny Williams climbed in, too. "Me will go with you, squire, lest him have another fit and maybe fall out."

Or step out, Peter thought as he put the jeep in motion. The way Edith would have stepped off the cliff's edge.

With his eyes closed and head lolling, Gerald Dakin appeared to be in a daze when they arrived at his mother's house in Look Up. The pig hunter helped Peter lift him from the jeep and walk him to the door. It was opened by the tall woman in white.

Peter explained what had happened.

"Put him on the bed, please," Mother Jarrett said.

When the two men walked the boy into the bedroom he shared with his missing brother, they found Bronzie Dakin on her knees there, polishing the waxed board floor with half a coconut husk. Anguish distorted her handsome face as she looked up at her son and realized he was still afflicted. Swiftly rising, she helped Mother Jarrett ease him onto the bed.

"Take his clothes off, please, Bronzie," the tall woman said.

Standing beside Manny Williams in the doorway, Peter watched Bronzie undress her son. At Mother Jarrett's request she brought a basin of water and placed it on a chair beside the bed. Using a washcloth, the white-robed woman then proceeded to bathe the boy.

It took time, the way she did it. Talking to him all the while, but in a voice so low that Peter could not make out what she was saying, she began at his feet and worked her way up to his head. Nothing she could reach was overlooked.

Through it all, Gerald lay perfectly still on his back, gazing wide-eyed at the ceiling. Not once did Peter see him even blink.

"Turn over, please," Mother Jarrett ordered when she had washed all she could.

"Huh?"

"Turn over."

He did so and she finished the treatment, while Peter recalled the time she had healed his own hands and face merely by stroking them.

"All right, Gerald, you can lie on your back again now."

The youth rolled himself over and looked up at her. "Feel better, do you?"

"Yes, Mother Jarrett." But his voice was barely audible.

"Can you tell us now what happened?"

His mouth began to quiver as it had in the coffee field, and he seemed to be reaching for words that would not come. But they came at last. "Me . . . did kill a man."

Bronzie gasped. Peter felt himself twitch with astonishment and heard Manny Williams, beside him, voice a low grunt of surprise. Only Mother Jarrett remained seemingly unperturbed.

Calmly the tall woman said, "Now, Gerald, you couldn't have killed anyone. You were working at Armadale, bushing coffee."

"Me did kill a man," the naked boy insisted in his barely audible voice. "Them make me do it."

"How could anyone make you do a thing like that?"

"Me . . . was so hungry. Them wouldn't give me nothing to eat till me kill him."

"Till you killed who, Gerald?"

"Don't know. Me never see him before."

"Who made you do it?"

"Them."

"Who do you mean by 'them'? Come now, tell me."

"Me never see them before, either. Two men. Them come and talk to me in a room all green where me naked and tied up. Them say if me kill this man, me can eat. So me do it because me dead from hunger."

"And you don't know who you killed?"

He shook his head.

"How did you kill him?"

"Them give me a jackknife."

"A jackknife?"

"Him was on the ground, like him dead already, but

them say no, him not dead and me must kill him. Them tell me to cut him head off with the knife."

At that, even Mother Jarrett voiced a gasp. Then the room filled with silence—a silence so vibrant it seemed to Peter more like a prolonged scream. Finally the woman doing the questioning said, "And did you do that, Gerald? Did you cut this man's head off?"

Gazing up into her black-opal eyes, Gerald nodded. "Yes, ma'am, but not with only the jackknife. It take too long. Them must had to give me a machete to finish it with."

She placed her hands on his shoulders. "Gerald, did you do all this while you were working in Mr. Peter's coffee field? Was the machete you used the one you were bushing coffee with?"

Apparently bewildered, he did not answer.

"You realize, don't you, that you've been sick? That all this about killing a man was just your mind playing tricks on you while you were working in the coffee?"

He only stared at her.

"Just one more question," she said. "This man you killed by cutting his head off—how was he dressed?"

"Huh?"

"What was he wearing?"

"Huh?"

"Did he have on a scout uniform?"

Gerald shook his head.

"An army uniform?"

Again, no.

"What, then?"

"Brown pants, ma'am, and a nice yellow shirt. Only the shirt wasn't nice after me finish. It was a ruin, all red with blood."

Straightening, Mother Jarrett stepped back from the bed. To Bronzie she said, "I don't know what to do. It has to be something he is getting from Georgie but not getting right. Like a telephone message when you don't hear correctly what the other person is saying."

"Dear God, I hope so," Bronzie said faintly. "I hope my boy Georgie did not kill somebody. Must I take this one to the hospital, Mother?"

The woman in white looked at Gerald again. "Well . . . why don't we wait one more day, Bronzie? See if my treating him helps. If it doesn't—"

Peter said quickly, "If he is no better tomorrow, I'll drive him to the hospital. You can send word to me by one of the men coming to work in the morning."

"Thank you, squire."

"I'll run along now. All I can say is, I'm sure Mother is right and this is only something he's imagining." With a "Coming, Manny?" to the pig hunter, Peter turned to the door.

On the way back to Armadale, Manny Williams broke a long silence by saying, "What you think about that boy, squire?"

"We know he didn't kill anyone, Manny. He was with you the whole morning."

"Something funny going on, all the same," Manny said with a deep scowl. "Something that have to do with the scouts-them, me thinking."

"How could the scouts have anything to do with Gerald?"

"Through Georgie. You know them two a long time, suh. You said yourself them is not like ordinary brothers. Squire," the pig hunter went on thoughtfully, "me think we should not tell the men what Gerald did say about cutting off a man's head. Me think we should just let them decide him a little crazy for some reason."

"Do you believe he's crazy, Manny?"

"No, suh, me don't. Do you?"

Peter decided not to answer, though his silence might be taken as a reply in itself. There was something he should have asked Gerald Dakin before they left, he realized. The strangeness of it all had dulled his thinking.

"Gerald," he should have said, "tell me something, please. When you were confronted by those two men who ordered you to cut off the injured man's head . . . were you seeing things clearly or was there a kind of mist of fog swirling around you, doing things to your eyes and mind?"

Yes, he should have asked that question. But perhaps the boy had already answered it. A green room, Gerald has said. His prison room was *green*.

18

EDITH CRAIG AND HER FIANCÉ HAD BEEN SERVED lunch and were waiting to question Peter when he walked into the Great House. They had had time to talk to each other about him, it seemed, and Preble was very much the barrister in search of answers.

Once again—please—why had Peter suddenly stopped in the middle of that dangerous bridge when it must have been obvious that to do so would imperil the person behind him?

Peter had anticipated the interrogation and already made up his mind how to respond. Any further attempt to hide the truth would only add to his troubles.

Seated with the two from England on the Great House veranda, he did his best, first, to describe fully what had happened to him at the John Crow's Nest—or what he thought had happened. How the green mist, whether real or imagined, had temporarily deprived him of his sight and confused him. How the hand-drawn map had become hot in his fingers, then begun to smoke, then burst into flames.

Holding nothing back, he went on to tell them of his eerie journey to the kitchen in the middle of the night, his disconnecting the gas pipes, and why he believed he had been directed by someone or something to set fire to the house.

Finally he described his feeling at the intake pool that something alien, disguised as mist again, had flowed over the brink of the cascade, from the unexplored gorge above, to attack him. And how it had struck again while he was crossing the tree bridge later.

Preble's icy scowl must have been employed often to intimidate witnesses in courtrooms. "Of course, you could easily have burned the house down without tampering with the gas line. With impunity, too. That's in your favor. Are you saying you have no explanation for any of this, Sheldon?"

"Does Edith have any for why she would have walked off the cliff's edge if I hadn't stopped her?"

"No, I don't." Shaking her head, Edith turned to Preble and added, "You must take that into consideration, Alton. Peter did stop me from destroying myself. If all this is a St. Alban plot to eliminate me as the owner of Armadale, as you seem to think, why would he have done that?"

"A plot to do *what*?" Peter was incredulous.

She shrugged. "Alton thinks—well, I've already said it, haven't I? Of course, I don't agree with him."

"What do you mean, a '*St. Alban* plot'?" Peter demanded of Preble.

"I dislike this country. I distrust its politics and its present government."

"What have politics and government to do with Armadale?"

"I can't answer that. I don't know. But, quite frankly, I'm suspicious."

"*I* think," Edith said, "that what's been happening to us is more likely to involve those missing boy scouts." She looked at Peter. "And that place—what do they call it?—the Devil's Pit?"

"It has several names."

"What a lot of bloody nonsense!" Preble snorted.

"No, you mustn't say that, Alton. What do you and I know about this island and its people?"

Preble silenced her with a flap of his hand and said in a voice sharp with challenge, "All right, Peter, suppose you *tell* us about your Devil's Pit, and what you think it or the scouts could have to do with what's been going on here."

Peter welcomed the challenge, if only because it would transfer him from the witness box to a tale-teller's chair. He was no match for Preble at the game of prosecutor and defendant. He knew that. But he did know something of the island after having lived and worked here for five years. He did know some of the superstitions of the country people.

He tried patiently to explain that most of the people who worked for him had had little schooling but were steeped in the Bible. "Nearly all of them attend their little churches and have the Bible read to them by people like Bronzie Dakin. They *believe* the Bible. So they believe in Satan."

"A devil with horns?" Preble sneered.

"Some think of him that way, probably. Others haven't an exact mental image but do know he's an evil and active enemy of God. And powerful. They're certain he's powerful."

"And he lives up here in these mountains?"

"I'm sure some of them believe that. Yes."

The barrister smiled in disbelief. "With the whole

world, the whole universe available to him, he has chosen a base of operations within a few miles of this house, on this insignificant Caribbean island? Is that what you want us to believe?''

Peter quietly tried to explain that most of St. Alban's country people, never having been off the island and having no true concept of the earth's size, looked upon their land as a world in itself.

"They migrate to England and America," Preble argued.

"True. But many of them, when they go to the airport and board a plane, have no notion of how far they're going or how long it will take to get there. England and the United States are just names of places. Hand some of those people a world map and ask them to point out their destinations—they'd give you only a blank stare.'' Peter shrugged. ''So you see, Mr. Preble''—somehow the man's given name eluded him at this moment—''it's perfectly logical to them that the devil should be here. They are told in church that he's to be feared; therefore he must live within striking distance. And what more probable place than these mountains, which to most of them are full of mysteries anyway?''

Preble's smile became scowl. "Does this have anything to do with the obeah I've been reading about?''

"No. Obeah is a kind of black magic brought here from Africa by slaves. If you want an obeah charm, I can get you one without any trouble. I can't take you to the Devil's Pit because I don't know where it is.''

"What do you think is really happening to that boy in Look Up?" Edith asked.

Peter hesitated. He had not told them Gerald's story of being forced to kill a man. "I don't know. You're the one who thought he might be getting a message of some sort from his twin brother.''

"Who is lost up there near the Devil's Pit," she pursued.

"Or somewhere."

"You did tell the soldiers about Gerald?"

"I did. And by now they should be somewhere near where the scouts became lost. If, that is, the scouts were where they thought they were," Peter amended. "Sergeant Wray said the two who were found were badly confused."

Alton Preble, apparently running out of patience, said sharply, "Well, what are we to do about all this? Do you have any ideas, Sheldon?"

"I'm afraid it's not up to me."

"Meaning?"

"Edith owns Armadale. I only work here."

"What if we weren't here?"

"I suppose I'd be trying to persuade Manny Williams to hike up there with me, to find out what's going on."

"Would you? I wonder."

The retort that leaped to Peter's lips in response to Preble's sneer certainly would not have helped to ease the tension, but it was not uttered. His housekeeper came onto the veranda at that moment, to tell him there was a report on the radio about the missing scouts.

Followed by the two from England, he hurried into the drawing room.

". . . was flying near Blackrock Peak searching for the missing scouts when its pilot, Lieutenant Kevin Bradley, looked down and saw a Defence Force helicopter in a forest clearing directly beneath him. There was scarcely room for two such craft to land there, but he did so and investigated.

"According to Lieutenant Bradley, the first craft had crashed and burned. Speculation is that it may have run into unexpected air currents or a sudden hard rain. Of its pilot and civilian observer, Lieutenant Bradley could find no trace. So now, along with the scouts, we have two more persons unaccounted for: Captain David Anderson of the Defence Force and Mr. Ronald Cripp, his observer.

"Lieutenant Bradley said that after searching for the two men for nearly an hour, he took off again and dropped supplies, as planned, to a group of soldiers, led by Sergeant Leslie Wray, who were making their way on foot along the ridge from Morgan Peak. With the supplies he also dropped a note advising them of his discovery of the burned chopper and requesting they look for the missing men.

"On the news this evening we hope to have more details of this latest puzzling event in the baffling mystery of the missing scouts."

"What did he mean by a civilian observer?" Edith asked after Peter had turned the set off.

"The army has been using some Forestry Department men to assist them."

"I see."

Do you? Peter wondered, recalling what Bronzie Dakin's boy had said about the man he had been ordered to murder. Brown pants and a yellow shirt, Gerald had said. "Only the shirt wasn't nice after me finish. It was a ruin, all red with blood."

The missing scouts would be in uniform, of course. So would any soldiers seeking them. But an observer from the Forestry Department would not be.

19

ALONE IN HIS ROOM, HOURS LATER, PETER WONDERED how he could find out what the missing forester had been wearing. If he went down to the police station in Cedar Ridge, would he be able to persuade young Corporal MacQuarrie to let him phone the capital?

He could almost hear the corporal's response. "You're telling me, Mr. Sheldon, that Bronzie Dakin's boy may have murdered the man without even being up there where the copter was discovered? One of us has to be crazy, Mr. Sheldon."

Anyway, to find out what the forester had been wearing, he would probably have to talk to someone who had been present when the chopper took off. That could involve a lot of telephoning at a time when the station phone should not be tied up.

Seated on his bed, staring at the photographs on his walls, he shook his head in defeat. It was nonsense, anyway, to think that Gerald Dakin's fantasy of killing a man might be based on an actual happening. The forestry fellow had not been found headless; he was simply missing.

Forget it, he told himself. Turn in.

He was certainly tired enough. All evening he had continued to talk with Edith and Alton about what was happening. Deeply interested in the subject of twins, Edith must have read everything about them that she could get her hands on. She had spoken of the mysteriously close relationship of certain pairs—how, for instance, some of those separated at birth and reunited years later discovered they had led amazingly similar lives, even to having pursued the same careers and married mates of the same name.

"There was an International Congress on Twin Studies in 1977, in Washington, D.C.," Edith said. "Your *Reader's Digest* had a story on it. All kinds of astonishing reports were presented. One, I recall, was almost unbelievable—how twin brothers taking the same school exam were seated far apart from each other. They simply couldn't have communicated in any way. Yet out of six theme topics given to the students to choose from, those two picked the same one and wrote almost word for word the same story."

"You think, then, that Gerald is communicating with his brother Georgie?" Peter had asked. "Do you really believe that's possible?"

"I really believe it is. As I told you, the subject of twins has intrigued me ever since the doctors operated on the wrong twin in the hospital where I was working."

But more than the possibility of telepathy between twins had been discussed there in the Great House drawing room. Alton Preble, obviously anxious to depart from Armadale at the earliest possible moment, had again bombarded Peter with questions about plantation affairs. For one thing, he was not pleased with Peter's bookkeeping.

"I concede, Peter, that a sophisticated system might not be possible here. But surely a more foolproof method than the one now in use could be devised."

Peter could only point out again that the tax people had not complained.

"At any rate"—Preble turned to Edith—"I'm sure you've seen enough of your father's folly here to know what you must do."

"Folly, Alton? Really, I—"

"Oh, I don't mean to criticize his judgment. But in view of what's going on here, how can you even think of absentee ownership? And as for the other suggestion in your father's will . . . well, my dear . . ." He shrugged and was silent.

What, Peter had wondered, was the "other suggestion" in Philip Craig's will? They hadn't enlightened him. Edith, in fact, had appeared to be annoyed at her fiancé's mention of it.

In his pajamas now, he stretched out on the bed and shut his eyes, trying again to think how he might find out if the man in Gerald Dakin's fantasy was the missing observer from the helicopter. Then he realized he had another problem in connection with Bronzie Dakin's disturbed son. He had promised to take the lad to the hospital tomorrow if he was no better.

To drive to Wilton Bay and back would take two hours. Probably longer, because he would have to spend some time at the hospital. Alton Preble would not be pleased.

Well, to hell with Alton Preble. To hell with his hints, his innuendos, his courtroom inquisitions.

Sleep, old buddy. Tomorrow may be a long, tough day.

His mind made up, he put out the light and lay there

gazing at a ceiling now silvered by a wash of moonlight from the windows. But instead of sleep came thoughts of the John Crow's Nest and the bits of burned map he had saved. A careful examination of the charred scraps had told him nothing, but the handkerchief containing them was still in a dresser drawer.

Maybe if he turned them over to a chemist . . . But the only chemist he knew was a professor at the university who had been here for a weekend a month ago, hunting orchids, and was not likely to come again soon.

Suddenly, staring at the dresser, he was afraid to go to sleep. What if that damned green mist crept up on him again? Nothing but luck had kept him from burning down the Great House last night. What if this time the mind in the mist simply commanded him to hold a match to a curtain?

What if it told him to take a kitchen knife and go to Alton Preble's room?

Or Edith's?

He sat up in a cold sweat, trembling.

Then, facing the problem, he groped for a solution.

It was a thing you had to do here all the time: find your own solutions to problems. Very early in the game he had discovered that. Carpenters, mechanics, plumbers, electricians—all such people, if professional, were miles away and not at all eager to respond to a summons, even when knowing they would be well paid. So if a boulder came crashing down the mountain onto the pipeline, you removed the shattered section of pipe and installed a new one yourself. When a high wind wrecked the power line between the generator and the house or the warehouse, you replaced the poles with new ones from the forest. If a plantation vehicle became temperamental, you patiently worked on it until you found the trouble, then did your best to fix it at least well enough to get it to a garage in town.

What to do now about guaranteeing one Peter Sheldon at least a few hours of trouble-free sleep?

He could think of only one solution, and it required a few feet of rope. That was no great problem: there was a coil of sisal rope, used for tethering mules and donkeys, on a wall of the storeroom downstairs. He went down, took a machete from the bench there, and cut off the length he needed.

Back in his bedroom he tied one end of the rope around his right ankle, positioned himself on the bed, and fastened the other end to one of the mahogany bedposts.

Now, by God, if the mist tried to send him prowling again on some ugly nocturnal mission, he would be awake before he got off the bed.

All right, old buddy, relax. Get some sleep now.

But when he awoke, with the room full of that eerie green mist, the first thing he did was sit up, lean forward with his arms outstretched, and untie the rope from his ankle. Then he slid off the bed, removed his pajamas, and as calmly as though it were time to begin a new day, pulled on his clothes. The small alarm clock on the chest of drawers said it was not time to begin a new day; it was only a quarter to four. Moonlight streaming through the windows infused the swirling mist with an eerie glow, as though the green haze were born of mother-of-pearl.

With sneakers on his feet he went silently out of the room and down the stairs again to the storeroom, not for rope this time but for a shotgun hanging on a wall there. Lifting it down, he opened a drawer of the workbench and took out two shells with which to load it, then four more that he put into his pocket.

He hadn't used the gun in months. Never, in fact, had he hunted the wild pigeons on the property as men like Manny Williams did. The only reason he had even bought shells for the weapon, after finding it here when he came as manager, was to cut down the mongoose population. Those wily, weasellike killers, originally brought to the island to war on rats in the cane fields, took a heavy toll of birds that nested on the ground.

With the 12-gauge in his hand he left the Great House by a lower door and, like a sleepwalker, paced down the path through the gardens, on his way to Look Up and the home of Bronzie Dakin.

Gerald Dakin had to be silenced.

It was an eerie journey on a night shining with moonlight. Every bush and tree, every boulder in the path, cast a clean-edged black shadow, as did his own plodding body and the shotgun held in the bend of his arm. The night itself was breathless, not even a whisper of wind to stir a leaf, yet it was far from silent. Stones clacked in the road when disturbed by his sneakers. Insects chirped and twittered, hummed and buzzed. High in a cloudless sky the moon was an unblinking eye recording his progress.

Gerald Dakin must be destroyed before . . .

Before what?

Before he revealed too much.

In the shimmering moonglow the house was white as milk against the brown of the yard and the dark green of the trees. He put his left hand on the gate and pushed it open. He stepped through. With his gaze fixed straight ahead, he advanced to Bronzie Dakin's door.

The door was locked. And there was a wooden bar inside, he remembered, that could be slid into place to make intrusion even more difficult. With the shotgun ready in his right hand, he made a fist of his left and pounded on the barrier.

"Bronzie, open up! It's Peter Sheldon!"

After seconds of silence he heard a slow shuffle of

sandals on the old board floor inside. Then, timorously:
"Who it is?"

"Peter Sheldon! Let me in!"

He heard the wooden bar grate through its slots.
Heard the key turn in the lock. The door opened a few
inches and he saw Bronzie Dakin's far-apart eyes peering out at him.

"Mr. Peter, it's so late. What you want?"

Lunging against the door, he thrust it open and all
but knocked her down. In fact, she did fall to one knee
and was still struggling to get up when he strode past
her to the room where Gerald would be sleeping. As he
bulled his way into the bedroom, he put both hands on
the shotgun and jerked it up in front of him. By the
glow of the lamp near the sick boy's bed, he saw that
his intended victim was asleep.

His finger curled against one of the weapon's twin
triggers. There was no need to aim at such close range.
But a low voice behind him interrupted.

"No, Mr. Sheldon."

He felt his body become rigid. Felt his trigger finger
stiffen as though turned to stone. The voice was not
that of Bronzie Dakin. It was Mother Jarrett's—deep
and calm as always, but now hypnotic as well. "No,
Mr. Sheldon," it repeated. Then, almost as an after-
thought: "Please hand me the gun. You will not use it
here."

Not altogether sure what he was doing, he turned to
face her, half expecting to find her changed somehow.
But she had not changed. Though wearing a white
nightgown now instead of a headcloth and robe, she
was still the same tall, dignified woman. And there
seemed to be no accusation in her voice or expression
as she extended her right hand toward him and said
again, "Please, Mr. Sheldon—the gun."

He put it in her hand. She knew about such weapons,

apparently, for almost without looking at it, she extracted the two shells before turning to place it against a wall.

"Come now," she said then, still not raising her voice. "We must talk about this."

In silent obedience he followed her into the front room, where he became aware that Bronzie Dakin, also in a nightgown, was staring at him in obvious terror. The Jarrett woman motioned Bronzie to a chair, then said to him, "You sit down, too, please, Mr. Sheldon," and found a chair for herself. Gazing at him without apparent hostility, she said, "Now tell me, please, what you meant to do just now."

"I was told to kill Gerald." Was it actually his own voice he was hearing? It sounded faint and muffled, and was the voice of a stranger.

"Who told you to kill Gerald?"

"My God, I don't know. I was asleep in bed. When I woke up, I just knew I had to do it." He looked helplessly at Bronzie, who had been one of his most faithful workers for so long, and his sense of guilt was all but unendurable. "Bronzie, believe me," he heard himself sobbing, "I don't know. . . ."

"It is happening," Mother Jarrett said calmly. "Bronzie, I told you. It is happening." Rising, she stood before Peter like something from an old Bible illustration, ruler straight and with her long fingers entwined beneath her breasts. In an even lower voice than usual she said slowly, "How did you fall under the power of Lucifer, Mr. Sheldon?"

He could only stare at her.

"You don't believe in the evil one, Mr. Sheldon?"

"Well, I—"

"Today so many don't, and I think that is why we are becoming so vulnerable. Because he exists, you know. I don't think we are learned enough yet to say whether he is a person, a thing, a place—perhaps even only a thought—but he exists, never doubt it. Just as God exists. And Lucifer, Satan, the devil—whatever one wishes to call him—is wholly evil.''

"But why me?" Peter heard himself whispering in the stillness of the lamplit room. "Why always me?"

"You have felt this force before, you mean?"

He told her of his experience at the John Crow's Nest. Of what had happened to him at the intake pool and the tree bridge. Of his nocturnal attempt to set fire to the Great House. It was a relief to tell her. He had a feeling she might be able to help him. Bronzie Dakin sat there watching him in a silence of horror as he spoke.

When he had finished, the silence seemed to last a frighteningly long time before the voice of Mother Jarrett dispelled it. "Mr. Sheldon," she said then, "I think you should leave here."

"Leave Armadale, you mean?"

"Leave the district. Perhaps even the island. Think. This evil has attacked you several times. Tonight it felt so confident of its control over you that it sent you here to kill Gerald. Who knows what it may do next?"

20

As Peter trudged back up to the Great House in the moonlight, the tall woman's words were a drumbeat in his brain, matching the thud of his footsteps. What, indeed, might his personal devil not force him to do next? What came after attempted murder?

But he could not leave Armadale. No way was he going to turn his back on the best five years of his life and his best hope for the future. Anyway, he hadn't been the sole target of what was going on, had he? Up there at the John Crow's Nest, Edith Craig, too, had been affected.

And the scouts. And perhaps the helicopter men. Mother Jarrett's "force of evil"—if such a thing existed—may have been at work there also.

Don't run, old buddy. But don't let your guard down again, either. Sooner or later, whatever is at work here will tip its hand and give you a chance to fight back.

Looming there above its own massive shadow in the

moonlight, the old Great House seemed hostile now, poised to pounce like something alive and monstrous. What was the time? he wondered. When dressing for his nocturnal murder mission, he had neglected to put on his watch. The alarm clock in his room had read quarter to four when he left, though, so it must be after five now. He would not be going back to bed. Anyway, he wanted to think, not to sleep.

On the Great House veranda he sank onto a chair and looked down over the moonlit metal roofs of the village from which he had just climbed. A nondescript cluster of peasant farmers' homes in the mountains of a Caribbean island, he thought. Until now, nothing more notable had happened there than the usual petty quarrels over wandering cows or goats. What had brought about the change?

The devil's work, as Mother Jarrett had hinted? She might believe that, if the tales about her were true. According to the people who praised her so highly, she had taught religion or proclaimed her philosophy— whatever it was she actually did—in parts of the world as far away as India and China. Certainly she was no ordinary woman.

But "the devil"? There had to be some less esoteric explanation of what was happening here, even if, as she had suggested, the word might be taken to mean something more than a mere person. There had to be something he could sink his teeth into.

The metaphor made him think of the ham again, possibly poisoned. Of the many poisonous roots, berries, leaves that grew on the plantation. He had lost donkeys to certain deadly weeds, and the poor beasts had seemed to go mad before succumbing, as though brain as well as body were affected. But would poison, however virulent, send a man in search of a shotgun in the middle of the night, then down the road half a mile to murder a youth who had never harmed him?

His head throbbed as he vainly sought answers. He watched the moonlight merge into daylight and saw a morning mist creep up the valley. Armadale had always been such a peaceful place. You could sit on this old wooden veranda with your feet propped on the railing and watch night turn into day and feel you had found your destiny. And now . . .

Startled by a sound of footfalls, he turned to see Edith Craig step from her bedroom doorway. She wore a dressing gown over pajamas, both garments the blue of the forget-me-nots in the garden. At sight of him she stopped short, as startled as he.

"Well, hello," she said. "I didn't expect to find you out here. When did you get back?"

"Back?"

"From your 4:00 A.M. walk with the gun."

"You saw me?"

She sank onto a chair beside him. "Alton did. He couldn't sleep, he said, and was standing at a window looking out at the mountains in the moonlight. When you suddenly appeared with the gun, he came and woke me." A smile made her attractive mouth even more enticing. "I really believe he thought you must be up to something, and wanted me to be a witness."

There was nothing to be gained by trying to hide the truth, Peter decided. She and her Alton were probably planning to leave, anyway. In fact, he would now be urging them to. "I was up to something," he said.

"I wish you'd be frank with me, Peter."

"You wish what?"

"You'd be honest with me. Because Alton wants me to leave here today, even if we only go to the capital and wait there for a flight out. To be truthful, he is convinced you're involved in something nasty."

Peter studied her for a few seconds. As the light improved and pushed the night back, she emerged as the most physically attractive woman he had ever known, and he already knew how he felt about her as a person. "Are you convinced of that, too?" he said. "You're not, of course, or you wouldn't be telling me this."

"I don't think you know what's going on here any more than we do, Peter."

"You're right about that, at least. But about last night, Alton is the one who's right."

"Oh?"

"I went out intending to kill someone."

"What?" she said with a gasp.

"It's true. The hypnosis—call it what you like—that got to us at the John Crow's Nest, and to me later at the river . . . All I know for sure is that a voice in my head ordered me to take the gun and go down to Bronzie Dakin's house and kill her son Gerald. I probably would have done it, too, but for Mother Jarrett. Her voice was more powerful than the one she says belongs to the devil."

Edith Craig looked at him. Finally she said, "I can't believe this, Peter. Not of you. I can't believe anything could make you want to kill someone."

"Then I hope you'll do what Alton suggests."

"What?"

"Leave here. Let me drive the two of you to the airport this morning."

"No. I intend to find out what's behind all this."

"Edith, leave. Please. I might have gone to your room with that gun!"

She could be a very stubborn person, he realized as she vigorously wagged her head and said again, "No."

"You're determined?"

"I'm determined. I have a decision to make about

this property, and I'm going to make it calmly and sensibly—after we've put all this ugliness behind us.''

"Then I'd better leave,'' Peter said.

"What?''

"Hasn't it occurred to you that I may be losing my mind?''

"Don't be ridiculous.''

"Why did I go down there to kill Bronzie Dakin's son, then? Tell me. I like the boy.''

"I don't know what made you do that, but you're not losing your mind. I tried to walk off that cliff, didn't I? And I know I'm not crazy.''

"The point is, how do we know what I may try to do next? You or Alton might be the target.''

The answer to that came unexpectedly from the drawing-room doorway, in Alton Preble's voice. "What's that about me?''

Edith and Peter both turned their heads. In the doorway, wearing a dark dressing gown over white pajamas, stood the tall, long-faced barrister from London. As he came along the veranda to a vacant chair, he said, "Hope I'm not interrupting. I heard voices out here and wondered what was going on so early in the morning.'' He sat. "Have you told him we want to leave today, Edith?''

She gazed straight at him. "I haven't said yet that I want to leave, you know.''

Preble looked annoyed, even angry. The argument about their leaving must have been a long one, Peter speculated. Perhaps even a bitter one. These two might hold hands while walking in the garden, but they obviously were not of one mind about everything.

The barrister folded his long arms now and scowled at Edith in preparation for what promised to be a stern statement of some sort. But it was never uttered. At that moment a noise in the driveway brought Peter to his feet.

Through the tree shadows there, two obviously exhausted figures stumbled uphill toward the house, one more or less supporting the other.

Still fully dressed from his visit to Bronzie Dakin's, Peter excused himself and ran to meet them.

The less weary of the two was sturdy little Sergeant Wray, leader of the Defence Force group whose truck still stood near the carriage house. The other, seemingly at the end of his endurance, was one of Wray's men. Peter helped them up the steps and guided them to chairs. Almost at once Edith Craig appeared at his side, saying, "They need water, Peter. I'll get some."

While she was gone, Peter simply stood and waited, unwilling to press the men for an explanation of their condition. Their uniforms were dark with sweat and nearly in shreds, their shoes all but destroyed. Hands and faces had encountered enough thorns of assorted kinds to transform them into puffy red horrors.

Seemingly filled with relief at having finished their journey, the two men simply slumped forward on their chairs, arms on knees, and stared blankly at the veranda floor. They gulped down the water when Edith brought it, though.

Turning to Peter, she said, "I'd better go to the kitchen for some food, don't you think? These men look famished."

He nodded, and she disappeared again. Alton Preble rose from his chair to lean against the railing.

Peter gazed at Leslie Wray and recalled when the jaunty little sergeant had so energetically led his men up the track taken by the missing scouts. Wray at last looked up at him.

"Sorry to come to you like this, sir. We've been

walking all night. Since four o'clock yesterday afternoon, in fact.''

The group had left the Great House Wednesday morning, Peter reminded himself. They had planned on spending that night near Morgan Peak and going along the main ridge to Blackrock Peak on Thursday—yesterday. "What do you mean, four o'clock? Isn't that about the time you expected to reach Blackrock?''

"Yes, sir. And we reached close to there with no problem. But then things went bad.'' Turning his head, Wray gazed sadly at his companion. "Look at Private Pennock here, sir. You see what's happened to him?''

Something had certainly happened to the man, Peter realized—but what? About thirty, taller than Wray, and well built, he must have been a fairly soldierly-looking fellow before his ordeal. But now, in addition to what the thorns had done to his face, there was a frightening emptiness in his eyes.

"Everything was in good order as we approached Blackrock,'' Wray said. "Not a thing wrong, except one man had turned an ankle and was limping. Then something really strange happened—something we were not prepared for. We were just hiking along, keeping an eye out for a helicopter supposed to have crashed somewhere near there, when the whole place filled up with fog.''

"Fog?'' Peter asked. "You mean a green mist?''

"Whatever. I say 'fog' because I go fishing a lot and this was like what sneaks up on you sometimes when the sea is extra calm at daybreak. But it was green, yes. Up there near Blackrock it closed around us and we could not see one another. I called out to the men to halt and stay together, but the order was disobeyed. It seems the fog did something to us like what those two scouts say happened to them, though I don't remember if they ran into any fog.''

141

"I didn't hear it mentioned on the radio," Peter said. "But go on. This fog or mist—I've had a brush with it, too. I know what you're talking about."

"You found you couldn't think or act proper, sir?"

"Something like that. What did you do?"

"I can only say what I alone did. After the fog came at us, I couldn't see the others. It did something to my mind, I believe. I was not able to think right. Instead of continuing to yell to the men to stay together and wait for it to clear, like how I should have done, what I did was go blundering around trying to get out into the sunlight again. And I could not. No matter which way I turned, that green fog was there doing this thing to my mind like as if I was drunk or going crazy."

The sergeant stopped talking and looked up. Edith had come with a tray. On it were two plates of sandwiches and two dark brown bottles of St. Alban's Strong Man Stout.

Peter placed a small table between the chairs on which Wray and his silent companion sat, and Edith put the tray on it. Murmuring "Thank you, ma'am," the sergeant filled his hands with sandwiches and began eating as though he had not seen food in days. But then he paused and, scowling at his companion, said sharply, "You don't see the food here, Paul? Eat, man!"

Peter glanced at Alton Preble. Still leaning against the veranda railing, the Englishman surveyed the scene with as little visible emotion as though he were a critic appraising a play.

The sandwiches, Peter noted, were not of ham. Edith had opened some tins of bully beef and used the local hard-dough bread and Armadale lettuce. Was she still suspicious of the ham?

"So, as I was saying, sir," Leslie Wray went on when his mouth was empty enough, "I behaved badly because of what this green fog was doing to me. At least,

I hope it was the fog and not bad soldiering. Then, after I don't know how long, the fog thinned and I started calling to the men again, but only one of them answered. That was Pennock here, and when I reached him, he was wandering about the same as I had been doing, not knowing where he was. And he was looking just about like how he looks now, sir. Not in full possession of his senses, I mean.''

Peter looked again at the vacant eyes of Private Paul Pennock. The man was not even very hungry, it seemed. Having taken a single corned-beef sandwich and eaten it at Wray's urging, he was again sitting there motionless, as though in a trance.

"Drink up your stout, man," Peter said.

The soldier glanced at him but did not respond.

"So I tried to find some of the others," Wray went on, sipping gratefully at his bottle of Strong Man. "But nobody answered, and I was not able to locate anyone. Then, just when I was thinking I must try to return here to the Great House with Paul before anything worse happened, we came upon the Forestry Department man from the helicopter.''

He looked at Peter and slowly shook his head. "Sir, I knew that man. All the time he worked out of the Royal Gardens for the Eastern Division, he was my good friend. His wife and mine are related. Excuse me, sir.'' He put the stout to his mouth and emptied the bottle, then saw that his vacant-eyed companion was not drinking, and emptied that bottle as well.

"Sir . . . somebody had chopped off his head and it was lying there beside his body. Somebody had done that awful thing to my good friend Ronnie Cripp, a nice man married to my wife's cousin. Cut his head off. Hacked it off with a knife, from the looks of it . . .'' Lowering his own head, staring now at the veranda floor, the little sergeant began to cry.

"What was he wearing?" Peter asked mechanically. Sometimes an idea simply would not go away.

"Huh?"

"Was he wearing a yellow shirt?"

"Yes, sir, he was. Just like a new shirt I have at home. His wife and mine, they were shopping together one day last month and bought them for us."

"Did you see the chopper?"

"No, sir. After finding Ronnie I didn't look for it, though I suppose it must have been somewhere nearby. I just decided Paul and I must get back here as fast as we could, and thank God there was a bright moon last night to make it possible. Now, what I feel I should do is go to the police station here and use the telephone to call headquarters. Could you drive me down there, do you suppose? I don't feel up to handling the truck yet."

"What about him?" Peter glanced at Pennock. "Will you need him to back you up?"

The sergeant hesitated, then shook his head. "Let him stay here and rest, sir. He's had a hard time of it."

21

Watching the jeep go down the plantation road, Edith Craig tried to sort out her feelings for the man driving it. She had never known a man like him before.

He was compassionate; his concern for Bronzie Dakin's boy Gerald proved that. He was a quick-thinking man of action, too. Had he been any less so, she would have stepped off the cliff up there at the John Crow's Nest and would not now be here trying to analyze her feelings for him.

He had worked hard and devotedly here to make Armadale what it was. Why? Not just for the salary her father paid him; that was obvious. A man with his talents and determination could easily earn more at some other job. He really did love the place, then. As she did. Or as she would like to.

Her glance went to Alton Preble, still leaning silently against the veranda railing. Alton did not like Armadale. That was equally obvious. He liked nothing at all about it. But he, too, was a man of compassion and courage. Anyone who had followed his career as a barrister had to be aware of that. And he loved her.

From Preble her gaze moved to the blank-eyed Defence Force man, Private Paul Pennock, and his zombielike behavior brought her back to the problems of the moment. What, dear God, was going on here at Armadale?

Think about it, she commanded herself. Put aside your feelings for Peter Sheldon and Alton Preble and think about it. Emotions have no place in this decision you have to make. Look at the facts.

Some scouts and their leader were lost in the mountains. Very well, she could accept that if these mountains were as wild as Peter said they were, and as they certainly appeared to be. It was a little hard to accept certain statements made by the two who had found their way back, but perhaps in time there would be an explanation.

Now then, one of the missing scouts was a twin who seemed somehow to be communicating with his brother in Look Up. All right. After seeing reputable doctors mistakenly operate on a twin who was not ill, she could accept that. And she could accept the downed helicopter. Helicopters were more dangerous than ordinary planes, weren't they? She had read that somewhere, or been told it. And weren't they especially dangerous in mountainous country where treacherous updrafts or something like that might be encountered?

But—and again she looked at Private Paul Pennock, sitting there less than ten feet from her with his eyes wide open, staring into space—what could explain the hideous beheading of the dead forestry man? Who would do such a ghastly thing? Why?

And who could explain the green mist that had caused

her to attempt suicide at the John Crow's Nest, and later caused Peter to behave as he had at the river crossing?

Suddenly Alton Preble broke the silence, and she looked at him again. Since the departure of Peter and Sergeant Wray, he had been leaning there against the railing and his face had been something of a mask, betraying no emotion—as if he were in a courtroom, coolly listening to and weighing the testimony of a witness being questioned by an opponent.

Now, with his eyes narrowed and a scowl on his lips, he had straightened from his slouch and taken two steps toward the man in the chair. And he had said—or at least she thought he had said—"Are you sure of this, Pennock?"

Puzzled, Edith said, "Is he sure of what, Alton?"

"That he can take us to those missing scouts."

"Alton, I didn't hear him say that."

Preble turned his head to look at her. "You didn't?" Again he scowled at the Defence Force man. "That is what you said, isn't it?"

Private Pennock nodded.

Something was wrong, Edith decided. Until Alton had broken the silence, no one had said a word. She was certain of that. Pennock had simply sat there, gazing into space.

But she, too, was hearing something like a voice now, and it was telling her she was wrong—telling her to look at Private Pennock and pay attention to what he was saying. And he was saying . . . what was he saying?

"I will take you to where the scouts are. Yes."

"Where . . . are they?" she heard her own voice asking.

"That is not important. I will take you there."

"If you know where they are, why didn't you and Sergeant Wray bring them back with you?"

He only shrugged.

She gazed at him. Except to turn his head toward her and move his shoulders in the shrug, he had scarcely moved on his chair. But that lost, empty look had gone from his eyes now, and they returned her gaze in such a challenging way, she felt they were seeing into her mind.

"I . . . shall have to put on some clothes," she said. She still wore the blue pajamas and dressing gown in which she had stepped from her room, half a lifetime ago, to find Peter Sheldon seated here on the Great House veranda.

"And I," Alton Preble said. He still wore his white pajamas and dark dressing gown.

"Very well." Private Pennock nodded as he put his hands on the arms of his chair and pushed himself to his feet. "But be quick about it, both of you. We are wasting time here."

She glanced at Alton and went to her room, knowing full well that something was happening to her mind. But was the man named Pennock wholly responsible? She felt the way she had at the John Crow's Nest with Peter—as though some implacable force were taking charge of her mind and would soon be able to make her do anything it wished. Pennock hadn't been there when that happened.

Another thing. The takeover obviously wasn't complete yet—it couldn't be—or she would not even be aware it was happening. But all too soon it would be, so if she were to leave a warning for Peter, she must do so at once!

Reaching her room, she ran to a desk Peter had provided for her and snatched pencil and paper from one of its pigeonholes. Desperately she tried to put her thoughts down before they might be driven from her mind. But after only a few words, the pencil fell from her fingers and dropped to the floor.

The paper itself fell to the floor, too, caught up by a current of air as she turned blindly to her clothes closet. But already she had forgotten about it. Discarding her dressing gown and pajamas, she mechanically put on slacks, shirt, and sneakers and returned to the veranda.

Alton Preble was already there, dressed as she was to go wherever Private Paul Pennock might lead them. Seemingly unaware of her presence, he stared at the Defence Force man as though awaiting instructions.

They came, those instructions, with something very like a sneer. "All right now. Follow me, the two of you, and don't bother talking to each other. There's nothing you can say that will change any of this, so just accept it."

With that, the man who had pretended to be what he was not, fooling Peter Sheldon and perhaps even his own sergeant, turned and walked along the veranda to the steps leading down to the Great House yard—so confident they had to obey him that he did not even bother to glance back at them.

At the Cedar Ridge police post, Peter lingered only long enough to be sure the sergeant had made contact with his superiors and would not have to be driven to some other phone. The island's rural telephone service could never be taken for granted.

As soon as he heard Wray begin to repeat the story of what had happened in the mountains, he nodded to the corporal at the desk and hurried back out to the Armadale jeep. Wray would not return to the Great House, they had decided. For a while, at least, he should stay close to the phone.

The little mountain village was just stirring from sleep. Mangy dogs yawned themselves into their day-long search for food. With buckets on their heads for water, half-awake children trudged barefoot to the nearest standpipe.

Driving through, Peter asked himself what the Defence Force would do in response to their sergeant's shocking report. Would they send more soldiers to search for those missing, as they had sent Wray's group to look for the scouts?

There may be no end to this nightmare, he thought. But he knew what he himself must do. His housekeeper would be at the house when he got back there. In a short time she would be serving breakfast. Over coffee he would announce to Edith Craig and Alton Preble that he was driving them to the airport, whether they approved or not.

Edith might not like it, but her fiancé would. And with Preble's help he should be able to persuade her it was in their best interest.

It would mean the end of his stay at Armadale, of course. Once Edith left, she would not return, and the plantation out of sight would soon be out of mind. Back in London she would marry her barrister and arrange for the property to be sold; Preble would no doubt be delighted to assist her in finding a buyer for it.

Recalling the barrister's brief mention of her father's will, though, Peter was again puzzled. Could Philip Craig have requested her not to sell the property? No, that was beyond reason. No matter how fond he had been of the place, he would not have tried to burden her with it. St. Alban had long since ceased to be an English colony.

End of the line, he thought glumly as he turned the jeep in at the gate and drove up the plantation road.

There was no one on the veranda when he walked from the carriage house to the steps. Edith must have taken Private Pennock inside to look after his macca-torn face. Alton Preble was probably helping her. Passing through the dining room on his way to the quarters he had assigned to the Defence Force men, Peter saw that Coraline had arrived and set the table for breakfast. In the kitchen, downstairs, her radio throbbed out a popular Jamaican reggae tune.

No one was in the soldiers' rooms, though. He looked in Edith's room—her door was open—and she was not there. He knocked on Preble's door, got no answer, opened it, and found that room empty also.

Puzzled now, he went down to the kitchen and found his housekeeper standing at a counter, turning the handle of a coffee mill.

" 'Morning, Coraline. Where is everybody?"

"Me don't know, suh. Wasn't them with you?"

"Me?"

Her face filled with sharp lines. "Wasn't the three of you at the river, suh? Me did see three people going along the river track when me coming from Look Up."

"You saw three persons going to the river?"

"Yes, suh. Me was not close enough to see who them was before them passed from sight, but me took for granted it was you and Miss Craig and Mr. Preble."

Peter felt something small with many cold feet crawl over his skin, and his body responded with a shiver. "Are you sure of this, Coraline? You couldn't have seen some hunters going after pigs or birds?"

"Mr. Peter, me did see three people on the track to the river. That's all me sure of. Is only one or two places you can see that track coming up from where me live, remember. Me was not close."

"Nobody was here when you got here?"

"Nobody at all not here, suh."

Pennock, Peter thought. That look in his eyes. That empty look, as though something had possession of his mind. But why would Edith and Alton have gone with him?

"Coraline, listen to me now." He caught her by a wrist and drew her away from the coffee mill, which she seemed determined to finish using. "Never mind about breakfast. Something has happened here—something bad, I think—and I'm going to the river. What I want you to do is go for Manny Williams. You know where he lives, don't you?"

"Of course."

"Tell him I've gone to the river after those three people, and I may need his help. Tell him to come as quick as he can. Tell him I'm counting on him. You hear?"

"Yes, Mr. Peter."

"Don't let him say no!"

"No, suh."

Thoroughly apprehensive, Peter strode from the room.

From the very start of his stay at Armadale, walking to the river in the early morning had been one of his greatest pleasures. It was no joy this morning. The pigeons and doves were present, colorful lizards eyed him from rocks and branches, orchid scents filled the air, but fear hurried along with him. Why, for God's sake, had Edith and her barrister followed a man who had just been through a severe ordeal and almost certainly was not in his right mind? What could they have been thinking of?

As he strode along, he studied the ground for footprints. What they might tell him he did not know; Edith and her fiancé had been wearing slippers when he last saw them, but would have changed to something more solid, surely. The soldier had worn boots, or what was left of them. But there were no prints of any kind here;

the ground was too hard. Perhaps at the river's edge . . .

His ears caught the sound of the stream and it was not so loud as when he had brought Edith and Alton here. They could have crossed the bridge, then, if that was what Pennock wanted. Who was Pennock, anyway? What was he up to? He had seemed almost a basket case after his experience at Blackrock.

Yes, the stream was normal. And there was no one on this side of it, so they must have crossed the tree bridge. Peter paused at the top of the descent, trying to see the steeply climbing path on the far side.

Nothing moved there. But then, the trees and bush were so thick he could see only parts of the trail.

He went down the steps swiftly, used to them now and having no pair of strangers to watch out for. And, yes, in the soft reddish earth at the river's edge were telltale prints, most of them smeared into smooth streaks where their makers had slid in the mud, but distinguishable here and there for what they were. Sneakers for Preble and Edith, it seemed. Boots, no doubt army issue, for the third person.

And there was something else. On a thorny wait-a-bit bush just short of the stream, where the macca must have tugged it from Edith's hand or pocket as she stepped forward to start across the bridge, hung a woman's handkerchief, small and white.

Or had she deliberately—perhaps surreptitiously—left it there for him to find?

Disengaging it from the bush's wicked thorns, Peter thrust it into his shirt pocket.

Then at the bridge he tensed himself. For five years the tree here had been as easy for him as walking the Great House veranda. Now, remembering the mist and his paralysis last time, he hung back.

But no green mist attacked him this time. His cautious steps carried him safely across, and through the forest's dark shadows he toiled upward to the intake pool.

Here, yes, he felt something. Something invisible but menacing, that caused him to stand trembling with his gaze fixed on the stream of water arching down from the unexplored gorge above. Something that chilled him with its threat of personal peril.

A presence? His mind was aware of it without even remotely being able to identify it. There seemed to be no mist this time, or if it existed, it was as wraithlike as a vapor rising from the pool itself. But something monstrous here was waiting to pounce. He was sure of it.

Get out of here, Sheldon! his mind silently screamed. Get out!

Only the thought of Edith kept him rooted there, rejecting the warning. Only the certainty that she had come this way and had to be somewhere ahead of him, beyond or above the fall of water, perhaps desperately counting on him to follow and help. Why else would she have left the handkerchief at the river crossing?

But how could she have gone beyond this point? He had tried it with Manny Williams, and there was no way up to the gorge above. Absolutely no way, at least from here.

He stood there scowling at the cascade, numbed by its roar, not knowing what to do.

Then the mist.

As before, it seemed to flow down over the lip of the cascade, transforming the falling water into a thing that resembled a giant, slow-moving, green slug. Terror shattered his resolve as he stood there for a moment staring at it, then not even the thought of the woman from England could hold him. Lurching about, he fled in panic down the track to the tree bridge.

The mist did not follow him. On reaching the bridge, he was able to cross over without stumbling. Slowly his fear subsided. Then as he ran along the track to the Great House, annoyance took its place and anger set in.

There had been time enough for Manny Williams to get here, damn it. Why wasn't he here? Had Coraline failed to deliver the message? Had she delivered the wrong one?

They did that sometimes. You patiently explained the need for something and took time to make sure they understood, then they thought it over and calmly decided you were wrong and they must save you from your folly by doing it their way.

It should not have taken her all this time to reach Grove Path and alert Manny. And not only was he the best mountain man in the district; he was the most loyal of Armadale's workers as well. He should be here by now.

Rounding the last bend of the track, Peter peered down at the house and saw no one—only the empty plantation road winding down through coffee and pine trees to the distant main gate. No pig hunter. Nobody.

"Coraline!" he yelled as he stormed into the house.

Only echoes answered.

"Coraline! Where are you?"

Again only echoes.

He searched the house, though all but certain it was empty. Only because Edith's door was still open did he enter her room and discover on the floor a sheet of scribbled-on paper he must have been too impatient to notice before.

He picked it up.

"Peter," she had written, "something is happening to me. The thing that took possession of my mind on the cliff is doing so again. I am being sent for and must go—can't help myself. Alton is, too, I think. Pennock is part of it. He is not what he seems. Try to follow if—"

Clutching the note, he walked out onto the veranda and looked in desperation down the plantation road again. This time Manny Williams was briskly striding up it. Over one shoulder the old man carried the shotgun he used when hunting wild pigs.

22

"I FOUND THE HANDKERCHIEF HERE," PETER SAID.

Halting at the stream's edge, he indicated the thorny shrub on which, he was now convinced, Edith Craig had deliberately left her handkerchief for him to find.

Manny Williams glanced from the shrub to the tree bridge. "If Pennock was in front, the lady most likely put it here whilst him watching him foot on the bridge." Moving on down to the bridge, he examined the soft earth there. "There was three of them, all right."

With a scowl Peter said, "But if they crossed here, Manny, where could they have been going except to the intake?"

"Nowhere, squire." The pig hunter shook his head. "But let we look anyhow." Crossing the bridge with the same care that marked everything else he did, he waited at the far end for Peter to join him. Then he plodded on up the path to the intake pool.

Remembering his headlong flight from the mind-bending green mist less than an hour before, Peter followed with trepidation. But there was no sign of the mist now as Manny and he stood at the pool's edge, gazing across at the waterfall.

"Did they reach here, Manny?"

The pig hunter lowered his head to peer at the ledge of stone on which they stood. He frowned, but that was to be expected—only rarely did his craggy face wear any other expression. Pacing slowly along the rock, he at last eased himself down on one knee, the shotgun still balanced in his right hand.

"Them was here, squire."

Peter stepped over to him. "How can you tell?"

"Look here at the moss."

Peter knelt beside him to examine the layer of bright green that blanketed most of the stone. It was always damp here, of course; the falling water flung out a spray, and the forest trees conspired to let in precious little sunlight. And, yes, there were marks in the shape of shoe prints where something had pressed the moss down so recently that it had not yet had time to spring up again. Three persons had stood here, it seemed, facing the cascade.

Manny placed his feet in a pair of the prints and looked across the pool. "We did try this before when the water was lower, if you remember," he said. "But me will try again." Handing Peter the shotgun, he stepped into the pool and waded slowly across toward the fall, the water rising to his waist as his feet felt their way carefully along the stony bottom. The pool was over one's head in places, Peter knew from having stepped into a deep spot one day while repairing the intake. But what Manny was doing was safe enough.

Halting just short of the fall of water, the pig hunter turned first to his left, then to his right, while Peter anxiously watched. *Could* there be some way of climbing to the top behind that veil of water? Anything was possible in a place such as this, no?

But, turning at last, Manny shrugged to admit failure, then trudged back through the pool and climbed out. "Me don't understand this," he said, shaking his head.

"You don't understand what?"

"Them was here, and there is no sign to show them returned back. So where them is now?"

"Manny, they got up into the gorge above here. I don't know how, but they must have."

"You say."

"Manny, hear me. When Miss Craig and I stood on the cliff above that gorge, something uncanny happened to us. When I stood here by this pool just a while ago, some god-awful misty thing came down out of that gorge to attack me. Pennock took these two up there into that gorge. I don't know how but, damn it, he must have!"

"It not possible from here," the pig hunter insisted.

"It has to be!"

"Well"—the shrug was eloquent—"if there is some secret way up there, we could be a long time finding it. Better we try to get down into the gorge from above."

"Can that be done? I always thought—"

"Me not saying we can do it, squire. Only that it more likely than from here. So come, huh? We just wasting time standing here talking."

To reach the coffee-field track to the John Crow's Nest it was necessary to go back past the Great House. Manny led the way and set a fast pace. Trotting along after him, Peter felt blessed in having such a man for a companion at such a time. Manny Williams represented the old, almost forgotten St. Alban of hard work, decency, and dignity. The island today was short of such qualities and far too long on politics and violence. Especially violence.

Emmanuel Williams at this moment wore patched, dark gray pants with a piece of rope for a belt, worn-out boots with tire-tread soles, an old, long-sleeved white shirt stained with a colorful assortment of bush saps—and Manny could tell you the source of each stain by its color—and, finally, a battered, gray felt hat without a band. But the same Manny Williams attended church on Sundays looking like the deacon he was, and the old shotgun in his right hand at this moment was "cared" as though for display in a museum.

Thank God he's with me, Peter thought as they arrived at the house.

In the backyard his housekeeper was roasting a breadfruit over charcoal, and the rich, dark smell in the air was like a blessing in its own right. Peter had not talked to her before leaving with Manny for the intake. The pig hunter had come so swiftly in response to his summons that Coraline had trailed far behind. Even then Manny had apologized for being late and explained that Coraline had had to climb to his own hillside coffee field to tell him he was wanted.

Peter halted before the woman now, and she looked up from her squatting position at the fire, waiting for him to speak.

"I'm going to need your help, I think," he said. Briefly he explained to her that in response to Sergeant Wray's phone call to Defence Force headquarters there might be more soldiers arriving, and she was to offer whatever hospitality was requested. "I don't know for sure, of course," he concluded. "They may go to Blackrock some other way. But if they do turn up here, please look after them."

She nodded, seeming a little frightened.

"Manny and I are going to the John Crow's Nest and

try to get down into the gorge,'' he said. ''We think that's where Miss Craig and Mr. Preble may be. If we don't return soon, you'd better send some men to look for us.''

''Yes, suh.''

''If the soldiers do turn up, please talk to the officer in charge. Tell him he ought to question Bronzie Dakin's Gerald about the death of that forestry man. Will you remember that?''

''Him must have to talk to Gerald. Yes, suh.''

Good Lord, Peter thought—I was going to take Gerald to the hospital this morning. Now I don't know what I'm doing or how it will end. ''All right, Coraline. We—''

''Squire,'' Manny Williams interrupted. ''We will need a rope.''

''That's right, we will.''

''A long one.''

''There's one in the storeroom,'' Peter said. ''Hold on while I get it.''

23

THEY STOOD TOGETHER ON THE FRIGHTENING PRECI-
pice called the John Crow's Nest, and Manny Williams
peered at the old juniper leaning out over its brink.
Scowling as usual, he said in a muted growl, "You
remember looking down from that tree, squire?"

"Yes, Manny."

"Me thinking this is the most likely place for us to
go down, but let I look around first."

"Can we get down here, Manny?"

"Maybe—with the rope."

So doubtful was he, the pig hunter used up half an
hour exploring the canyon's rim before deciding the almost sheer wall beneath the leaning juniper was indeed
the best the gorge had to offer. Even then, after he
picked up the coil of sisal rope, he shook his head while
striding across the table of rock to a sturdy young tree
at its inner edge. "This not going be easy," he said as
he finished making one end of the rope fast to the tree.

Back at the cliff's edge he tossed the coil of rope over the brink, then went to the leaning juniper and laid himself against it, peering down. Peter stood watching him. For a suspiciously long moment the old pig hunter was silent. Then he stepped back from the juniper and let his breath out in a noisy gust and shook his head again.

"The rope not long enough, squire."

"What?"

"It short by the length of this table of rock we standing on. Unless me go back to the house for more, we must have to fasten it to this old juniper here."

"Oh God." Peter thought of Edith Craig and what might be happening to her. "Manny, we can't go back. It would take too long!"

"So me think, squire. This old juniper good enough anyway, me think. If we careful." Hurrying back to the younger tree, he untied the rope.

When he had made the rope fast to the juniper, Manny peered down into the gorge again. "But better me do this alone, squire," he said with a frown. "You not used to such things."

"How old are you, Manny?"

"Old? Seventy, maybe, or a little more."

"I'm a little younger. But, anyway, we'd better go down one at a time. If you want to go first, go ahead."

"In a minute, squire."

Manny turned away and strode to a clump of saplings near the cliff's edge. Placing his shotgun on the ground, he took a jackknife from his pocket and stripped off a length of light brown bark. In his gnarled hands the thin, supple bark became a sling for his shotgun. When he turned again to the cliff, the sling was over one shoulder and fastened to his rope belt, holding the gun securely against his back.

With a glance at Peter he lowered himself to a sitting

position on the canyon's rim and took hold of the rope with both hands. His feet groped for the first outcrop. Peter lay belly-down at the edge of the rock and watched, with an apprehensive glance now and then at the old tree to which the rope was fastened. Not forgotten was the time when he, Peter Sheldon, had leaned against that tree and been almost afraid to breathe, lest any sudden movement tear its roots out of the rock and send him plummeting to his death.

Far below, the white water in the canyon's depths looked like a length of white string dropped from above. Sunlight never wholly penetrated this deep rift in the mountainside, he guessed. Not even ordinary daylight could do so with any brilliance.

Slowly, very slowly, the old pig hunter descended into that near darkness. Then his voice came back up, triumphantly shouting that he had reached the bottom.

It was Peter's turn.

Like Manny, he sat on the edge and reached for the rope. Like Manny he swung out into space and struggled to turn himself so he would be facing the canyon wall. He was heavier than the pig hunter, he reminded himself. He must be even more careful not to put the old tree to any sudden test.

The cliff was not less vertical here than elsewhere, he presently decided. What had caught Manny's attention was its comparative irregularity. Other sections had been too sheer. Here, ledges a few inches wide at least appeared to be arranged in a pattern vaguely suggestive of a ladder. When his feet found those, his fear subsided a little. But each time he swung out in space again with his full weight on the rope, the terror returned.

Below, when he found nerve enough to chance a downward glance, the thread of white water appeared to grow more distinct. He was only sixty or seventy feet above it now, he guessed. Manny Williams stood there, gazing up at him.

Fifty feet to go now. Forty. He was almost there, thank God. Suddenly he heard a sound above him and felt himself falling. And heard, from below, a shout from his companion.

"Squire! Watch out!"

Some thirty feet above the canyon floor, he could not swing himself out of danger with the rope; it had gone limp. His only hope was to grab at the cliff wall somehow and hope the thing that was crashing down on him would miss him. He let go the rope and clutched an outcrop of rock. Missed and clawed at another as he slid downward. This time his fingers caught and hung on.

The tree came down past him like some pursuing monster in a nightmare. One whipping branch, like an outflung arm, slashed across his back as it went by. Then he felt himself sliding half-conscious down the last few feet of stone. Felt the upthrust arms of the old pig hunter, Manny Williams, catching him. And heard Manny saying, "Easy now, squire. You is going be all right."

He must have passed out, either from the tree's blow or from fright. The next thing he knew, he was seated on the canyon floor with his back against the wall. Manny Williams gently stroked his face, as if he were a child.

"You is better now, squire?"

Peter turned to look at the tree. It had crashed with its nearest branch tip not four feet from where he sat. Had he not made his move when he sensed his peril, he would have been under it when it landed. "I'm all right, Manny—I think."

"Let we rest a few minutes, then, before we go on."

165

There was a new warmth in the older man's voice. "You a good man, squire."

"We can go now, Manny. We mustn't waste time."

They had been talking loudly because of the muffled roar of the stream. The old-timers of the district called this stream Wild River, Peter remembered. How many could have seen this portion of it, where the water that gave it that name was almost certainly wilder than anywhere else along its course? Reaching for Manny's hand, he pulled himself to his feet.

They should go downstream now, Manny suggested, and look for some sign that the three they sought had come this way. Downstream they went, circling the fallen juniper that had so nearly brought the venture to a sudden end.

It was slow going. The canyon walls were but twenty yards apart here. The river transformed most of that span into a roaring rush of foam over a bed of boulders.

Where, Peter wondered, had the boulders come from? Not from the walls, obviously; those were solid rock. Had the gorge once been a cave, or part of one, and the boulders part of the cave's collapsed roof? According to geologists, that kind of thing had happened many times in this land of caverns and underground rivers.

As they picked their way along, trying to avoid the angrier rapids and deeper pools, Manny Williams never stopped looking for what he called "sign." When asked what kind of sign—"so I can help you, Manny"—he shrugged and said it was not possible to tell a man what to look for.

"If them did come this way, me will know it, squire. People's boots do things to rocks and weeds that water don't do."

But he discovered no sign, and after half an hour they found themselves at a place where the walls of the gorge closed to within ten feet of each other, and the river leaped into space. Gingerly feeling their way out to the funnel through which it leaped, they gazed down on the pool from which Armadale drew its water. The same pool from which, earlier that morning, Manny had peered up at this same cascade and said there was no way to reach the place where they now stood.

With a shake of his head the pig hunter said, "Them never did come this way, squire. Them never could climb up here."

Peering down at the pool, Peter thought of how close they were to the Great House as a John Crow might fly, and how very long it might take them to get there from where they stood. "I agree, Manny. They couldn't have climbed up here. But we can't get down there, either. So how do we get out of here?"

"We must have to go back up the gorge, squire."

"To where we came down? We can't climb that cliff without the rope, man!"

"There must have to be some other place." Manny leaned over the fall's brink for one last look at the pool below, then turned away and began walking upstream. There was nothing for Peter to do but follow. Again thinking of Edith Craig, he did so with a feeling of hopelessness.

Where was Edith? How was he to find her?

The journey upstream was harder. By the time the pig hunter first stopped to rest, Peter was bone weary and soaked with sweat. Shaking his head, he sank onto a streamside boulder and looked up.

Against the strip of blue sky overhead—so far overhead it seemed to be in another world where the ever-present gloom and river roar of this one did not exist—the place where the old juniper tree had leaned out over the brink seemed strangely naked. The cliff wall below it would have posed problems for a lizard.

If the ancient tree had appeared to be a nightmare

monster when it came plummeting past Peter, it was a dead monster now. They went on by it, Manny again feeling his way with extreme care around the more dangerous pools and whitewater runs. Tiring again, Peter had to stop a second time. Again seeking a place to sit, he looked at his companion in disbelief.

"How old did you say you are, Manny?"

"Squire, it not a man's age that count. Not him color, either. Plenty people younger than we not going to be down here doing what we doing this minute. Not for all the money in St. Alban."

It was meant to be a compliment, Peter realized. But the fact that a man in his seventies was still reasonably fresh while Peter Sheldon was close to collapse did not make it seem a valid one. Then he glanced up at the cliff wall they had conquered in descending to the stream and changed his mind. It was a compliment. Not many men of any age would have accepted that challenge.

Why, really, had he done it? He was not one to take crazy risks. Had he allowed Edith Craig to become that important to him despite her being engaged to marry someone else?

Manny, peering upstream, said in a voice just audible above the river's snarl, "Squire, now we must hope the Lord good to we."

Peter was not sure he had heard it right. "What, Manny?"

"Me know the rest of this gully from the top, and me don't recall any place we can climb out without a rope. Let we hope this old man wrong for once."

He peered at Peter, awaiting a reply. On getting none, he turned and continued upstream.

Peter followed in silence. What if the old man was right? he thought. If they had to return to the waterfall that plunged sixty feet to the plantation's intake—if the only way out of this gorge was to ride that savage chute of water down to a shallow pool full of boulders, what would be their chance of getting out alive?

The thought of it made him shiver.

Peering at the canyon walls with the total dedication of a cat watching for lizards, the old pig hunter now continued upstream so slowly that he seemed scarcely to move at all. Behind him, Peter, too, desperately sought a way out of the trap they were in. But the walls were even more vertical here. They were smoother. With every bend of the gorge they were higher.

Peter's faint hope for a miracle gave way to despair. What was this kind of thing called in the old American West? A box canyon? A cul-de-sac? Here it could only be called a grave. A three-sided grave with its open end suspended sixty feet above a drowning pool.

Rounding still another bend, they saw the end of it.

Manny Williams sat on a flat stone at the river's edge and looked at the right-hand wall and shook his head. He looked at the left-hand wall and rubbed his jaw. In front of them the canyon had widened, yes, but into a barrier of stone, unbroken except for a narrow, dark slit that seemed to end a few feet farther in. The stream boiled up from a hole in the canyon floor.

"Lord Jesus, we in trouble," Manny said. Then with a low growl of defiance he pushed himself to his feet. "But, squire, we must go the whole way before we return to we death at the fall of water. You hunting a hog, you must have to follow him track to the end."

Trudging the last few yards of the cul-de-sac, he stopped within reach of the wall and looked first to his left, at the stream rushing up from some underground passage. Then, pushing forward, he put his hands on the sides of the vertical slit in the rock face and leaned forward, trying to see into it.

"Well now, look here, squire!" he called.

Peter splashed forward to his side and peered into the slit with him. "A cave, Manny?"

"It sure do look like one. A passage of some kind, for sure. And it seem wide enough for skinny men like we, anyway. And no water to stop us, you notice. The river come up from the ground there. Squire, let we find out where this go to!"

24

THE DARKNESS WAS FULL OF SMALL SOUNDS, AND THEY had brought no flashlights—a mistake, Peter realized now, but how could he have foreseen a development such as this? Most prominent of the sounds, and most disturbing, was that of flowing water, although, as Manny had pointed out, no water flowed in the narrow passage through which they advanced.

Was there a parallel passage beyond the wall on their right, where the sound seemed to come from? Everything about the place seemed threateningly wet.

Water dripped from the ceiling here. Peter could hear the drops striking the floor and feel them on his head. Other sounds pushing back the silence were those made by Manny and himself as they blundered forward, slipping on the rough floor, careening into the walls, and by their increasingly heavy breathing as forward progress became more uphill and difficult.

Now and then Manny's voice drifted back, and the

sound was comforting even though the tunnel distorted it. "Watch you step here, squire. The floor truly rough rough rough rough. . . ." Or, "It truly wet here, squire. Be careful you don't fall all all all all. . . ."

Time passed. Surely twenty minutes. Then Peter saw a crooked slit of daylight ahead, with his companion's moving figure outlined against it.

The pig hunter stopped, and Peter caught up to him. "It seem we will get through, squire, if that opening is big enough to let we out," Manny said with a grin in his voice.

But as they groped toward the light, the ceiling sloped downward and the walls closed in. Still more than fifty feet from their goal, Manny had to drop to hands and knees, then flatten himself and proceed on his belly. With the shotgun now thrust ahead in one hand, he then seemed to be trapped by the narrowness of the passage, but after a prolonged struggle managed to squirm on through.

From the sliver of daylight his voice came back in a yell of triumph. "Me is out, squire! Come!"

Flattening himself to begin the crawl, Peter was apprehensive. He was larger than Manny; he weighed more. On reaching the place where his companion had become wedged, he felt the walls squeezing his shoulders. The more he squirmed, the more the grip tightened. He struggled until his feet and knees ached from pushing, his fingers bled from clawing the stone, his shoulders felt black and blue.

"Manny." He knew he was trapped. Knew he would die here. "I can't get through."

"Squire, just hold still a minute. Me soon return." The pig hunter disappeared from the opening, leaving Peter to lie there staring helplessly at a tantalizing glitter of sunlight that was so close, yet out of reach.

In a few minutes Manny was back. Headfirst he came

wriggling into the tunnel, holding not the shotgun now but a three-foot length of green sapling an inch or so in diameter. Propelling himself forward like a salamander, he stopped with his face close to Peter's and said quietly, "You not to worry you'self now, squire. Old Manny going get you out of here."

One end of the stick had been stripped of its bark, Peter saw in the dim light from the opening. Manny thrust that end against a wall of the passage and methodically rubbed it back and forth, pushing each forward stroke to the point where the stone held Peter fast. When he was finished, the wall was coated with a layer of slime, as though a giant slug had slithered over it.

After performing the same operation on the other wall, the pig hunter studied his handiwork. "All right," he said, and wriggled backward. Discarding the length of sapling, he positioned himself to grip Peter's wrists.

"You ready, squire?"

"What must I do?"

"Me going pull. You push with both you foot. The stick will do the rest."

"What?"

"Never mind, squire. Just push."

But it was not Peter's boots that provided the forward motion. They could find no secure hold on the wet floor. What freed him from the tunnel's grasp was the pull of Manny's powerful hands on his wrists and the remarkable new slipperiness of the walls. First his shoulders, then his hips slid past the pressure points, and a few minutes later he was at the end of the passage, with the pig hunter grinning at him as he emerged.

"Thanks, old buddy," Peter said.

"No problem, squire."

"What was that stick you rubbed the walls with?"

"Pudding whisk, squire. People use it for soap sometimes. All the same, we lucky it grow here."

Peter looked around. This was a wild part of the plantation, one he had not been in or even seen before. The river descended into it over a narrow, boulder-strewn bed, through a wilderness of tall trees and massed undergrowth, to disappear underground at the base of a barrier cliff through which Manny and he had just crawled from the gorge.

"Where are we, Manny?" A place as dramatic as this was probably noted on that old map of Armadale.

Manny shrugged. "Me see it from above whilst pig hunting a few times, squire, but don't believe it have any name. Tell the truth, me never have any reason to come down here and never knew the river go underground like this."

"Can we get out?"

"More'n that, squire. If you believe Miss Craig been taken to Blackrock, we can get there quicker from here than the soldiers will."

"I don't understand."

"Look up there." Manny pointed to a ridge gleaming in the late-morning sunlight. "To get there from the house is hard. Is just no track. But we did save miles of walking by coming up the gorge and crawling out through the tunnel here. Now we can reach Blackrock by a shortcut whilst the soldiers must have to go to Morgan Peak and along the ridge."

Still suffering mentally from their experience in the gorge and tunnel, Peter needed time to think about it. Right now, nothing seemed more desirable than a long sleep on the four-poster in his room at the Great House. Then he remembered what Edith had written in the note he had found in her room there.

"Peter, something is happening to me. . . . I am being sent for and must go. . . . Try to follow. . . ."

"All right, Manny," he said. "Lead on."

25

Hour after hour, not knowing where he was, Peter struggled to follow in the steps of the veteran pig hunter.

He should be hungry by now, he supposed, but he was not. When Manny and he did need food, the old pig hunter would know what they could eat and where to find it—trust him for that. As for being thirsty, they had walked in enough water for Peter to feel he would never want a drink again.

These tropical mountains were densely wooded and for the most part without trails. Manny and he had clawed their way up almost vertical slopes by using the dry beds of old watercourses or the wet ones of streams presently flowing. They had slid down into seemingly bottomless gullies by using their boots for brakes and their butts for toboggans. Almost never had they arrived at a point from which they could obtain a clear view of anything. Peter had been forced to rely almost completely on his guide.

Manny Williams employed wild-pig runs for trails, too, and seemed to know where they would lead him. To follow him was to take an advanced course in woodcraft. It was also raw, hard work. By the end of the day Peter was silently screaming for rest.

Manny sat and looked at him. "Last night, squire, Sergeant Wray and the man we trying to find had a moon. We not so blessed tonight."

There had been no clouds in the sky during the late afternoon. Could Manny be wrong for once? But when the moon should have risen, it did not. And the pig hunter had been so certain it would not, he was already sound asleep on a bed of leaves, with his old felt hat folded under his head for a pillow.

With conflicting emotions Peter, too, sought a bed. A moonlit night would have allowed them to keep going, perhaps to find Edith Craig sooner. But he hadn't the pig hunter's endurance and knew he needed sleep.

Resuming the hike at daybreak, they trudged on again through the same killing terrain, and at midday, according to Manny, were at the junction of Blackrock Peak and the ridge. It was here, if the reports of the two rescued scouts and Sergeant Wray were accurate, that first the scouts and then the men of the Defence Force group had encountered some inexplicable peril—some horror that had left the forestry man headless.

But there seemed to be nothing unusual here. Nothing different. Only the same high mountain trees and dense undergrowth, now all too familiar.

Peter sank onto a fallen juniper to rest for a moment, and Manny Williams said, "Is supposed to be that helicopter here somewhere, squire. Suppose you get you breath back whilst me look for it."

"Oh, no you don't," Peter countered quickly. "We stay together, man!"

"You don't trust me, squire?"

"Of course I trust you." Peter rose, wishing he could have rested a few minutes more. "But things have been happening to people here, Manny. Let's not get too far apart."

Half an hour later the pig hunter found his first sign.

To Peter it would have been nothing—merely a cracked green branch on a sapling. He would have guessed that the wind or an animal had split it. But Manny pointed out that the tree was a tough young bulletwood, and there had been no strong winds in the past few days. And the only animal large enough to do such damage would be a wild pig. "Pigs-them don't climb trees, squire."

With his gaze on the ground, Manny plodded on, grunting every now and then to indicate he had found something. The trail led him through a jungle of vine-draped trees to a black rock cliff that remained hidden until he burst through to it. At the base of the cliff he stooped to pick up a piece of a broken pop bottle. It was the neck, and it was black. He held it out to Peter. "You know what this was, squire?"

Peter rubbed a finger over the blackness and found it greasy. "A bottle lamp?"

"Right. But the scouts-them would have flashlights, no? The soldiers-them, too."

"And wouldn't have carried kerosene, Manny."

"True. Me wondering if is a cave here somewhere, squire. Maybe hunters from some other district using it for shelter."

"From some other district, Manny?"

"Nobody from ours don't come this far up, squire. The only time me was ever here before was once when me and young Witford Cushie did track a hurt pig up

177

here.'' Manny shook his head. ''Something queer happen to Witford that day.''

''Queer, Manny?''

''Well, me did leave him to rest a little when him too tired to seek the pig further, and when me return, him did gone. Then when him turn up quite a while later, him was like in a daze. Of course''—Manny shrugged—''him never was too bright anyhow.''

''Is this the boy they call Witless?''

''The same, squire.''

''I see.'' Knowing about the lad—having, in fact, once tried to give him work—Peter dismissed the matter and went on to something he considered more meaningful. A cave, Manny had suggested. A cave here?

Well, why not? There most certainly could be one; these mountains were honeycombed with them. Not all the caverns in St. Alban had been explored, either. According to the university's geology department, there were probably some that hadn't even been discovered yet.

The existence of a cave here might explain some of those puzzling reports, Peter thought. What if the scouts had stumbled on one and become lost while investigating it? And after the scouts, the soldiers? It was dangerous to explore a wild cave with only flashlights, and neither the scouts nor the soldiers would have carried anything more suitable.

But there was no time for further speculation; Manny Williams was in motion now along the base of the black cliff. Trailing him, Peter had to step over rocks and rubble that must have fallen from above. Even when close enough to the wall to brush against it, both men were forced to thread through a labyrinth of vines and tree roots.

If a cave did exist here, Peter thought, it must be one

of those least likely to be stumbled on, for the cliff face was almost wholly curtained.

Suddenly Manny Williams held up a hand and halted.

Just ahead was an opening in the base of the cliff.

No more than a yard wide and four feet high, the aperture was still large enough for a man to crawl into. Out of it came a sighing sound and a current of air colder than the midday heat of the forest.

"Seem like we has found something, squire," the pig hunter said. His voice was low, with a note of apprehension. "Me should go in alone, me think." Reaching to his shoulder, he unslung the shotgun and grasped it in both hands. "Is only me have one of these."

"We stay together, Manny. No argument. But we won't be able to see in there."

"Well, now—"

"We need a light. You're a woodsman. Isn't there some tree or bush we can use for torches?"

Manny looked thoughtful. "Well—is one or two, if them grow here. You wait for me, squire."

He and the shotgun disappeared.

Time crawled while Peter angrily asked himself why he hadn't had the sense to bring flashlights. But, of course, neither Manny nor he had anticipated spending a night or nights in the mountains. Then, while leaning against the cave entrance—if it was a cave entrance— he heard approaching footsteps and tensed to defend himself.

It was only Manny Williams returning with a fistful of slender, pale brown sticks.

"Bamboo, Manny?"

"If it dead. And is almost always some dead where you find a live root, squire."

"But for torches?" Peter had expected something like pine.

"It easy to burn and give a good light. Let we use two of these, eh?" Thrusting the rest into his rope belt, Manny held two close to the cliff for shelter while Peter struck a match.

The sticks caught quickly enough, and when Peter crawled after his companion into the cave, he discovered Manny was right about the light they provided, too. It was even adequate when the tunnel widened some hundred feet in and they were able to stand up and walk abreast under a ceiling ten feet high.

Had the missing scouts stumbled on this place? Had the soldiers found it and asked themselves that very question, and then become lost, themselves, while seeking an answer to it? With every forward step, Peter became more convinced that that was what had happened.

It wouldn't explain the disappearance of Edith Craig, of course, or the note she had left saying she was being sent for. How could she and the other two have reached here from the intake pool? How could she be here now?

But the answer to that might well be here, too, Peter decided.

Then, when they had advanced through the tunnel for five minutes or so, a warning hiss from the pig hunter stopped him in his tracks.

He saw Manny snuff his torch out against the passage wall. He put his own out. For a few seconds the blackness that filled the tunnel was frighteningly solid. Then, to his surprise, a faint green glow became visible ahead as his eyes adjusted.

He felt he should be very careful now to make no noise. "What is it, Manny?" he asked in a whisper.

"That a strange kind of light, squire. Let I find out what go on there."

So silently that he might have been a mere wraith against the green glow he was investigating, Manny went on down the passage. Peter stood without moving, hearing the pounding of his own heart as he waited. Then, just as silently, the pig hunter ghosted back to him.

"Squire," he said in a hoarse whisper, with his mouth close to Peter's ear, "the light is in a big room down there. Me don't see what making it; it just seem to be there. But in the middle of the room is a man on a cross, like our Lord when them crucify Him, only this man naked." Moving back a step, he peered wide-eyed at Peter's face. "What you think we must do?"

"A man on a cross?"

"Yes, squire. A cross made of two pine tree, with a base to hold it up. Him tied on it, not nailed like Jesus. Him alive, too, for him struggle and make moanings."

The Devil's Pit, Peter thought. Or was something going on here that used the legend of the Devil's Pit as part of some hellish ritual?

26

Soundlessly they stole through the passage, Manny Williams holding his weapon ready for action. The green glow puzzled Peter. No power plant that he knew anything about could be providing a light so unnatural. It seemed to be alive, not the product of a machine.

Was it really pulsing with some mysterious power, or was his imagination tricking him? Just as the mist earlier had caused him to do weird things—to shut off the gas in the Armadale kitchen and go after Bronzie Dakin's Gerald with a gun, for instance—this green glow was having an effect on him, he realized with alarm. It was making him feel stupid, as though he were drugged or drunk. He stumbled. Manny reached out to steady him.

Peter froze. There was a sound in the tunnel now. It must be the moaning Manny had mentioned. Just ahead, where the glow seemed to become a more intense shade of green, must be the entrance to the room the pig hunter had spoken of.

As Manny inched forward again, Peter followed closely with a hand on the man's right shoulder, and could feel him trembling. And why not? This was not a situation in which a man like Manny Williams could be expected to display his usual composure. A mysterious underworld in a place rumored to be an abode of the devil? An unearthly light? A man crucified, perhaps in some grisly reenactment of the death of Christ?

Manny must be badly frightened.

He, Peter Sheldon, certainly was. If his heart drummed any louder, someone was likely to hear it.

Suddenly the tunnel opened up before them and he found himself staring into a room as large as a country church, with a ceiling as high as the usual church roof. But there was nothing of a religious nature in it—unless the presence of the man on the cross could be considered such through association.

The man was naked, as Manny had said. He was black. He appeared to be fairly young, perhaps in his twenties. The cross on which he hung consisted of two young pine-tree trunks held upright on a crude stand. Near it stood another crude piece of carpentry: a table some six feet long, with a top fashioned of saplings laid crosswise.

Because of the way it was constructed, the table looked like a xylophone, Peter thought, and he found himself wondering if someone would come and play it while the crucified man died. A kind of devil's requiem, perhaps. When three other men suddenly appeared from the far side of the chamber, this fanciful notion seemed actually to make some sense.

Two of these were naked also. The third wore the dark brown uniform of a scout. On the table he placed an iron rod four feet long, a bundle of sticks, and what appeared to be a long leather thong with a wooden handle. A man in his late thirties or early forties, he was at tall as Peter and at least ten pounds heavier, with a handsome, bearded, medium brown face.

Linford Grant, Peter thought. The leader of the scout group that disappeared. The one who did most of the talking when they were asking permission to go up through the plantation. But with that strange green glow causing distortions and perhaps affecting his judgment, he could not be certain.

In any case, the man was apparently in charge here. The naked two who had entered with him now stood motionless by the table, gazing at him in silence as though waiting to be told what to do.

"You," said Grant, if it was Grant. "Make a fire on the floor. Heat the rod."

The one spoken to took the sticks from the table and carried them to a spot only a few feet from the cross. Kneeling, he arranged them and put a match to them without even glancing up at the man being tortured.

The latter had stopped moaning and was gazing at the fire builder as though mesmerized by fear.

Grant turned to the second man. "You will use the whip. And I warn you, use it the way you have been shown or you will take your friend's place on the receiving end of it!"

Peter glanced at Manny Williams. What was happening before their eyes in this underground room with its eerie light was having its effect on the pig hunter. His tight-pressed lips quivered. The hands clutching the shotgun seemed to be all knuckles. The taut look on his face said he was about to do something reckless.

Peter touched him and warned in a whisper, "Careful, man."

Manny's voice was a low growl. "Mr. Peter, them going kill that man!"

Peter peered again into the green glare that seemed so hideously alive here. The man who resembled the scout leader stood with his arms folded, watching the one he had told to use the whip. That one advanced toward the figure on the cross. There was a weapon, Peter noticed—a handgun of some sort—in a holster at Grant's hip.

"Have you changed your mind, soldier?" Grant asked the intended victim.

No answer.

"You can save your foolish life if you want to, you know. All you need do is prove you can be one of us, the way these other two have. Are you better than they?"

The man on the cross raised his head very slowly, as though it had become almost too heavy to be lifted. When his gaze finally focused on his tormentor, he said in a rasping voice, "It too late, damn you, Grant."

"Perhaps not." The scout leader shrugged. "Don't you owe yourself the benefit of the doubt?"

"Me say it too late. Me dead already."

"You are still able to talk, soldier."

No answer.

"He will whip you worse than before, you know, if you persist in refusing to join us. He will whip you until there is very little skin left on your body, I promise you. Then your other friend here will take the iron rod from the fire and blind you with it." Grant spoke as calmly as though he were addressing students in a classroom. As though, Peter suddenly thought, he had been doing this for a long time and was perhaps even bored by it. But the evenness of his voice did not detract from the horror of what was happening.

Getting no answer from the man on the cross, the scout leader motioned to the one with the whip. That one obediently took a step forward and drew his right arm back. His shoulder muscles rippled. The leather thong whistled as it flashed forward to its target. Wrapping itself around the belly of its victim, it wrung a groan from his lips.

"There is still time to change your mind, soldier," Grant said. "You have a wife and children, don't you?"

"It because me have them me not serving you," the victim mumbled. "We is church people, damn you!"

"Very well, then." Grant turned to peer at the man kneeling by the fire, which now blazed brightly. The smell of it told Peter the sticks were pine, which would soon turn the iron bar crimson.

God in heaven, no! he thought.

The whip whistled again, this time opening a line of pink across the victim's dark hips, barely missing his genitals. Again he groaned. The pink deepened to red as blood oozed out.

The next cry was Peter's, as he snatched the shotgun from Manny Williams and lurched forward. "No!" he yelled. "Stop it!" But he took only four steps before stumbling to a halt.

The green light had been waiting, it seemed, just as the green mist had before. He felt as though he had lurched into an invisible web, soft enough to let him struggle but too thick to be bored through. It held him squirming like a trapped insect, while an unseen giant spider swiftly spun more strands to hold him fast.

"Manny!" he sobbed. "Help me!"

The shotgun fell from his grasp and he followed it to the floor. Then the room with its tableau of torture became merely a sea of green in which he knew he was drowning, and the voice of the man in the brown scout uniform said calmly, "So at last you have found us, have you, Mr. Sheldon? Welcome, friend, to the Devil's Pit."

27

For three days he had been a prisoner.

The watch on his wrist told him that. It was one of those that told the date as well as the time. Without it he would not have been able to keep track of the passing hours, for his prison cell was illuminated by the same green glow he had seen in the torture room. In fact, most of the cavern appeared to be so lighted, and by now he must have seen nearly all of it. Enough, at least, to know it must be one of the largest caves in the island.

When his captors were not walking him about, one end of a chain only three feet long encircled his left leg above the ankle. The other end was attached to a rusty iron ring in the wall of his cell.

"With you, Sheldon, we are in no great hurry," the man in the scout uniform had said. "We think you are worth a prolonged effort."

"What is that supposed to mean?"

"Well, now, in a way it's a confession of my personal

inadequacy. You see, when I first met you at Armadale, I scarcely gave you a second thought. I asked one of my scouts about you—his mother had worked at the Great House under a former owner—but he knew almost nothing. Then Georgie Dakin and another lad volunteered information that made me change my mind.''

"What information?"

"That you are much admired in the Armadale district. That almost all the people employed by you are fond of you. In short, that I could use you."

This conversation had taken place soon after Peter's blackout in the room of the cross and his return to consciousness in his prison cell. The scout leader had been standing over him when he opened his eyes.

"If you thought you could use me, why did you try to destroy me?" Peter said.

"Ah—you mean at the John Crow's Nest?"

"That was one time."

"A mistake," Linford Grant said with a shrug. "When you—or rather the woman with you—picked up that little map I had drawn to show the boys where we were going, I was afraid it might lead to trouble for me."

"Because the map stopped here at Blackrock?"

"Which wasn't very bright of me, was it? But I was in a hurry and told them that when we reached here, the route to the north coast would be clear to them. I should have realized, of course, that anyone finding my sketch after we disappeared might think . . ." He shrugged. "So when it was picked up and I did realize the danger, I had to destroy it."

Incredulous, Peter returned the man's gaze. "You mean you saw us looking at that map and were able to make it burn?"

"You have much to learn about me, Mr. Sheldon. We who serve Lucifer are not without certain abilities."

There had been other conversations, interspersed with walks through the cavern. On most of the walks Grant had been his guide, wearing the holstered handgun and casually carrying a second weapon. Peter had seen a photo of such a weapon in the island's leading newspaper, after police in the capital had shot dead one of two gunmen who attacked them. Taken from the dead man, the gun was apparently the first of its kind to fall into police hands, and the photo caption had described it as a submachine gun only nineteen inches long, yet capable of firing thirty rounds of .30-caliber ammunition. Called an M-1 Enforcer, it was made somewhere in Florida. Grant carried it, Peter supposed, to discourage any panic-inspired attempt on his part to escape.

On a few occasions the task of walking him about had been delegated to others, one of them a soldier from Sergeant Wray's group. All were naked—as, it seemed, were all the inhabitants of this sinister underworld except Grant and himself.

By his guides he had been led along tunnels of green light to rooms wherein he was made to watch things happening. What Manny and he had witnessed in the first torture chamber was no special event in this den of horrors, he knew now. There were many ways of inflicting pain.

"Who are you, Grant?" he had demanded on one occasion after the leader returned him to his cell. Seated on the floor, with his leg again chained, he looked up at his captor and prayed for some shred of information that would help him.

Grant smiled down at him. "One of the chosen ones, friend. But still only one of many."

"Chosen by whom?"

The heavy shoulders moved in a shrug. "Your Bible refers to him as Satan. Or the devil."

189

"You're a servant of Satan?" The man was mad, of course. But perhaps by humoring him . . .

"Let's say I am a colleague who is given certain tasks to perform, Sheldon, as are many others throughout the world. Or even, I suspect, throughout the universe. This is war, Sheldon. It may be the final confrontation. The Armageddon your Bible talks about."

"How long have you been doing this?"

"I was selected when I chanced upon this place several years ago."

"As a scout?"

"No, not as a scout. I was not a scout then. There were three of us, three adventurous sons of the St. Alban elite, if you will, and we were on a wild-pig hunt. Not for food, you understand. Purely for the pleasure of it. And I became separated from the others—not by accident, I know now—and was guided to the cave here."

"Guided by whom?" Peter demanded, more to keep him talking than with any hope of being given an intelligent reply. That was the way to deal with insane people, wasn't it? Make believe you thought them sane?

Grant's gesture this time was not a shrug but a lifting of his hands, palms upward. "By *whom*, you say. You see, friend, you persist in thinking of a person. I have never met any such person. It was a mind that reached out to me. The contact has always been mental."

"All right. But how?"

"The same way my mind nearly caused your destruction at the John Crow's Nest and later instructed you to burn the Great House. The latter was stupid of me, of course. But, as I've explained, I was not then aware how valuable you could be to us."

"The Great House." Peter frowned. "How did you know about the gas line in the kitchen?"

"I've told you. The mother of one of my scouts used to work there. Her son knew the house well."

"So you picked his brain."

"I asked questions."

"If you wanted me to burn down the Great House, why didn't you have me splash some kerosene around and strike a match, for God's sake?"

"My powers are limited, Sheldon. You, too, have a mind, you know—or you had—and at that time it might have alerted you against any instructions so obvious. I had to take that into account."

A mind of his own? That, Peter thought, might explain why the man on the cross had been able to say no despite being tortured. And why others were being put through various degrees of torment. But, obviously, there came a time when this disciple of Satan felt he was more firmly in control of his victims' minds. Following the incident with the gas line, he hadn't seen a need to be devious in instructing Peter Sheldon to commit murder, had he?

"You say there are others like you, Grant?"

"Oh, many."

"Where?"

A smile of satisfaction flickered across the man's face. Perhaps even one of triumph. "Wherever what the uninitiated call 'terrorism' is becoming a way of life, friend. Here in little St. Alban we haven't machine-gunned an airport yet, of course. Or bombed churches. Or thrown grenades into crowded markets. Or murdered an Olympic team. Or seized an embassy and taken its people hostage. We're young yet. We don't send our soldiers after protesting college students and slice the girls' breasts off with machetes, as was done in Uganda, nor do we yet execute political prisoners by bashing their skulls in with iron bars." Grant chuckled. Describing atrocities obviously gave him intense pleasure.

"That bus that went off the road when it was bringing a church group out to Armadale," Peter said. "You were responsible for that?"

"Of course, Sheldon."

"Then the *Post* columnist is right about what's happening in St. Alban. What he calls the increase in violence. The senseless brutality of it."

"The *Post* columnist? Ah, yes, we have plans for him."

"What about Private Pennock. Is he one of you or did you just get to his mind when he was weakened by his ordeal?"

"He has been one of us for a year or so, Mr. Sheldon. I recruited him when he and his older brother came up here on a holiday hiking trip. The brother refused to cooperate, I regret to say, and died here in one of our persuasion rooms."

"You bastard," Peter said.

Grant chuckled again. "You understand, of course, that this unit of Lucifer's organization was here before I was placed in command of it," he continued. "But before me, the ones selected to be in charge were incompetent. About all they accomplished was the creation of a Devil's Pit legend when they caused a few persons to disappear."

Stepping to the wall, he idly examined the iron ring to which Peter's ankle chain was fastened. "Still," he went on with another of his shrugs, "we are not doing too badly now, I would say. We're improving."

Peter had to suppress a surge of revulsion as the man turned and smiled at him. "But why?" he demanded hoarsely.

"I told you, this is war. The ultimate struggle. And you will soon be in the front line of it."

"Not if I can help myself, damn you. Where is Miss Craig?"

"Who?"

"Edith Craig! The woman you lured away from the Great House. Don't tell me you don't know where she is. You've just admitted you sent Pennock back with Sergeant Wray to bring her here!"

But the man in the brown uniform had decided to answer no more questions, it seemed. "You know," he said, peering down at Peter, "winning you over is going to be an interesting diversion, I think. And when I've enlisted you, we should be quite a team. Think what we can do with an army of your uneducated plantation workers." Again the smile Peter had learned to loathe. "Ignorant people are our brightest prospects everywhere, Sheldon. Lucifer thrives on ignorance. I'm sure you appreciate that."

The man was totally mad, Peter told himself on being left alone—except that on several unforgettable occasions he had indeed displayed dark powers. But even if Grant were insane, there was no comfort in the thought. Escape still seemed impossible.

They had fed him since his capture, but not well. Twice a day he was given a chunk of hard-dough bread and a battered aluminum bowl half-full of lukewarm gruel or watery soup. At times the soup contained a few small freshwater crayfish, probably caught in some nearby mountain stream, or bits of dark red meat that appeared to be wild pig. He was hungry now, though at first the meagerness of the rations had not seemed to matter. Fear evidently had a way of dulling one's appetite.

For the rest, it was simply a situation to be endured while he waited for whatever might happen next, though the agony of not knowing what had happened to Edith Craig was always with him. He had been given a bucket to use for a toilet, and kept it as far away from him as the length of the chain allowed. The smell was annoying but endurable. Every now and then one of the naked people came for the container and brought it back empty.

Where, he wondered, was the old pig hunter, Manny Williams? He had not seen Manny since they were seized.

Other questions hammered at his mind while he sat there in the green glow hour after hour, his back against the cold stone wall, contemplating some of the things the scout leader had said to him. What must the plantation workers and Miss Coraline be thinking of his disappearance, not to mention the disappearance of the new owner and her fiancé? What must Bronzie Dakin be thinking? He had promised to take her boy to the hospital, and she knew him to be a man who kept his word.

"I have something interesting to show you," Linford Grant said on his next visit.

Peter had been dozing and had opened his eyes on hearing the footfalls approach his cell room. He sat up now. For the first time, Grant was not in his scout uniform. Perhaps it was being washed for him—certainly the devil's advocate would not do his own laundry. This time he wore a khaki shirt and pants probably stripped from a captured soldier.

He really was a well-built man, Peter thought. In a one-on-one encounter Peter Sheldon would probably come out second best. But the scout leader had not come to provoke a fight, and in any case was again armed with an M-1 Enforcer.

"Come," Grant ordered, releasing Peter's leg iron. "I've decided to let you watch a former worker of yours in training."

Peter rose stiffly from the floor. A former worker? Georgie Dakin came to mind but had to be dismissed when he remembered that Georgie, through his twin brother Gerald, had already reported an act of ghastly violence and must therefore be already "trained." Dear God, had they won Manny Williams over? That deacon of the church and rock-solid man of God? The prospect filled him with dread as he trudged out of the chamber ahead of his captor.

The passage down which he was guided this time was one of the longest he had traversed—wide enough, too, for Linford Grant to have walked beside him had Grant wished to. The man seemed content, however, to stay behind and voice directions. "Turn left at the fork ahead, Sheldon." "Keep to the right at the next junction, Sheldon."

The so-called Devil's Pit must indeed be one of the island's largest caverns, Peter decided. The largest he had been in before was an underworld called Glowrie Cave in the parish of Dorchester, a river cave some five miles long with passages on several levels and a number of "ducks" where one had to crawl under long stretches of low ceilings.

But this cave was not dark, as Glowrie had been. That eerie green glow was as omnipresent as the air itself, and neither flashlights nor torches were necessary. As he proceeded quietly along one of the easier tunnels, where the floor was level enough to require no really strenuous effort, he said experimentally to the man at his back, "Where does this light come from, Grant?"

"From him, I suppose. A product of his will. It was here when he brought me here."

"You keep saying 'he' but insist you're serving a mind, not a person. Others have had that notion, you know—that all of us and the world we live in are merely an idea of some great mind."

"So I've read."

"You believe it?"

"I have not yet been instructed on that point. But it occurs to me that if our world is merely a thought, the universe itself may be the same."

"God's thought," Peter said.

"You say. And who knows—maybe it was in the beginning. But whose mind will control it in the end? Take the passage on your left here."

Peter did so, and after only a brief stretch of new tunnel found himself in yet another torture chamber. Or training room, as Grant called them.

"Stand against the wall, please, and observe." His captor motioned with the rifle. "I've brought you here because I want you to see how well your friend has responded to instruction. Also because I plan to begin your own instruction tomorrow, and this should persuade you not to be foolishly stubborn."

The room was a duplicate, though smaller, of the one in which Peter had been captured, containing the same kind of cross and table. On the table lay another of the automatic rifles. Within reach of it stood a man Peter thought he had seen before—perhaps one of the missing soldiers.

On the cross was a naked figure he recognized without question—one of Grant's own scout group, a youth no more than fifteen or sixteen years old. He had had a camera, Peter recalled, and had promised to bring back a picture of the Devil's Pit if they found the place.

There was no fire in this chamber, thank God. But there was a whip, in the hands of a naked man who stood before the cross, awaiting the command to use it.

"Manny," Peter said. "Don't do it."

The pig hunter turned slowly toward the sound of his voice and looked at him. Simply looked, without comment. Then without a word he turned back again.

"Please, Manny. For God's sake," Peter begged. "Don't do it. He's just a boy!"

"One of my scouts," Grant supplied without emotion. "They have surprised me a little. Two have been real problems."

Peter said dully, "This one and who? Georgie Dakin?"

"No, not Georgie. Hunger and cold soon put an end to his scruples."

Even as he numbly watched Manny Williams, Peter recalled what Georgie Dakin's twin brother had said about being desperately hungry in a cold prison that terrified him. "So you starved the boy into submission," he said bitterly.

Grant shrugged. "Hunger is a most effective weapon, friend. Keep that in mind." His gaze shifted bleakly to Manny. "You with the whip—you may begin now."

"Manny, no!" Peter cried out again.

This time the pig hunter did not even turn toward his voice. On the cross the young scout shut his eyes and voiced a low whimper in anticipation of pain. The whip flicked forward and stroked his waist.

He cried out. But Grant, intently watching every move, was not satisfied.

"I think you failed to give that your best effort, Williams," he coldly accused.

Manny would not look at him. "No, suh. Me hit him hard."

"Show me again."

The pig hunter braced himself. The whip straightened out behind him, then leaped forward again. This time it seared the chest of the bound boy and drew blood.

"Very well," Grant said calmly. "Continue until you are told to stop." To the man at the table he said with a scowl, "I am losing patience with this boy, Coleman. You understand?"

"Yes, sir."

"Convince him quickly."

"Yes, sir."

"Or destroy him. We have better things to do with our time." Grant's rifle nudged Peter again. "Come, Sheldon. You have seen enough of this for my purpose. Now let me show you another phase of our training before I return you to your cell and let you think about it."

Sick at heart, Peter allowed himself one last glance at the man who for so long had been his trusted companion—the man without whose courage and cunning he would not even have found this underground hell.

On heavy feet he turned away.

28

As Peter left the training room, the man at the table glared at Manny Williams and snarled, "You heard our leader! Get on with it now!"

His whip hand dangling, the snake coiled on the floor next to his right foot, Manny turned to face the fellow. "Me arm hurting me." His voice was a whine.

The man reached to the table for his rifle. Holding it in both hands, he halved the distance between himself and the pig hunter. "Is you trying provoke me, man? 'Cause if you is—"

"All right, all right." Manny turned back to the youth on the cross. "Who being trained here, anyway?" he muttered. "Me or him?" It was a question he had asked himself ever since being marched to this chamber at gunpoint and having the whip thrust into his hands.

"Both of you," was the snarled answer. "Now get to work!"

Manny flicked the whip out over the floor to straighten it. Both of them? The system here, insofar as he understood it, was to use the truly stubborn captives as victims. He had been one of those in the beginning, until he figured things out. Those who accepted the ways of evil early were made to work on the stubborn ones until the leader was convinced they enjoyed what they were doing. Then, as the devil's disciples, they were sent out to commit acts of evil elsewhere.

From one of his jailers he had learned, too, what had happened to Witford Cushie the day he and Witford had followed the hurt pig. Discovered resting there near the cave mouth, the lad had been taken inside.

"And what did happen then?"

"Him was rejected."

"Him was what?"

"Rejected. Mr. Grant don't have no use here for people like him, so him was let go."

"But something did done to him mind, no?"

"It was emptied, is all. So him would not remember him was here."

Emptied, Manny thought—and the easy way the fellow said it had made him want to kill the man. Granted, young Witford Cushie had not been too bright to begin with, but the lad could have got by. He could have learned farming or something and had a half-decent life. Now, because these followers of Satan had "emptied his mind," he would forever be just Witless Cushie, the village dummy.

Damn them.

But to the business at hand.

Do me look as if me enjoying this? the pig hunter asked himself. He had better, or his instructor might be annoyed enough to play rough. The fellow was a sullen brute, anyway. In sessions when Manny had been the one on the cross—before he had figured out the system and devised a desperate plan to defeat it—the same man had twice had him whipped unconscious.

As he braced himself to use the whip again, the pig hunter allowed himself a quick glance at the man. The rifle was being held horizontally across the fellow's ribs, not aimed at him. The whip came off the floor and flowed backward a foot above the stone. It hung straight and level in space. At that moment Manny spun on the bare but leather-tough sole of his backward foot and shot the lash at a new target.

He had been forced to use the whip many times since the start of his plan to beat the system. A fast learner at almost anything, he was adept with it now. It whistled straight at the man with the gun and wrapped itself around his ankles.

Manny spun to face away from him. With the snake over his left shoulder and both gnarled hands on its wooden handle, he bent low and lurched forward, jerking the gunman's feet out from under him.

The man went over backward with a howl of rage. The part of him that hit the floor first was the back of his head, and it hit with a sound like that of a slammed-down melon. His yell could not have ended more abruptly if sliced off with a machete.

Manny walked over to him and looked down. He saw the puddle of blood forming under the man's head and was satisfied. Picking up the rifle, he looked at it and said aloud, "Lord Jesus, me don't even know how to use this thing." But he hung on to it all the same as he turned to the youth on the cross.

"Now how we going get you down from there, son?" he said, shaking his head. "Nobody here have no knife."

He scowled at the ropes holding the youth—one at each wrist, a third securing both ankles. Dragging the table over to the cross, he climbed onto it and went to work on the wrists first, while the boy gazed at him in silent amazement.

"Me sorry me hurt you so much," Manny told him. "But me couldn't risk making them suspicious, sonny."

"Yes, sir." The boy's voice was barely audible.

Manny finished freeing the wrists. "Now you feet. Hang on while me untie them. But you know something, boy? Me have no idea how we going find the way out of this place, with so much tunnels. Has you?"

"Is more than one way out, sir."

"Me name Manny. What you mean, is more than one way?"

"Is the way them bring us in from Blackrock," the boy said as Manny finished freeing him and eased him to the floor, "and is a longer way that come out somewhere on the Armadale property. Me hear some of them talking about it."

Manny paused to consider. Precisely where they were at the moment he was not sure, but he had some idea. The part of this twisty underworld that he knew most about lay above them, and their chances of reaching the entrance near Blackrock were nil with people constantly using the corridors. It might be just as hopeless the other way, of course. But he favored trying for Armadale.

"Son, does you know which passage lead to Armadale?"

"Them say is the main one, Manny."

"You can show me?"

"Come."

As they left the training room, Manny glanced again at the man whose gun he carried. The fellow had not moved. With the amount of blood now pooling around his head, it seemed unlikely he would ever move again. Maybe me should make sure him won't, though, Manny thought. But no—if me do that, me no better than him. Anyway, him not likely to trouble we soon.

St. Alban had been such a peaceful place before the violence began, he reflected. Sure, there had been hold-ups in the capital now and then, and a few break-ins and some thieving. Probably any big city was cursed with such problems. But now when a gunman held up a shop and demanded money, you never knew if he would be content just to take the money and run. Today he might shoot the poor shopkeeper dead, along with his wife and kids if they were unlucky enough to be there.

Only a short while ago two such gunmen, perhaps two of those trained here, had held up a young woman who was to have a baby. After taking her money they had slashed her belly open with a knife, thrown the baby into the gutter, then cut the woman's throat and left her dead. The devil's doing, without a doubt. Or Lucifer's, to give the fiend the name favored by Linford Grant.

Manny scowled at the weapon in his hands and wished he knew how to use it. Of course, if he pointed it at someone and pulled the trigger, something most likely would happen. But what then? He had nothing to reload it with, even if he knew how. He wished he had his old shotgun, but he had not seen that since being captured.

"What you name, boy?" he asked as they left the training chamber behind.

"Cornelius Dennis, sir."

"That a mouthful. What them call you?"

"Mostly Cob."

"All right, Cob. You a brave lad to be doing this after you hurt so bad. How you feel?"

"Me body sore, sir."

"Me name Manny," the pig hunter gently reminded him.

The narrow tunnel they had been following joined a wider one now, and Cob halted. "This the main road, me think, Manny. But which way we must go?"

Manny peered right, then left. "Well now, Armadale a long way below here. So let we try go downhill to the left here, huh?"

It was the beginning of a long, long hike.

Though it was steep at times, the passage itself did not trouble Manny. But he feared being followed. Every little while he signaled his companion to stop while he listened for pursuing footsteps. He should have removed the dead man from the training room and hidden the body somewhere, he told himself. Then Grant's people wouldn't have known exactly what happened, and pursuit might have been delayed for a while.

What he liked least about the tunnel was its wetness. This whole underworld must have been a river cave once. Maybe streams still ran through some of its passages. None flowed here, but perhaps after a hard rain one would.

Please God, don't make it rain, he prayed. Anyway, the tunnel was choked with boulders, and where the now-vanished stream had formed pools, Cob and he had to find ways around them because the holes were deep. And all the while the walls dripped, and the rough ceiling kept swooping down to force them to bend low or even at times to go forward on hands and knees.

What if the roof were to come down too far and block their escape entirely?

The rifle was a nuisance. He kept having to shift it from one hand to the other when the passage presented problems. His nakedness bothered him less. As a child in Grove Path he had been given a sore bottom more than once for taking his clothes off and throwing them away, he recalled wryly. Now he was cold but otherwise indifferent.

How did his companion feel about it? Probably the only thing Cob was aware of just now was that he hurt from the whippings. His body was marked by blood that had oozed from his wounds and dried like painted-on stripes.

It was me put some of those there, Manny thought unhappily.

Suddenly the boy halted. They were about six feet apart and had been watching their bare feet as they picked their way down a cluttered slope. "Manny," Cob said in alarm, "me can't see good no more!"

"Huh?"

"Is something wrong with me eyes, Manny! Everything gone misty here!"

Manny peered both ways along the tunnel and saw nothing but the green glow that by now seemed almost normal. To be sure, it was less bright than before, but there was no sign of any mist. "Me no see nothing, Cob."

"Manny, help me!" The youngster's voice was a scream that broke like glass against the walls. "Help me, please! Something calling me to go back and me don't want to be tied to a cross again! Help me, Manny . . . please help me!"

As he cried out, he turned and lurched back up the passage. But before he could take more than a few steps in that deadly direction, Manny Williams rushed across the rocky stream bed and caught him fiercely about the waist.

29

"REMOVE YOUR CLOTHES, PLEASE, SHELDON."

Peter was not startled by the command. Not forever could he have hoped to be the only one in this green hell, other than its director, who was not naked. Rising from his prison floor, he proceeded to obey. Linford Grant had already unlocked his leg iron.

"Where are you taking me? To one of your damned torture rooms?"

"We call them training rooms, Sheldon. And you'll see."

His clothes in a heap on the floor, Peter eyed the weapon in the leader's hand. "How did you come by that thing, Grant?"

"We have no trouble obtaining weapons."

"The marijuana planes?"

Grant's only answer was a brief smile, but Peter was sure he had hit the mark. Planes clandestinely landing on the island's noncommercial airstrips for St. Alban's marijuana brought in all sorts of contraband, he had heard. Was Grant involved in that trade as a means of financing his operation here? The money had to come from somewhere.

"Walk ahead of me," Grant ordered, motioning with the strange-looking weapon toward the corridor. "Turn right."

To the right was away from the training room to which Peter had expected to be taken. Was there something even worse in store for him? He had already made up his mind not to follow Manny Williams's lead if handed a whip and told how to use it. They could put him on a cross, damn them, but he would not torture someone else.

For ten minutes he paced in silence up a slightly up-hill passage, with Grant's boots thudding behind him over the rough stone floor. Then his captor ordered him to turn left, and a short side passage led him to a chamber he had not seen before.

It was a strange room, almost a perfect circle in shape, with walls that rose twenty feet or so to a roof nearly as smooth as its floor. In the center of the floor an iron ring had been set in the stone—an operation that must have required hours of work with a drill of some kind. To the ring was attached a short length of chain terminating in a leg iron like the one he was now so familiar with.

But—and this puzzled him—there was nothing else in the chamber. Nothing at all.

"Walk to the center, Sheldon. Then sit, and close the iron around your ankle."

In his nakedness Peter found the floor unpleasantly cold and damp. "Which ankle?"

Grant briefly smiled again. "You know, I find your sense of humor interesting. Are you really so un-afraid?"

"I can't believe any of this is happening. I expect any minute to wake up and find myself in bed in the Armadale Great House."

Grant stepped forward to make sure the leg iron had locked itself when Peter closed it. "Aren't you forgetting that when you got out of that bed not long ago, you went to the Dakin boy's house with a gun?" Backing away, he leaned against the wall and for some time gazed at Peter in silence.

Not eager to hasten whatever was about to happen, Peter, too, remained silent. Presently he became aware that the green light in this oddly shaped room appeared to be more alive than elsewhere. Even more alive than in the first training chamber, where it had been the cause of his being captured.

In fact, this room was somehow like a monstrous green eye malevolently watching him. Yes, watching him . . . even though he was chained in the center of it.

"Have you guessed where you are, Sheldon?" the director asked.

"If this underworld of yours has a center, I suppose this is it."

"Not bad for one who can't believe any of this is happening. This is the chamber I was brought to."

"What?"

"This is where it all began for me, after I became separated from my companions and found myself selected. He brought me here. Sorry—you dislike that word, don't you? It led me here, then. The mind that took charge of me."

"And then?"

"Now we shall find out if what happened to me will happen to you. I think it might."

"Don't bet on it, Grant. You must have been insane to begin with."

Grant shrugged. "I am in no hurry. You are important to my plans. To his plans. I could use the usual methods on you—we have some you haven't seen yet—but I think if I leave you alone here as I was left . . . Well, we'll see." Walking back to the entrance, he turned there. "After a while, Sheldon, you will feel the presence here."

"You mean I'll be hungry, and this damned floor will get harder and colder."

"Those too. But mainly you will feel *him*. With me it never fails."

"You still come here, you mean?"

"Whenever I am in doubt about something. Because he is here. His power is greatest in this room. And when you leave here, you will be my most valued assistant. Never doubt it." Grant smiled. "I should tell you—if you haven't already figured it out for yourself—that I don't bring every stubborn recruit here to this room, Sheldon. I wouldn't think of bothering him with, say, people like the man you first saw on the cross. Only very special recruits come into this room, believe me. You should consider yourself privileged." Then, turning again, Grant disappeared into the passage, leaving Peter alone.

"So I'm to become a disciple of your Lucifer, am I?" Peter said defiantly to the silence. "Oh, no, you bastard—you're wrong. It isn't going to happen."

But as he sat there naked on the cold stone floor, he again had the terrifying feeling that he was chained in the center of a huge, living eye that was watching his every movement.

30

With the trainer's automatic rifle in his left hand and his right arm around the waist of his naked young companion, Manny Williams swung Cob Dennis around. In the eerie light of the passage, the boy's face looked like a fright mask painted green.

"Help me, Manny!" Cob still sobbed. "Don't let them take me back!"

Manny peered up the tunnel and saw no sign of pursuit, though he guessed it was bound to come. "Let we go on, sonny," he urged fearfully.

But it was not to be that simple. Though the boy obviously did not want to return to his tormentors, he seemed determined to do so. His struggles to escape the pig hunter's grasp increased, and for his age he was stronger than Manny had suspected.

Manny could see a genuine battle developing—one that could use up much precious time. There was but one solution. Lowering the rifle, he made a fist of that hand and drove it against the youth's jaw, silencing still another plea of "Help me!"

Cob went limp in his embrace.

"It seem me can't stop hurting you, sonny," Manny said as he stooped to work the limp form over his right shoulder. "Me truly sorry."

More slowly now because of his burden, he picked his way down the boulder-strewn tunnel again. There was no sign of the mist Cob claimed to have seen. When he stopped to listen—a precaution he thought it wise to take every few minutes—he heard no sound of following footfalls.

The young scout remained unconscious. Seem like me lick him too hard, Manny thought anxiously.

Narrowing now, the tunnel became more difficult. Its ceiling dipped to a mere seven or eight feet. Its walls closed in so much that when a larger-than-usual boulder choked the dry stream bed, squeezing past it was sometimes a bruising struggle. The downward slope, too, had become more acute. With one hand holding the rifle and the other arm encircling Cob's legs, Manny at times had trouble keeping his balance.

He stopped to get his breath. This time his sharp ears caught a sound other than the ever-present drip of the walls. Startled, he turned to look back.

Near the limit of his vision, where the passage disappeared around a bend, human shapes seemed to move through the green glow. It was hard to be sure because the glow itself so frequently appeared to be alive. Lowering himself to one knee, Manny eased his burden to the floor and took the rifle in both hands. His finger curled around the trigger as he waited.

He had confidence in his eyes. If anything really moved up there, he would see it despite the shifting light.

Something did move. He squeezed the trigger and the

M-1 startled him by firing a burst that filled the cavern with thunder. Whatever had moved became still again, though with no outcry that could be heard through the echoes of the burst.

With difficulty in that confined space, Manny lifted Cob to his shoulder and continued his flight.

Lord Jesus, how much longer?

Half an hour must have crawled by before he heard sounds of pursuit again. He had no watch, so could not be sure. This time what he heard were not footfalls but a rumbling sound produced by a dislodged stone. Perhaps he himself had loosened it. Even so, it might not have fallen of its own accord. A pursuer could have moved it while squeezing through a tight spot.

He stopped to look back again but saw nothing. Should he try another squeeze of the trigger? No, he decided, not yet. Stumbling on at a pace he knew was reckless in such a treacherous place, he heard a sound of water.

Water *falling*.

In a moment the sound became a roar and he knew the fall could not be far ahead. It must be a big one, too. Was it thundering into the passage from some high-up opening, to fill the tunnel with water and bar his flight?

He turned again to size up the situation behind him. With the water making so much noise he could hear no footsteps, but the green glow revealed three distinctly separate human shapes hurrying to overtake him.

Once more he lowered young Cob to the floor and squeezed the trigger of his remarkable weapon. And again the sound of the burst filled the cavern, though this time the thunder of the unseen cascade was almost as loud.

One of his pursuers performed a wild, arm-waving dance and disappeared from view among the boulders.

Manny gathered up his burden and hurried on into the ever-more-frightening roar of falling water. Rounding a bend in the tunnel, he saw the cascade crashing down in front of him.

Puzzled, he stopped. It was not in the passage as he had expected. It did not come from any opening high up on either wall. The tunnel apparently ended here, and the fall was outside the exit.

Blocking the exit? Shutting off his escape?

A fall of water that powerful had to block the exit, he decided. If he pushed on and tried to bore through it, it would drown him and the boy he carried.

Unless . . .

This passage came out on the Armadale property, Cob had said. Could this be the place where Edith Craig and her fiancé, along with Grant's man, Pennock, had disappeared? The cascade at the intake pool, viewed from inside the cliff?

He went closer, with a glance to the rear that revealed two human figures still moving down the passage toward him—ghostly green shapes in the ever-present glow. If this was indeed the intake fall, there was a thing he had to know. Just what part of it was he standing behind. If he stepped out near the top, he and Cob would be slammed down into the shallow pool and mangled among the boulders there. But if near the bottom . . .

He pressed close to the curtain of water and could not see what he needed to see. It was a seemingly solid, plunging wall. But, carefully listening, he thought the sound of water crashing into the pool was only a little distance below.

Once more he turned to peer back up the corridor. There was no time to lower his burden and use the gun again. The two pursuing shapes were close now. But he hung on to the rifle as he stepped to the curtain of water, preparing for the worst.

"Lord Jesus, have mercy," he prayed aloud.

With the spray from the cascade soaking him, he halted. To his astonishment, the wall on his left curved to reveal a vertical slit of daylight between the cliff and the cascade. A way out?

With the boy still draped over his right shoulder, Manny pressed his left side against the wall and squeezed along it. He reached the crack of light. "Lord Jesus!" he murmured, this time in a voice husky with gratitude as he looked down.

The surface of the pool was so close it lapped the ledge he stood on. Now he knew where those three had vanished to when their trail seemed to end at the pool. But unless a man knew this opening existed, he was not going to notice it from the pool. Not ever. Even peering in behind the waterfall here, with the light blocked by the cascade itself, he would have to think the cavern entrance was only a dark stain on the cliff face.

And what if he, Manny Williams, had reached here when it was night outside, and no daylight to show him there was a way out? What then?

Easing himself into the pool, which was only a little more than waist-deep here, Manny avoided the holes he knew about while wading to the opposite side. There he laid his burden down still another time and knelt with the rifle, aiming at the edge of the fall where he would first see his pursuers if they followed.

Would the weapon fire again? It was wet now, and he had no idea. But if those two meant to follow him any farther, they had better think twice about the chance they were taking.

He waited. No one appeared. The boy beside him moaned softly and struggled to sit up.

"So you coming back to give me an ease, huh?" the

pig hunter gently chided. "You suppose you can walk now, man?"

After being helped to his feet and swaying a moment, Cob succeeded in steadying himself. "What happen, Manny?"

"Some other time. Right now we in a hurry."

Cob looked around, bewildered. "Where we is?"

"Where you did say we would be. Armadale. But is not here at the pool we going to find what me want, so come." A final glance at the waterfall satisfied the pig hunter that their pursuers had stopped in the cavern. "Come, sonny," he said again, gently, and led his young companion down the streamside path to the tree bridge. The time, he guessed, was about seven o'clock in the morning. The day was cloudy, with no sunlight, but he was an old hand at telling time without a watch. After so long in the green twilight of the Devil's Pit, he could not say what day it was, though.

When they reached the Great House a short time later, Peter Sheldon's housekeeper came rushing across the yard behind a stream of shouted questions. Even before Manny held up a hand to silence her, she froze in her tracks to stare at them, shocked by their nakedness.

"Is no time to make you understand, Coraline," Manny said. "Where Mother Jarrett is? You know?"

Still wide-eyed, the housekeeper said faintly, "She at Bronzie Dakin's yet."

"Thank the Lord. We not fit to walk to Pipers now. But we need something to cover us. You can find pants?"

"Me think so—yes. But where Mr. Peter is, Manny? What happen to Miss Craig?"

"We got no time for talk, me tell you," Manny insisted. "Is nothing you can do for them, anyhow. Fetch the pants-them, please."

Totally bewildered, the woman hurried back to the

house, to return in a few minutes with slacks from Peter's clothes closet. Manny and Cob drew them on. Then Manny reached for the youth's hand again.

"Come, Cob," he said. "We going to find Mother and get you healed. Quick, too, because me, Manny Williams, must have to go back to that place in a hurry and get Mr. Peter and them other two out of there."

31

LINFORD GRANT HAD NOT LIED. IN THIS ROUND CHAMBER where the green glow was so bright and alive, Peter felt a presence.

Not a physical presence. Except for himself the room was empty, and he entertained no notion that some invisible being had come into it to torment him. The intrusion was solely in his mind.

He still wore his watch. It had not been taken from him when he removed his clothes. For more than five hours now it had marked the time for him while he sat naked on the floor in the center of this malevolent green eye, struggling to keep his sanity. The sluggish passing of the hours was a form of torture in itself.

No, there was no one in the room with him. There was only that pulsing green glow. He was sure of it. Yet his mind was being assaulted.

"Peter Sheldon, are you hearing me?" It was not a voice, but he was aware of it. Had been for hours. To keep himself or his mind from responding, he gripped his upthrust knees so fiercely that his fingers slowed the flow of blood to his legs and his feet seemed encased in ice.

He had tried other defenses, too. Had commanded his mind to concentrate on things beyond the reach of this alien presence that seemed so insolently confident of being able to enslave him.

First, his family. By squeezing his eyes shut and thinking about the pictures in his room at the Great House, he had been able for a time to create a mental barrier the voice could not penetrate. Tenaciously he clung to a vision of his red-haired father riding a favorite roan across a great sunlit sea of grass on the Florida cattle ranch where he, Peter, had grown up.

Then when that picture began to fade, he switched to one of his mother in the ranch-house kitchen, his mind cataloging all her familiar movements as she moved from stove to sink to counter, preparing a meal. Never demanding any special reward for her love and loyalty, she had always been there when needed and was there now when he so desperately needed a mental picture of her.

When his grip on that memory began to weaken, he put himself at the table with his parents and sister Laura, who even now still called him "Petey" in her letters, enjoying the meal his mother had just prepared.

Oh God, if I could only be there, he thought, then forced his mind to concentrate on precisely how, on his last trip home, he had reached there.

From St. Alban City he had flown to Miami on Eastern, after a trip to the capital the week before to buy his ticket and make a reservation. For some reason, forgotten now, his father had not been able to drive to Miami to meet him, so he had taken an airport taxi to the Greyhound Bus terminal and fretfully waited two hours for the right bus. Then the long ride north.

To block out the voice that kept saying "Peter Sheldon, are you hearing me?" he gripped his knees harder now and rode the bus a second time, reaching for details of what must actually have been a journey filled with boredom and impatience.

Again he saw the acres of sugarcane, with darkskinned West Indian workers harvesting the crop, as the bus neared Lake Okeechobee. Again the lakeshore country towns of Clewiston and Moore Haven were half-asleep in the heat, and again the ride north along the edge of the huge lake was frustrating because Okeechobee itself was almost everywhere hidden by dikes.

Think of the citrus now, he silently screamed at himself as the journey began to slip away from him, leaving him chained again in the center of the great green eye, vulnerable to the insidious persistence of the voice. The citrus, man!

So his mind fastened on the acres and acres of orange and grapefruit trees in that part of the state—how green they were, how the sweet scent of them filled the air when they were white with blossoms. In Lake Placid he climbed the observation tower to gaze in wonder at a dark green sea of them so vast he could not discover its shores. But the image receded like the others, leaving him alone in the eye again, and he frantically sought an anchor with more holding power.

Edith. Edith Craig.

The power of his mind to conjure up her face startled him. He was sure he could not have described her in that detail, yet he saw every separate feature—the wideset eyes, the soft and sensuous lips, the golden brown hair, even a little mark or mole on her left cheek that he had scarcely noticed before. And he saw her not static as in a photograph but in motion, alive. The eyes speculatively gazed at him. The lips smiled or frowned.

It was good and it lasted, giving him hope that he would survive the intrusion of the voice, after all. But at this point a sound of footfalls disturbed his concentration and drew his attention to the chamber's entrance. Linford Grant walked in.

Standing over him, the leader said quietly, "Was I right about the presence, Sheldon? Have you felt it yet?"

"Hell, no. You're crazy." How could Grant know he was lying?

"I'm not crazy. And you will feel it, friend. Be sure of that. Hungry, are you?"

Again Peter thought it best to be defiant, because a sign of weakness would indicate surrender. "Not for the slop you've been feeding me."

"Thirsty?"

"I could use some water."

"When I come back, I'll try to remember to bring you some." With a taunting smile the leader departed.

After the interruption, Peter found he could not rebuild his remarkable vision of Edith. The visit from Grant had made him too much aware of his surroundings again—even caused him to peer again into the shifting green glow to be sure it contained no alien physical presence.

"Sheldon, are you hearing me?" It was not Grant's voice but the other one, slipping through his defenses to speak to his mind again.

In panic he groped for something to think about that would keep his mind occupied. Baseball. He had played the game in college and retained a keen interest. Who were the major-league teams? The New York Yankees. The Pittsburgh Pirates. The Boston Red Sox. The Chicago White Sox. Get them all, Sheldon, or go back and do it over and over and over until you do! Concentrate now! You *know* them! Put your mind to work on it!

"I think it is time we talked about what I want from you, Sheldon," the voice intruded.

Exhausted by his struggle, Peter heard himself whisper, "What *do* you want? Who are you?"

"You know who I am. And where you are. And what you must do."

"If you mean become one of your—your people—I won't do it!" Wildly Peter looked around him again, seeking something in the mist that would explain the sound in his head. Some electronic trickery. Some man-made answer. But was it a sound? Or was the voice only a thought, with some hellish power behind it?

"I have a plan, Sheldon. Here in this small, backward country it is only just beginning. But we have made progress elsewhere, as my advocate has already pointed out to you."

The green light was more in motion now, swirling around him like a whirlpool slowly gathering speed. But it was still an eye, vast and mysterious, and he was in the center of it, being observed and made to listen.

"Let me add to what my advocate has told you," the voice went on. "Think back a little. Do you recall a report about the massacre of a hundred or more children in an African prison?"

"I—no."

"You disappoint me, but never mind. I am always especially pleased when the victims are children. He, my adversary, was fond of children, you may recall. You do know about the so-called boat people of Asia, of course—so many drowned, so many plundered and raped by pirates."

"I know," Peter whispered.

"My people played a significant role in that, as they have in many other such triumphs. I like it when they leave headless bodies for the authorities to find, as they have been doing in that Mediterranean country. And when the bombs are thrown into schoolhouses full of children. It makes things pleasantly lively, don't you think?''

"For God's sake, leave me alone!" Peter heard himself whimpering.

"We have had some notable successes throughout your world, Sheldon," the voice continued in the same even tone. "And I am stepping up the pace as we near our goal of total domination. Almost every day now, some project of mine happens somewhere. Are you aware of that?''

Still clutching his upthrust knees, Peter bowed his head and squeezed his eyes shut. It was impossible now to hold back the voice by thinking of his family or Edith Craig. The pressure was a drill applied to his brain.

"I could go on and on," the voice in his head continued. "I keep records of what you call atrocities, and the list daily grows more satisfying. I am not referring to the stupid violence inspired by political or religious differences, mind you. That childish idiocy occurs throughout your world without any help from me, though of course I turn it to my own use at times. An atrocity, by my definition, is purely and simply an act of evil for its own lovely sake."

Hearing footsteps at the entrance again, Peter raised his head. Linford Grant stood there watching him, but came no closer and did not speak.

"So, do you see now, Sheldon, how I work?" the voice persisted. "Do you understand why I have special plans for intelligent souls like you? Answer me, please."

"Go to hell," Peter tried to say, but it came out a moan, almost inaudible.

The voice laughed. In the entrance, Grant calmly watched as though fully aware of what was happening.

"I shall leave you for a time now, Sheldon, but with a warning," the voice said. "Have you heard about the condemned souls who are put to death by stoning in your Middle East? Do you know how it works? They bury you up to your neck in the ground and hurl stones at your head until it is reduced to pulp. Not a pretty way to die, I assure you. But, of course, you won't anger me to that extent, will you? You will do as I wish. And, believe me, you will enjoy working with me when you know me better, Sheldon. I promise."

32

Manny Williams sank to one knee and lifted Mother Jarrett's long black fingers to his lips. "Reverend Mother, this poor boy hurt bad. Me beg you lay you hands on him."

Standing in the front room of Bronzie Dakin's house, the tall woman in the white robe frowned at Cob. "Don't I know you?" she asked. "Aren't you from Seaclose?"

"Yes, ma'am."

"Dercy Dennis's boy?"

"Yes, ma'am. Me name Cornelius."

"Of course." She stepped past Manny and took the lad's hand. "What is wrong? Oh-oh, I don't need to ask, do I?" As she looked at the horizontal welts on the boy's bare chest, her black-opal eyes flashed with anger and her voice became steely. "Who did this to you?" There was a growing evil abroad in St. Alban, she told herself, and the time had come for it to be dealt with.

"Them did whip me, ma'am."

"Who whipped you? What for?"

"It a long story, Mother," Manny muttered, rising. "You can help him first, please?"

"Of course. Come into the bedroom, both of you."

She was alone in the house, Mother Jarrett explained as she instructed Cob to remove his borrowed pants and lie on the bed. Bronzie had gone to a shop in the village, taking her son Gerald with her.

"And how Gerald is?" Manny asked.

Mother Jarrett sat on the bed to examine Cob's wounds. "He knows who he is again, and what he is doing. But about Bronzie I am worried, Manny. If Georgie is not found soon, it will break her heart."

"Me don't sure she should want him found," Manny said sadly.

"What?"

"Please, Mother—help this boy here. Then me tell you all me know."

The hand that healed Peter Sheldon's face worked on young Cob now, while Manny looked on. For half an hour Mother Jarrett gently massaged Cob's body, concentrating on the marks left by the whippings—some of them inflicted, had she but known it, by the man standing there watching her and silently praying for her to demonstrate her power again. When she finished, the lad was asleep.

She walked back into the front room then, motioning Manny to follow. Respectfully the pig hunter waited for her to sit before easing his tired body onto a chair.

"So, Manny?" she said. "You know where Georgie is?"

He told her what he knew of the missing scouts, the missing soldiers, and the place called the Devil's Pit.

"And you think Georgie is one of the devil's disciples now?"

"Him was not on no cross being tormented, Mother. Him was one of those with the guns."

"You saw this?"

"The first time me was made to whip Cob, the one holding the gun on me was Georgie, Mother."

Mother Jarrett gazed at him in silence for a few seconds, then said in a low voice, "I must think what to do about this, Manny. Go back into the bedroom, please. Shut the door. Wait there with Cob until I call you."

"But, Mother, me must do something quick about Squire and the English lady!"

"I need a few moments alone, Manny."

With a shake of his head Manny turned and went into the bedroom, obediently closing the door behind him.

Still seated, Mother Jarrett clasped her long-fingered hands in her lap and lowered her head. She closed her eyes. It was one of the positions she habitually assumed when meditating, but the exercise she engaged in now was more than mere meditation. She sought to call into play a power she had acquired years before, in India, at the feet of a certain Maharajji who was one of that country's most revered holy men.

As she willed herself into a trancelike state now, her face slowly lost its anxiety and acquired an expression of euphoria. It began to shine, as though from an inner brilliance. Then a smile appeared upon her lips.

The room in which she sat—this room in Bronzie Dakin's small house in the mountains of St. Alban—slowly filled with mist and expanded. Its fading walls fell away and it opened into a vast, gleaming world of space in which Mother Jarrett moved so swiftly she felt dizzy. When the dizziness passed, she found herself striding along a dusty mountain road that smelled of flowers and wore a pattern of purple tree shadows.

But these were not St. Alban's mountains. High peaks in the distance were white with snow, and never had there been snow in her Caribbean island. Below the road, too, were railroad tracks, and along them ran what looked more like a toy train than a real one. Its little locomotive belched black smoke that drifted back above a flatcar and two passenger cars that it struggled to haul up the grade. Behind the grimy windows of the two passenger cars were faces—far too many for so little space!—and to the roofs and outsides of the cars clung additional riders. And the sound of the train's passing, the constant bleat of the locomotive's whistle, stirred memories in Mother Jarrett's mind.

She had ridden this very train on her first visit to the man whose counsel she now sought. It was one of several that had brought her here from Calcutta. That had been many years ago, long before she learned from Maharajji how to travel from place to place by other, swifter means.

How much easier had been her visits to him since that first one! At least half a dozen times, with no endless waiting in airports, no more riding on India's always crowded trains, she had come here to pay her respects or to ask for his help. Now here she was again. Just ahead, snug against the hillside on her right, was his ashram.

The time here was not the same, of course. In Bronzie Dakin's house, where her other self still sat with closed eyes, the time had been—still was—early morning. Here the hillside and ashram were bathed in soft evening light. It was because of the difference in time that she had chosen to make the road her destination rather than the ashram itself. Maharajji changed gatekeepers often and might have one now who would not know her. If so, the man might be upset by the sudden appearance of a stranger inside the grounds.

Lengthening her stride as she approached the temple-school itself, she recalled how she had once tried to describe it to a friend in St. Alban, after telling the friend about her being one of Maharajji's pupils. Impossible, of course. You could make a simple St. Alban person understand that certain of India's people were revered as saints and had supernormal powers. No problem there, in a country whose ancestors had brought with them from Africa a belief in powerful voodoo gods. And even the statement that certain higher saints could will themselves to be in more than one place at the same time—even that her friend had accepted. But that a ''Great King'' would be content to live out his life in a plain, peasant-style building in a far wilderness, with only oil lamps for light and a well for water . . . no, no! Great Kings dwelt in palaces!

Mother Jarrett smiled at the memory as she stopped at the ashram gate and knocked. For the last hundred yards of her journey the gatekeeper had been watching her, she knew. Now he rose from a chair on the veranda and came along the path toward her. Not the chaukidar she remembered, but an older one.

Not, of course, as old as Maharajji himself. He was said to have known Christ—which was yet another thing her friend in St. Alban had refused to believe, though many here were convinced. Certainly he talked with Christ now. One of India's most revered saints would not lie about such a thing.

''Good evening. I am Mother Jarrett, and I have studied under Maharajji. Now I need to talk with him.''

The gatekeeper peered at her face. ''Mother Jarrett? Ah, yes. Maharajji is expecting you.''

''Expecting me? How—''

''Please follow me.''

He opened the gate for her, then led the way to the house. Off the veranda were four doors, all of them closed. He led her to the third one and tapped it lightly with a knuckle. At a word from within he opened it and motioned her to enter, then closed the door behind her.

The man she sought was alone in the room's semi-darkness. Garbed in only a dhoti and a blanket, he sat cross-legged on one of the wooden platform beds they called tuckets—almost the only furniture the room contained—and gazed at her with the understanding eyes she so well remembered.

"Greetings, Mother."

"And to you, Maharajii. How did you know I was coming?"

"I felt you thinking about me." He motioned to her to come and sit beside him, then waved toward a tray of food that must have been placed there on the tucket for her visit. She should have brought a gift of food to him, of course. But if he had felt her thinking about him, he would know how little time she had. She even dared to shake her head when he urged her to take some pomegranate seeds.

She did lean forward, though, to place a gentle hand on his bare feet. To touch the feet of such a saint was to touch those of God.

"Maharajji, I need your help."

He frowned. "You need my help? You who are so much closer to God than I am?"

"I am not closer, Maharajji."

"I say you are. I merely taught you a few things you did not know." His frown said he meant it. "Tell me, are you wholly here or is my India sharing you with your homeland?"

"Only sharing, good friend." She smiled. "I came without a railway ticket this time, as you taught me."

"But not hanging on to the outside of the train, eh?"

229

He referred, of course, to those who came to him that way because they had no money for the fare, and his old, withered lips could still smile at the thought. "So tell me, Mother, how can I help?"

"You talk with Christ, Maharajji."

"He talks with me."

"I need his help. I face a struggle that will be too much for me without it.'

"Tell me," he said, and eased his frail body back on the tucket to listen.

She told him what Manny Williams had told her—about the Devil's Pit in the mountains of her island, and what was going on there. Not once did he interrupt.

When she had finished, he reached out to touch her hand. "Go back while you can still help those people," he said. "When your time of need comes, I will be there for you in spirit."

"And—will His spirit be there with yours, Maharajji?"

"Do not doubt it."

"Then farewell, good friend."

"Farewell, Mother."

The walls of the Maharajji's room dissolved in mist, and again Mother Jarrett felt herself moving swiftly through a shining world of space. When the sensation of dizziness passed and she opened her eyes, she was back in Bronzie Dakin's cottage. Giving her head a shake to clear it, she rose stiffly from her chair and called, "Manny! Come now, please!"

The bedroom door opened and Manny Williams stood there gazing at her.

"Manny, tell me. Can you find your way back to that place you told me about? Through the waterfall?"

"Yes, Mother. But if them on guard—"

"Never mind that. Can you take me there?"

The pig hunter looked down at his hands, and they

were clenched. "Mother, don't is supposed to be some soldiers here? Some that Sergeant Wray did send for?"

"No soldiers have come here, Manny. If any went into the mountains, they went some other way. The sergeant himself has gone to the capital."

"And you would dare try alone to stop what happening in that place? You would stand up to Satan by you'self?"

Mother Jarrett moved her head slowly up and down. "With God's help, Manny, yes."

"And Mr. Grant?"

"As for him—"

The front door opened then and Bronzie Dakin came in, followed by the boy who for so long had lain in torment on the bed where young Cob was now peacefully sleeping. Mother Jarrett acknowledged the woman's entrance with a mere nod, but gazed with strange intensity at the son.

Then, "Yes, Maharajji!" she whispered, moving her head up and down again. "Ah, yes. Thank you!"

33

"You must be hungry, Sheldon."

It was Linford Grant's fourth or fifth visit to the room in which Peter was being indoctrinated. Peter had lost count and knew only that with each appearance he hated the man more. Loathing was an acid in him now, corroding his reason.

According to the watch on his wrist he had been chained to the ring on the floor for sixteen hours. Was that why they had allowed him to keep the watch? So he would know the full length of his torment?

Sixteen hours of being forced to sit or lie naked on cold, damp stone in a room where that hellish green glare had etched itself on his eyeballs. There were certain positions he could no longer endure even for short intervals because of the soreness in his bones. As for hunger, he had suffered acutely for a time but was now consumed by thirst.

"Give me some water," he begged his tormentor.

"I keep forgetting to bring any. But if you would be more reasonable, I might go for some." Wearing his brown scout uniform again, Grant hunkered just out of reach and peered at Peter's face, perhaps searching for a sign of surrender. He was unhappy, it seemed. He had not expected Peter to resist for so long.

But Peter knew his resistance was nearing an end. The presence in this room kept making itself felt, no longer with mere recitals of its accomplishments, but with far more subtle pressures. He even wondered whether his increasing hatred for Grant might not be part of the plan. Certainly if he were handed a whip and told he could safely use it on the scout leader, he would do so with furious pleasure. And wasn't it one of their objectives to make him delight in violence?

There had been one shining moment in the endless hours of despair and pain. Four hours ago Grant, striding into the room, had stood over him seething with rage and said, "I have something to tell you, Sheldon. Your friend, Emmanuel Williams, has escaped."

"What?" Peter had almost forgotten the pig hunter, but his tired mind reached out to recall the time, ages ago, when he had seen Manny whipping a boy on a cross.

"Escaped, damn him! He has escaped!" Grant shouted.

"So you hadn't won him over as you thought you had. He was fooling you."

"So it seems. But this is a small island. He won't hide for long. And let me tell you, Sheldon—before he dies, he will wish he had never challenged me."

"Is he the first ever to get out of here?"

"The first since I took charge. But don't entertain any false hopes. If the men who discovered his flight had come to me quickly instead of trying to overtake him, I would have stopped him."

"How?"

"By persuasion, Sheldon. You should know."

"The way you got to me a time or two?" The dialogue, Peter felt, was doing him good, giving him strength. He made a real effort to keep it going. "What I want to know, Grant, is how you've been able to reach me the way you do. Why am I so damned easy for you when, obviously, an older man like Manny Williams is not?"

From a pocket of his brown shirt the devil's advocate produced a small yellow cylinder and held it out between thumb and forefinger. "Do you know what this is?"

"A film?"

"Several of my scouts had cameras, if you remember. One, while taking a picture of the Great House, asked you to stand on the veranda steps."

Peter was incredulous. "You mean you're able to reach into my mind because you have a photo of me on an undeveloped film?"

"Not only of you. Preble and Miss Craig were standing just behind you, and the lad caught them as well." The scout leader's lips curled in what was no doubt meant to be a smile of triumph. "Many things help, Sheldon. You will learn.

"Edith and Preble were not that close to me," Peter challenged. But Grant had gotten to Edith at the John Crow's Nest, hadn't he? She would have killed herself there if—

"The woman and you were closer to each other at that moment than you know." Grant shrugged.

"I say you're wrong. She was standing at least—"

"I don't mean physically closer, Sheldon."

Unable to think of an answer to that, Peter said after a slight hesitation, "You get to me through the photo, then. But you couldn't stop Manny Williams from escaping.''

"I didn't know he had escaped until too late."

"I'm glad to hear that. I'm glad to know you have your limitations, damn you. I'll beat you yet, Grant."

"Will you?" The leader's twisted smile had faded. His tone was ominous. "When I come again, perhaps I'll be sufficiently out of patience with you to find out. You've just given me an idea how to do it."

That had been four hours ago, and for a time the knowledge that Manny had escaped had been for Peter both food and drink. But his despair, when it returned, was even greater than before because of the all-too-brief reprieve.

Unable to concentrate on anything but his thirst and hunger now, in agony from his long confinement in this circular prison where the green light never ceased its whirlpool motion, he at times became totally confused and even forgot where he was.

And every little while the voice in his head sought to win his cooperation by promising power in place of suffering. Power and the endless delights it would win for him.

Then Grant returned, followed by two naked men leading a woman whose wrists were bound behind her. And the woman was Edith Craig.

Peter struggled to his knees and fixed his gaze on her. All these hours he had clung to the desperate hope that she might be safe somewhere. He had last seen her with her fiancé on the veranda of the Great House that early morning, an eternity ago, when Sergeant Wray had told what happened to the soldiers and the Judas named Pennock sat there pretending to be in shock.

Edith had been wearing a robe over pajamas then. Now she wore the khaki shirt and slacks in which she had walked about the plantation with him. She and Alton Preble must have changed when Pennock persuaded them to accompany him. But she was not now the same woman he had left at the house when he drove Wray to the police station. Obviously close to total exhaustion, she appeared ready to sink to the floor if the two men holding her arms let go their grip.

Returning his gaze, she seemed not to know who he was. Perhaps she was not even seeing him.

"You bastard," Peter whispered to Linford Grant.

Again Grant shrugged. "You gave me the idea yourself, when you asked why she responded to the command I sent you at the John Crow's Nest. Now, friend, I believe you will cooperate."

Sensing the terms about to be offered him, Peter clenched his hands and remained silent. His gaze, though, would not leave the exhausted figure standing there.

Grant was right on one point, without argument. He, Peter Sheldon, had feelings for this woman that went far beyond her being the owner of Armadale and in charge of his future. If, indeed, he had a future anymore.

Because she had brought a fiancé with her from England—because she had appeared to be fond of the man and not unhappy about her commitment to marry him—he had refused to allow his personal feelings to surface. But they were there and now had to be acknowledged. And, he guessed, the devil's advocate in the scout uniform was about to make the most of it.

In a moment he would hear Linford Grant saying, "Unless you capitulate, Sheldon, be prepared to see this woman on a cross, being whipped."

But Grant said something else. In a casual, almost conversational tone, he said, "You do understand the extent of our training here, do you not, Sheldon?"

Peter looked at him in silence.

"I mean to say, there are many forms of violence. I expect you haven't thought about that, really. Our whipping is a mere beginning. Actually, when they graduate and go forth to carry on the master's work, they seldom use anything so simple as a whip. Explosives, firearms, knives—those are faster and more effective. And there is one weapon that particularly terrorizes women, of course. That is one of our most effective tools." He was smiling now. Peter had never seen a more evil smile. "No pun intended there, Sheldon. I refer, of course, to rape."

Even had he wanted to, Peter could not have responded. His mouth dried, his throat contracted, his nails bit into his palms. Naked and helpless, his left ankle fastened by a chain to the iron ring in the floor, he began to tremble and presently was shaking all over. In exchange for one moment of freedom to go for the throat of the man before him, he would gladly have given the rest of his life.

"So, then, Sheldon," Grant was saying, "I now offer you a choice. Either you cease your resistance at once, or I instruct these two men to undress this woman and rape her here and now before your eyes. Your answer please. Now."

Peter had a voice after all. "Don't," he heard himself say.

"You will do as I command? Without further defiance?"

"Yes."

"I warn you, you will be taken from here to a training room and will find there a man on a cross. You will be given a whip and will use it on him until you are told to stop. Do you agree?"

Peter looked at Edith Craig, but her head had drooped. If she was seeing anything, it could only be the floor at her feet. "Yes," he repeated, "I agree. Don't . . . don't do it to her."

The leader motioned to his two aides, and they led Edith away.

The chamber Peter was taken to first was not a training room but a dormitory. As before, Grant paced close behind him with a gun, instructing him which way to turn.

There were twenty beds in a line along one wall. Made of mountain grass piled upon pine boughs, they must have caused their naked users to itch intolerably. Obviously the comfort of his trainees was not high on Grant's list of priorities.

Along the opposite wall were stacks of firewood and circles of stones for cooking. At one such arrangement, pine logs blazed under a large, soot-blackened pot. Peter was ordered to halt, and Grant handed him a battered aluminum cup full of water.

"You must be hungry, too," Grant said, and called to a naked young man who sat on one of the cots, cleaning an Enforcer. The youth came across the room and, when told to do so, ladled out a bowl of gruel and gave it to Peter in silence. He was a boy Peter knew well. Gazing at him while wincing over the sour taste of the porridge, Peter recalled the night he had gone to Look Up with a gun to kill the lad's brother.

Experimentally he said, "Georgie Dakin, do you remember me?"

The boy looked at him with what appeared to be total indifference. "Me 'member you."

"Is that all you have to say?"

"Me no business with you now. Me work for Mr. Grant."

The food was a kind of cornmeal mush and rancid, but Peter was too nearly famished to refuse it. While struggling to swallow it, he looked at the other occupants of the chamber. There were five. Two seemed to be sleeping. Two played with a pack of cards. The fifth was cleaning a rifle, as Georgie had been doing.

"How many do you trust with guns, Grant?"

"At the moment, four." Grant shrugged. "But all have to be trustworthy before they leave here, or they don't leave."

"How many are here? Are all these beds in use?"

"All but a few. With my scouts and the soldiers, we're busier than usual."

Peter looked at Georgie Dakin again. "Georgie, have you forgotten you have a mother? And a brother?"

"Me no business with them again," the boy mumbled.

"Give me some more water, please."

Sullenly the youth walked over to a table and refilled the cup from a square kerosene tin. Taking it from him, Peter said "Thank you, Georgie" but received no answer.

The muzzle of Grant's rifle touched his bare back. "We have things to do, Sheldon. Finish your food."

"I'm finished."

"Come, then. Dakin, lead the way."

"Where to, sir?"

"Number-three room. Bring your rifle."

Georgie went across the chamber and took up his weapon. With a hostile glance at Peter he walked toward a tunnel. Grant said, "Follow him, Sheldon," and Peter did so. With the leader bringing up the rear, they continued along the tunnel for a hundred yards or so. Then Georgie turned left into a narrower, more crooked passage.

Peter followed mechanically, no longer caring.

He would be forced to whip some poor fellow tied to a cross, he supposed. Someone courageous enough to accept torture rather than inflict it on others. In the end what difference would it make? Some of those here would die, one way or another, and the others would join Grant's gang of terrorists. By abandoning his resistance, he had perhaps saved Edith Craig from rape, but he could not buy her release from this underground hell. They would never let her go to tell what she had seen here.

Ahead, Georgie Dakin had reached another of the many underground chambers and stepped back against the wall to let Peter pass. While doing so, Peter for just a second or two entertained a wild thought of grabbing for the boy's gun and turning with it to destroy the man behind him. The notion fled when he saw who was on the cross in the room he had entered.

He trembled to a halt. "No. I won't!"

At the sound of his voice the man on the cross moved, raising his head with what seemed to be a great effort. His gaze fastened on Peter, but his eyes appeared to have trouble focusing in the chamber's green haze.

"Peter?" He could barely talk. The marks of the lash on his white skin explained why, perhaps. "Peter Sheldon? They've got you, too?"

Peter turned from staring at the Englishman and said in barely controlled fury to Linford Grant, "I will not whip this man, damn you!"

"You will do as you agreed to," Grant replied calmly, "or the woman will be raped. Come to think of it, she is engaged to marry this man, isn't she? So I will have her raped here, where both of you can watch."

On the cross, Alton Preble said, "Do what he wants, Peter."

"No!"

"It makes no sense to refuse. They're going to kill me anyway. As an outsider, I'd be no good to them here even if they could win me over."

It was true, Peter realized. The barrister was merely

a visitor to the island, lacking even the papers needed for him to remain. He looked around the room in an agony of indecision. It was like the other training rooms he had seen—the cross, the table, the whip on the table. The only difference was that the naked man on this cross was white and the welts on his body were scarlet.

"I am not a patient man," Grant warned. "You made your choice before we left the Eye, Sheldon."

"Peter, get on with it," said the man on the cross. "What difference can it make? I'm dead anyhow."

Peter looked at the gun in Grant's hands. At the one in the hands of Bronzie Dakin's son. He felt tears running from his eyes as he took the whip from the table. Moving woodenly toward the cross, he tried twice to speak before at last saying, "I'm sorry, Alton. God, I'm sorry."

"You're forgiven."

Peter drew back his arm. The whip snaked out behind him and quivered in the air. He shut his eyes as he brought it forward. He heard it crack against Preble's body and heard the man gasp.

"Nine more like that, Sheldon," the voice of Linford Grant intoned.

"God forgive me," Peter whispered, and swung the whip a second time.

The man on the cross gasped again, but still did not cry out.

"Eight more," Grant said.

Peter drew back his arm once more. The whip whistled forward again. But now his whole body was trembling and his knees buckled as he leaned forward into the stroke.

As he pitched to the floor, he wondered whether Grant would think his blackout a pretense, and whether Edith would pay the price for his weakness.

34

HE REGAINED CONSCIOUSNESS IN THE ROOM WHERE HE had first been imprisoned, with his left ankle again chained to the ring in the wall. But the assault on his mind in the room called the Eye, and his physical suffering there, had taken their toll.

He only dimly remembered using a whip on Alton Preble and blacking out while doing so. His recollection of talking to Georgie Dakin in a large chamber used as a dormitory was unclear. Somewhere, too, he had seen Edith.

He was so very tired. If only he could sleep, and wake up in the Great House. But if he did that, he might be going down to the kitchen to open the gas line again. Or to Bronzie Dakin's house with a gun, to kill the twin brother of the boy who had just said, "Me no business with you again. Me work for Mr. Grant."

He did sleep. But for how long, he had no idea. When

he awoke again, his watch had stopped. He lay there in the green haze, trying to think things out.

According to Linford Grant, this underworld was a domain of the devil—the biblical devil, archfiend of evil, adversary of God, and ruler of hell. The Bible said that Jesus had been forty days tempted of the devil but triumphed over him. The fiend was still very much alive and active, though. Anyone reading the world's headlines must know that. And this unknown cavern, this long, complex river cave in the Morgan Mountains of St. Alban, was one of his spheres of action.

Only one. According to Grant, he had many others and was embarked on a campaign to take over the earth—perhaps more than the earth. Ahead lay a final confrontation in which evil would emerge victorious and he would rule all.

Nonsense. Grant was simply mad. Yet how had Edith Craig been persuaded to walk to certain destruction at the John Crow's Nest? Why had Peter Sheldon tried to drown her at the tree bridge? And how . . . but the list was too long to review now. He lacked the ability to concentrate that much.

Anyway, even if the scout leader were mad, he had certainly acquired hellish powers and passed some of them on to his followers. How else could Private Pennock have lured Edith and her fiancé here from the Great House?

And where—oh God, where—was that grand old pig hunter, Manny Williams? After escaping, was he on his way back here with help? Would he get here in time, with the right kind of help?

What was the right kind of help? Surely not more soldiers who could be made to believe they were groping blindly in a mist that could destroy their minds. Manny would have to do better than that. Otherwise, what happened next would only feed the fires of Grant's vile ambition by repeating what had gone before.

Peter slept, and awoke to find Grant standing over him, nudging him with a booted foot.

"Feel rested, do you?"

He sat up. His nakedness had long since ceased to bother him, but in sleep he had turned so that the iron made his ankle ache. While gazing up at his captor, he rubbed the hurt. Having no idea what to say that might help him, he remained silent.

"When you passed out, I thought at first you were pretending," Grant said. "I had Dakin use his knife on you to find out—the same knife with which he tried to cut off the head of that forestry fellow. The forester, by the way, was unconscious and dying at the time, from the crash of the helicopter. You know about that. Dakin's brother told you."

Peter said, "How do you know what Gerald Dakin told me?"

"You forget his twin is here."

"And by reading Georgie's mind, you knew what Gerald was telling me?"

"Not all, perhaps, but enough."

"Is that why you sent me to kill Gerald?"

"And you would have, had it not been for the Jarrett woman." Shifting the gun he carried to his left hand, Grant leaned forward with a key to unlock the leg iron. "A most remarkable woman, that one, from what I've heard. Know her well, do you?"

"No."

"I wish you did. Nothing would please me more than to have her here. Perhaps when we have finished your indoctrination, you will think of some way to entice her."

Still rubbing his bruised ankle, Peter looked up.

"What do you mean—when you've finished my indoctrination? Haven't you done that?"

"Not quite."

"Damn you, I whipped the Englishman for you, didn't I?"

"Until you fainted. And perhaps you might have continued. Who knows? But I need further proof of your commitment. You are very important to me, Sheldon. And you held out in the Eye for a long time."

And would still be holding out, you bastard, Peter thought, if you hadn't come in with the woman I love. But the problem now was to keep this monster in the scout uniform talking. To postpone for as long as possible the resumption of the "training."

"Tell me something, Grant. After you finish indoctrinating the people you have here, and turn them loose on society like a pack of mad dogs, how do they explain where they've been?"

"How what?" Grant appeared to be genuinely puzzled by the question.

"You and your scouts disappeared. The soldiers came here looking for them. By the time you turn them loose—those you do turn loose—they'll have been missing for days. How will they explain it?"

"There is no problem."

"They'll simply go home and say they've been wandering for days in the mountains, and how nice it is to be back?"

Grant shrugged. "In the first place, they won't go home. Georgie Dakin said it all when he told you he has no further interest in his mother and brother."

"That isn't what he said."

"It's what he meant."

"Where do they go, then?"

"The city has its crowded slums where people are never questioned. All our West Indian capitals do. And it suits us to be in large cities, of course. The opportunities are more numerous there than in the country towns and villages.''

Peter said, ''What happens when one of your gunmen is caught? Isn't he identified? Suppose Georgie Dakin is caught a month from now in the slums of the city. 'Well, well,' they say to him, 'you're one of those scouts lost in the mountains a while back. What happened to you?' ''

''Our people are not caught, Sheldon.''

''Oh, come on. The police are not that inefficient. They catch thieves and holdup men all the time.''

''Not our people. When ours are apprehended, they either escape or die trying; never are they taken alive to be questioned.'' Grant allowed himself a smile of self-congratulation. ''Like many others, Sheldon, you probably wonder about police reports that certain criminals, when cornered, open fire on them and have to be shot dead. Police brutality, you may have told yourself. Their way of getting even for the trouble these lawbreakers cause them. Also their way of ensuring that the criminals, when brought to trial, won't be let off through the wiles of clever lawyers who make a reputation by defending them. But you're wrong. Our workers are *trained* not to be caught. I have lost some good men that way.''

''So your people melt into the slums of the capital. But you don't. You're a respected scout leader. How do you explain your own disappearances? Where do you live, anyway?''

''I live in Wilton Bay.''

''Are you married?''

''I've never been married, Sheldon.''

''But what will you say when you return to the Bay? How will you explain your absence? Even more to the point, how will you explain your missing scouts?''

"I won't be going back there, Sheldon. Not this time."

"What?"

"I'm organized here now. Bringing my scouts to this place was the final step of a grand plan, don't you see? Now I have them and the soldiers who came looking for them, and soon Sergeant Wray will be returning with even more soldiers."

"You let Wray escape on purpose?"

"Of course. So my preparations are nearly finished, and in a short while the master's campaign to control this island will be in full swing. With you, I might add, playing a major role in it."

Aware that he was to be led to a training room and probably forced to use a whip again—perhaps even on Alton Preble again—Peter desperately sought ways to gain time. "Tell me how you brought Miss Craig and her fiancé here, Grant. I know how you recruited Pennock; you've already told me that. But how did he persuade them to—"

"He was instructed to bring *you* here, Sheldon. But when you got away from him by taking Sergeant Wray to the police station, he anticipated complications and made his move too soon. He should have waited for you to return, of course. Can you think of any other questions to postpone your training?"

"Yes. Why did you bring two foreigners here? You can't use them in St. Alban, for God's sake."

"I've just told you—Pennock was instructed to bring *you* here. He made a mistake."

"So what are your plans for me, if you ever get to carry them out?"

"Oh, I shall carry them out. Never doubt it. As I brought my scouts here, you will bring some of your plantation workers. We need a few more people. But that phase will be completed shortly. We are nearly ready to begin Lucifer's work in earnest."

Unable to think of any new way to postpone the inevitable, Peter at last was silent.

"So come," Grant said. "Quite a few of my people are waiting to watch you. Let's not try their patience any longer."

With a gun at his back, Peter trudged along a short corridor to a room he had not been in before. Smaller than the other training rooms, it had no cross, no table, no whip. But before he could feel any relief at the absence of those props, he saw half a dozen of Grant's naked followers standing against the walls. And in the center of the room lay a bed similar to those in the dormitory.

No, not quite similar. This one consisted of the same mountain grass and pine boughs, but they were laid within a frame of heavy pine-tree trunks that made the bed nearly immovable. Ropes were attached to the frame's four corners.

Were they going to lay him on it and torture him? What would that tell them except the extent of his capacity to endure pain?

He turned to Grant just in time to see the leader motion to two men near the entrance. On bare feet the pair padded from the chamber like animals on a hunt.

Peter gazed at those left against the walls. They were all animals, he decided. He looked down at his own naked body. Was he one, too? He had not been allowed to bathe since coming here. Had not once been given even a bucket of water to wash away some of the grime and sweat. He felt filthy. Was that part of the indoctrination—to reduce a man's self-respect to absolute zero?

He turned back to the bed, aware that it was the center of attraction for the men against the walls. Then, hearing sounds behind him, he twisted himself about and crouched in a posture of self-defense, expecting the worst.

Into the chamber came the two who had left, and this time Edith Craig walked between them with their hands gripping her arms. More alert than when she had been dragged into the Eye room, she looked at Peter and faintly spoke his name. Her once lovely brown hair was a tangle. Her khaki shirt and slacks were as soiled as Peter's body.

He took a step toward her, but rifles were instantly leveled at him, one in the hands of the leader.

"I would not advise it, Sheldon," Grant said coldly. "She would die with you." With his weapon he motioned Peter back. "Remember, her only value to us is in helping us convert you."

Peter heard his own voice shouting in fury, "Let her go, God damn you! I'll do what you want!"

"Of course you will. The master attended to that in the Eye room."

"Then let her go! Now!"

"But we need her for what you will do next, Sheldon." Grant's voice was so matter-of-fact it was hypnotic. "Just be patient, please."

The rifle in his hands motioned Peter away from the bed, and the two men led Edith to it. The room seemed to hold its breath as they unbuttoned her shirt and removed it. The green light played over her bared breasts, and rigid in her terror, she became a statue of Aphrodite. They pulled down her khaki slacks and white brief, forcing her to step out of them, and in Peter's eyes she became the central figure in *The Birth of Venus*, Botticelli's paint still wet.

Forcing her onto the bed, faceup, the men secured her wrists and ankles to its corners. Then the man in the brown scout uniform stepped forward to look down at her.

"Very nice," Grant said. "This should be a pleasure."

Dropping to one knee, he extended a hand. His fingertips caressed the victim's body, and she moaned. They moved to the insides of her thighs and she strained against her bonds, arching herself in violent protest.

The rifles in the hands of the watchers kept Peter at bay, though he was close to a kind of madness that could easily make him defy them.

"Yes, very nice," Grant said, rising to face him. "Enjoy yourself, Sheldon."

"What?"

"As I told you, rape is one of our most effective tools. Prove to me you enjoy it, and I'll know better what to do with you."

35

WITH THE ROAR OF THE WATERFALL IN HIS EARS, Manny Williams stopped at the pool's edge and frowned at his two companions. Why, he asked himself again, had Mother Jarrett insisted on bringing Gerald along? How in the world could a mere boy—a sick one, at that—be anything but a burden to them?

He thought again of what Mother had said: that if everything else went well, Gerald could be a big help in persuading Georgie to come out with them. But, in his opinion, nothing Gerald might say to his twin brother would do any good. It was too late for that. Georgie belonged to the devil now.

The truth was, having Gerald along with them would only increase the danger of their being discovered.

"Mother, you sure you want this boy along?" Manny turned at the pool's edge to shake his head at the tall black woman beside him. "It going to be bad enough in there for just you and me, Mother. If him is along with us and do something stupid . . ." He had to shout the words to be heard above the thunder of the falling water.

"Manny, please," Mother said.

Now that was strange, Manny thought. She had certainly not yelled the way he had. Her lips had scarcely moved. Yet the words had found their way into his head somehow.

"Well, all right. Follow behind me in a single file so you don't step in any holes." With the automatic rifle in a sling on his back, he lowered himself to a sitting position, slid down into the water, and started for the tunnel behind the cascade.

But when he looked back after taking a few steps, he saw that Mother Jarrett and Gerald were not following him. They still stood there at the pool's edge, facing each other now with the woman's hands on the boy's shoulders. Again he could see no movement of Mother's lips, yet Gerald seemed to be listening to something she was saying to him, and after a while the boy nodded. Only then did the two turn to the pool.

Strange, Manny thought. But then, without further hesitation, they followed him across the pool and into the cave.

Manny did not speak again until the roar of the waterfall was behind them. Then in the tunnel where he had used the rifle to hold his pursuers at bay while he and the boy named Cob had made their escape, he stopped and spoke in a whisper.

"Mother, you has got to warn this boy here not to make no noise now. Every little noise in here sound like a conch-shell trumpet in the mountains."

The tall woman turned to Bronzie Dakin's boy and said in a whisper, "Did you hear that, Gerald?"

"Yes, ma'am."

"And him must stay close to us," Manny warned.

"Do you understand what Manny is saying, Gerald?"

Wide-eyed, Bronzie Dakin's son turned to look behind them at the route they had followed from the cascade, then swung about to peer into the greenish glow ahead. In the cavern's damp silence, the chattering of his teeth was louder than the words he uttered. "Y-yes, Mother Jarrett," he managed. "M-me will stay real close and not say nothing."

"So come along, then," the pig hunter said with a shake of his head. "Come quiet, so when we reach the part of this place where people is, we will hear them before them hear us. Otherwise we dead."

As before, the green haze showed them where to put their feet as they groped forward, and there were sounds of water dripping. And Manny had to admit to himself that he was scared.

What chance, he thought, did the three of them—an old, ignorant pig hunter, a woman, and a boy who was not right in the head—have of getting Georgie Dakin and Squire and those two people from England out of this place? How in the name of Jesus could they ever do it? But Mother believed they could, and who was he to argue with a woman who had studied in far-off countries and could heal people just by putting her hands on them? Was he supposed to tell such a woman she was wrong? Lord, have mercy.

Stop thinking about that part of it, he told himself. It only taking you mind off more important things like being real quiet and listening for sounds of danger.

Behind him, either Gerald Dakin or Mother Jarrett kicked a stone and sent it chattering into a wall. Manny froze, feeling his heart stop beating and thinking it might not start up again. But the silence returned and so did the thudding in his chest.

He swung around and could tell by the look of guilt

on Gerald Dakin's face that the boy was the one responsible. "Mother," Manny whispered, "him must be more careful! We is getting close to where things happen here!"

"He is trying, Manny. It was an accident."

"Him must try harder!"

"Of course. I'll warn him." And again Manny noticed that her lips did not move as she answered him.

She turned to Gerald then. Manny did not hear any words spoken, but when she walked back down the tunnel a few yards, the boy followed her. There she put her hands on his shoulders, the way she had at the pool, and seemed to talk to him, though again her lips did not move. The boy's did as he answered her, but Manny could not hear what he was saying. They talked longer than before—if talk was the word for it—and when they returned to Manny, young Gerald seemed different. It was as if he had grown older in those few minutes.

"You needn't worry about this one anymore, Manny," Mother Jarrett said with confidence. "He's a very special boy, you know. You've seen how he is able to receive his brother Georgie's thoughts."

Manny looked closely at the boy. Something had happened while Gerald and Mother were talking, he decided. Gerald might still be frightened—who wouldn't be, in a place like this?—but seemed to have his feelings under control now. Maybe he would not do anything stupid, after all.

"We can go on now, Mother?"

"Yes, Manny, we can go on."

And again Manny wondered how she could speak to him—when she wanted to—without moving her lips.

Puzzled about that, he went on again even more slowly now because he was certain they had come far enough in from the waterfall to be in real danger of being discovered. They had passed a number of side tunnels that seemed familiar. Not far ahead, he was sure, was the room where he had been forced to whip young Cob.

And now his nose, that could smell pig droppings in the forest or even fresh-turned earth where a wild pig had been rooting, detected a familiar odor.

Porridge. The thin, half-sour gruel he had been forced to eat in the room they called the dormitory. Someone nearby was cooking it, yes. Holding up a hand in warning, he stopped in his tracks, then turned around and stepped close to Mother Jarrett and put his lips next to her ear.

"Someone fixing the food them feed these people, Mother," he whispered. "Let I sneak on alone and see what we up against, whilst you and Gerald wait here."

A frown took hold of that handsome face, and Manny saw Mother Jarrett's nostrils quiver as she sought to confirm what he had said. "Yes, I smell something, Manny. Go on. But be careful."

And again her lips had not moved.

With the rifle at his hip, ready if he should need it, Manny went on with great care, one slow step at a time. The smell became more noticeable, and the green glow in the tunnel was brighter now. He recognized another side passage. The dormitory chamber was ahead on his right.

Georgie Dakin had seemed to spend most of his time in that room, Manny remembered. If by some piece of extra-good luck he was there now, alone, and Mother could talk to him . . .

He stopped to look back, and did not like what he saw. He had left Mother and Gerald together. Now they were no longer so. In her eagerness, the tall woman had left the boy and forged ahead on her own. It was not possible to judge distance in this green haze, but she seemed to be about midway between Gerald and himself. She must have told Gerald to wait.

Manny hesitated, not knowing whether to go on or not. Removing one hand from the rifle, he raised it in a gesture he hoped would tell the woman she should go back. But if she saw the movement, she ignored it.

Reluctantly he went on, around a bend in the passage that brought him to the dormitory chamber. Approaching its entrance with the same caution he would have used in stepping to the cliff's edge at the John Crow's Nest, he looked in.

Two men. One, with his back to the entrance, stood by a small cookfire, stirring a pot of the porridge. The other, seated on one of the grass beds, was busy cleaning and reassembling a rifle.

That one was Georgie.

With a nod of satisfaction, Manny turned away. He would tell Mother how things stood so she would not blunder into this and put the two on their guard. Then he would come back here. With luck he should be able to sneak up on the man at the cook pot and attend to him without having to use his gun. Georgie he would take back to Mother so she could talk to him.

But when he rounded the bend in the tunnel, the green haze between him and the distant figure of Gerald Dakin was empty. Mother had disappeared.

Disappeared how? Where? He had passed only the one side passage after leaving her and Gerald. Why would she have turned along that?

Scared, with some kind of sixth sense warning him of danger, Manny ghosted back down the tunnel to the passage in question and looked along it. Nothing. It curved, though, a short way in, and if Mother had gone that way, she could be beyond the curve now and out of sight. What should he do? Try to find out if she had done that, or go back to Gerald?

Gerald, he decided. Because if left alone much longer in a place like this, the boy might do something foolish.

Swiftly but silently Manny returned to the boy, to find Gerald with his back pressed against the tunnel wall and a look of panic on his face.

"What happen?" the pig hunter demanded in a whisper. "Where Mother Jarret is?"

"She gone, Manny!"

"Gone where?"

"She did tell me stay here whilst she go see what you doing. But some naked men did jump out of a tunnel up there and grab her! Manny, that not what she did tell me would happen!"

Manny let go the boy's arm and turned to look back toward the tunnel he had thought of investigating. His voice now more a groan than a whisper, he asked, "How many of them?"

"Me couldn't tell from here, Manny. Three, maybe four. It happen too fast."

"She didn't cry out?"

"Uh-uh. It look like them did knock her down before she could yell."

"All right." Manny shook himself like a rained-on dog, and in the process seemed to overcome his shock and get his thoughts together. "All right. Now listen me. You is to stay right here, sonny, whilst me try find out what did happen to her. It could take me quite a while, but you is not to move from here, you understand? Don't make no noise. Don't do nothing foolish. Just . . . What?"

Gerald scowled at him. "What you mean, what?"

"What you did say just then?"

"Me never say nothing, Manny."

Manny turned to look along the tunnel, and remained

in that position, twisted at the hips, so long that his companion's scowl became a look of alarm.

"What you doing, Manny?" Gerald said.

"Shh."

"But—"

"Shh!" the pig hunter repeated. Then the look of intense concentration left his face and he nodded. "All right, boy," he said. "Me know what to do now, me think. So come!"

36

LIKE A MAN FACING A FIRING SQUAD, PETER GAZED AT the guns. Then he looked at Grant.

The scout leader said calmly, "I've already warned you that I'm not a very patient man, Sheldon. Not even where you are concerned. And if I have to put you on a cross for lesser trainees to work on, she will only be raped by others. So why tempt me?"

His voice had shed its bantering tone and was dark with threat now. Peter sensed the time for games was over.

Aware that his mouth had gone dry and his body was soaked with sweat, he stepped toward the bed. The woman bound there looked up at him. Her lips moved slowly, as though with great effort.

"Don't let them hurt you," she said almost inaudibly—certainly not loud enough for those against the walls to hear. "Do as he says, Peter."

Gazing down at her, he shook his head. "My God,

I can't.'' Nor could he. To rape a woman you had to have an erection. In his state of mental anguish it was simply not possible.

"Lean over me," she said.

He knelt by her side instead.

"Lie on me," she whispered. "Pretend." This time not even Grant, closer than the others, could have heard her.

Peter shook his head again.

Studying his face, her eyes were thoughtful. "Peter." She barely breathed the name. "They will rape me themselves, so how can it matter? Please. Don't let them torture you for nothing.''

He could not answer.

"Obey them," she begged. "Please, Peter . . . don't give up while there's a chance!''

She was right, probably, about being given to others if he refused. They would never waste such an opportunity. After he satisfied them they might let others have her anyway. But could he postpone it, perhaps? If they came no closer than they were now—if they did not stand right over him—could he fake it with her? If she helped?

"We're waiting, Sheldon," Grant warned.

Rising from his knees, Peter turned his head to look at the man. In the room's green haze the leader's face, though still handsome, was contorted with impatience strained to the snapping point. There was no time left.

Peter looked again at the guns along the walls. If Grant became angry enough and decided to end the game altogether, a signal from him would cause them to fill the room with thunder, no?

He turned away from them. Kneeling again, this time between Edith's legs, he bent himself to lie on her.

"Forgive me," he whispered. No one could have heard. Perhaps not even she.

He had to kiss her, he supposed. They would expect that. Before feigning fierceness to satisfy them, he brushed her mouth with his lips in a gentle caress to let her know his true feelings. To his surprise her own lips responded with a message of affection even while she moaned in apparent terror and her body seemingly writhed to escape his assault.

"Dear Peter!" She breathed the words into his mouth. "Pretend!"

He could have an erection, he realized. He actually could go into her and make it real. In fact it was happening, and the warm body under him was responding.

Responding, for God's sake? At a moment like this?

But suddenly he became aware that the room had filled with loud, excited voices. Pushing himself up, he turned to see what was happening.

In the entrance, flanked by two men who held her arms, stood a tall black woman in a white, robelike garment. And Linford Grant, no longer even slightly interested in watching Peter Sheldon commit rape, was striding toward her.

With a glance at the woman he had not raped but had made love to, Peter rose to his feet.

"Mother Jarrett," Grant said, halting before the trio in the entrance. "You are Mother Jarrett, aren't you?"

The woman stood tall and looked at him with disdain. "I am called that."

"May I ask why you are here?"

"I have come for Georgie Dakin."

"How did you get here? Did Emmanuel Williams bring you?"

"He showed me how to get here," Mother Jarrett said.

"And where is he now?"

"I have no idea."

"Did you think for one moment, woman, that I would allow you to come here and take the Dakin boy away?"

"You are not all-powerful, Mr. Grant."

"But you are?"

"God is."

To the men holding her, Grant said sharply, "Did you see anyone with her?"

"No, sir," one replied. "She was coming up the passage from the waterfall and we did see her when we coming from the tunnel-four training room. We just grab her and bring her here."

"Did you look for others?"

"Well, no, sir. We thought we should bring her straightaway to you, her being such an important catch. But if you say so, we—"

Waving him to silence, Grant stood there gazing at the captive, rubbing his palms together as though fate had brought him the greatest possible prize. For a time he seemed content to peer into her face as though searching for the secret of the powers he had heard about. Finally he stepped back.

"Take her to the Eye," he instructed the two who held her. "Strip her. Chain her there." His gaze traveled over the others in the room, and still his tongue kept sliding over his lips as though in anticipation. "The rest of you go, too. Take every candidate. Take Sheldon. Tie his hands. All of us must be there when the master makes this woman one of us. For when he does, she will be our leader—even mine. Never doubt it!"

37

In the center of the Eye, Mother Jarrett was naked on her knees. Her eyes were shut. She held her hands pressed together before her breasts in a posture of prayer. Her lips moved but made no sound. She was a statue carved from black ivory, seen through clouds of emerald green vapor.

Peter had never seen a black woman naked before, except from a distance. While driving the rural roads he had sometimes glimpsed women and girls bathing in the island's streams, but not this close. He was impressed by this woman's dignity, as he had been on every other occasion. Being stripped of her robe had not reduced it. If anything, she was an even more commanding figure now than before. Nor had being chained to the ring in the floor shaken her incredible calm.

Peter stood at Linford Grant's left along the wall, some thirty feet from her. Around the same circular wall of this strange room with its intense green light were lined up men enough to fill nearly all the beds he had seen in the dormitory. Evidently all those now undergoing training were here.

Most of them watched the kneeling figure in restless anticipation, but a few still looked curiously around the room itself. Those were seeing it for the first time, perhaps, though they must have heard of it even if they had never been brought here before. There had been a constant whispering and murmuring until Grant angrily demanded silence.

Four of those along the wall were armed. That was the number Grant had mentioned, wasn't it? Four could be wholly trusted now. The others were still undergoing indoctrination at one stage or another. One of the select four was Georgie Dakin, standing a few yards to Peter's left. Another was the man who had brought Edith and her fiancé here, Paul Pennock.

Grant had not brought a gun, not even the conveniently small submachine gun Peter had seen him with earlier. If my hands were free, Peter thought, and I could just catch Georgie off guard . . . but Gerald Dakin's twin was too far away to be taken by surprise. And, anyway, Peter's hands were bound behind him. Before marching him from the room where he had been ordered to rape Edith, they had removed one of the four ropes that held her to the bed, and used it on him.

The last he had seen of Edith, when he looked back while being led away, she had still been lying there naked, with both wrists and one ankle fast to the immovable bed. With the revered Mother Jarrett having stumbled into his hands, Grant evidently no longer cared what became of the woman from England.

Grant cared what was happening here, however. Leaning toward Peter, he whispered excitedly, "Look at her, Sheldon! Observe the light!"

Peter stopped trying to think of some way to reach

Georgie Dakin's rifle and saw that the naked woman in the center of the Eye had slightly changed her position. She still knelt, and her lips moved, but her long, thin arms were now folded over her breasts, exerting pressure as though to hold back some inner pain. Her body trembled now.

She was feeling the presence, he guessed, just as he had. She was hearing the voice that for so long had insinuated itself into his mind. But—and this startled him—she was apparently more susceptible than he had been. She was already weakening.

Grant saw it, too, but had an explanation. "The master really wants this one, Sheldon," he said in triumph. "He merely toyed with you here, but there is no way this woman can escape him!" Hoarsely he added, "Look, man! Look at her!"

Yes, the woman in the center of the Eye was under attack and in trouble. Around her the green light was more intense than it had been. More alive. She was caught in a whirlpool of color. The whole room, in fact, was filled with an ever-more-luminous green mist. Peter heard cries of alarm from the men along the wall.

"He has her!" Grant was gloating. "He could have had you the same way, Sheldon, but wouldn't stoop to exert himself."

It must be true, Peter thought, for the cries of alarm from those about him were matched by his own sensation of dread as the glow increased. Nothing he had experienced while chained here could be compared with this. The voice he heard in his head now was not one of mockery and banter. It was a thunder of command, demanding immediate capitulation. And though he felt his mind being torn and twisted by its impact, it was aimed not at him, but at her.

He saw the kneeling shape stiffen to a thing of stone, seemingly too rigid even to tremble. Her head high, eyes still closed, arms fiercely enfolding her breasts, she moved only her mouth. No sound came from it, but it moved as though in prayer.

The green whirlpool of light raced faster and still faster. At its outer edge Peter felt it as a hot wind searing his body and sucking away his breath. In a futile effort to escape it he pressed back against the wall and saw that the others were doing the same. Even the man in the scout uniform did so.

Then the pressure eased, the light began to lose its evil glitter, and Peter saw the woman in the center of the Eye slowly become less rigid, as though relieved at least temporarily of her agony.

He, too, felt a physical relief and was able to breathe again without gasping. He looked at Grant beside him. The scout leader gazed at Mother Jarrett and seemed puzzled, then angry.

"All right," Grant muttered. "It only proves she is worth having. She can't deny him again."

No, Peter thought, she can't deny him forever. She will become weak from thirst and hunger, as I did. Besides, what was happening to her was not the simple game of cat and mouse that he had endured. The green light had never been a seething whirlpool for him, or so blindingly intense. And she was older than he. Much older.

How long would she be able to hold out? That was the only question yet to be answered.

Time passed, but he had not wound his watch since letting it stop and so could only guess how long he had been standing there against the wall. His legs ached. He was cold. Enough time had crawled by since Georgie Dakin had given him food and water in the dormitory for him to be hungry and thirsty again. Especially thirsty.

With his hands hidden behind him, he worked on his

bonds. Had, in fact, been doing so since the rope was first twisted about his wrists. He had good wrists, strong hands, and could even reach the hurriedly tied knots with his fingers. In time he would be able to slip one wrist through a loosened loop, he was certain. Then . . .

He kept an eye on Georgie and hoped the waiting would dull the boy's attention. No one else with a weapon was nearer. But it seemed hopeless. Some of the other trainees appeared to be mesmerized by what was happening to Mother Jarrett, but not the ones with the guns. Those four did not relax their vigil for even a moment. Their attention shifted constantly from the kneeling woman in the center of the room to the men around its perimeter, and the four automatic rifles never once drooped.

A shame, Peter thought as he watched Georgie. The twin brothers had been fine boys, good workers. Their mother, Bronzie, was a decent woman. How many other terrorists here in little St. Alban and throughout the world had been good people once?

The light was intensifying again. Was moving more swiftly. In the middle of the room the intended victim braced herself to endure a new assault. Peter saw her shoulders stiffen, her arms tighten against her breasts, her long fingers dig into her sides. Her lips were in motion again, if they had ever stopped. Had they ever stopped? He did not think so.

What was she saying? A prayer, probably, or many prayers. But what kind? She was known to have carried God's word to remote parts of the world. She must know a number of tongues and more than a few ways to pray. He wished she would pray aloud.

"This will end it, Sheldon," the man beside him said confidently, and even smiled in expectation. An ugly smile. Had Peter's hands not been roped behind him, he would have been tempted to wipe it off and accept the terrible consequences. He could never escape from this hell, anyway. Nor could Edith.

This time he had to force his eyes to stay open against the glare as the light grew more brilliant. Even its hue changed, from the assorted greens of shallow tropical waters to a blazingly bright viridian. It was as though the room were indeed an eye, a hideous green one that was being narrowed to focus its owner's fury on a mote that annoyed him.

Once more the watchers around the wall cried out in fear and huddled back against the stone. Once more Peter felt his mind battered by the commands being aimed at the kneeling woman.

"She can never stand up to this," Linford Grant muttered. "But what a woman we shall have, Sheldon! What a prize!"

Braced against the wall, Peter watched her while the viridian cyclone tore at his senses. If he stopped watching her, he must be destroyed by what was happening, he felt. She was his anchor, his one hope of survival. He tried to think of the way she had healed him by touching his torn face with her hands. Of how she had helped Gerald Dakin when Gerald, through some mysterious bond between twins, endured the training inflicted here on his brother Georgie.

He watched her and prayed she would find the strength to go on resisting. If she yielded, he knew he would in total desperation make an attempt to reach Georgie Dakin's rifle, whether his hands were free or not.

It would be a suicidal effort, of course. How in God's name could a man, even with free hands, snatch a weapon away from anyone so alert and hope to live long enough to use it when others, too, had guns and would cut him down?

The color storm continued, all but blinding him. His body felt touched by a blowtorch. He could not think anymore. Immeasurable by any senses left to him, time flowed on. Then when his sight slowly returned and his mind could again absorb what his eyes were seeing, he could scarcely believe it.

The storm had passed. The woman in the center of the Eye was still in the same defiant position. Her head was still high. Her lips still moved.

Again there was an aeon of calm and waiting. Peter looked at Linford Grant. The man was unconcerned, even elated.

"I have a feeling it will not be necessary to train this woman as a terrorist before accepting her as our leader," Grant said. "In fact, if we had to, we probably could not. But the master will do it for us."

Peter said, "I'm beginning to believe one thing you told me, at least. There is a presence in this room, and it isn't a person."

"A power, Sheldon. A thought."

"Something like that. Producing this light and using it."

"Using it, yes. You'll see. She will yield to it."

If I leap at Georgie and smash the rifle out of his hands, Peter thought, I might have a chance of reaching it on the floor before he does . . . if I fall on it just right, in a position to grab it and swing it up and use it. But can I reach him before he cuts me down with it? Even with my hands free?

He had almost succeeded in loosening the rope enough to liberate one wrist. The waiting went on.

He studied the others who had guns. Georgie, standing a little forward from the wall, seemed a shade more alert now than they. Perhaps they suffered from leaning naked against the wall too long, with their feet planted on the equally cold stone floor. Just as I'm so stupidly doing, Peter thought, and took a step forward to change position.

Still, the target for any attempt at escape had to be Georgie. The others with guns were too far away.

Mother Jarrett knelt with her eyes closed and her lips moving, awaiting the next assault upon her mind. Where was Manny Williams, who must have shown her the way here? Why hadn't Manny come with her and been caught with her?

"We've been here eight hours, Sheldon," the man in brown said, frowning at his watch. "Not once has that woman moved from her knees. What endurance!"

And not once has she stopped praying, Peter thought.

"She is thirsty now, though," Grant said. "Probably hungry, too, for she must have been in the cavern a long time before she was discovered. I don't believe we shall have much longer to wait."

Peter heard himself say in anger, "Turn your damned light on, then, and get it over with!"

"It is not my light, Sheldon. I have no control over it."

"The hell you haven't. You've got a power plant here somewhere." Peter did not believe that; it was simply something to say. If the light came from a power plant, there would be wires. Anyway, no light such as this could be produced artificially, he was certain.

Grant gravely shook his head. "The light was here when he first brought *me* here, Sheldon. Haven't I told you that? It's part of the force here. A part of him that he projects to indicate his presence."

"Well, then, tell him to rev it up and put an end to this comedy!" And this time I'll be watching Georgie instead of Mother Jarrett, Peter promised himself.

"I don't tell the master what to do," Grant said. "He tells me."

Peter resigned himself to waiting. Watching the

woman in the center of the chamber, he wondered how much longer she could endure the agony of kneeling on that brutal stone floor. Her whole body must now be full of pain. He remembered how he had suffered here, and he had not forced himself to assume her posture of supplication but had changed position constantly in search of relief.

In so many, many ways she was a remarkable woman.

Now the light was brightening again. He heard Grant draw a deep breath of satisfaction and say, "This will do it, Sheldon. Watch!"

As the whirlpool built up speed, the light blazed with a new, more terrible intensity. Peter's naked body felt alternately caressed with frigid slime and cooked on a spit. Concentrating on the movements of Georgie Dakin, as he had planned, required every atom of energy he could muster. Surely what was happening would make all those with the guns less vigilant and give him the opening he sought!

"Look!" Grant cried out in triumph. "Look at her, Sheldon!" His right hand shot out to point.

Intending only to snatch a glimpse of whatever was happening, then to watch Georgie again, Peter responded. So much for a man's desperately thought out plans, even with his life at stake. When his gaze touched Mother Jarrett, he could not look away.

She was on fire.

No, not really on fire. There were no flames. But the swirling green light, incredibly bright there at the core of the maelstrom, appeared to have drilled its way into her. She was no longer a kneeling woman but a statue radiating an unearthly luminescence.

"He has her!" Grant shouted.

Mother Jarrett's arms had been folded over her breasts. She moved them now and raised her hands in front of her face, with their palms together. Her face appeared to have been transformed into a mask of green metal, so fiercely glowing with inner heat that it must at any moment begin to melt.

But, incredibly, her lips still moved.

The fire began to fade.

It dimmed first in her face, allowing her handsome features to come through as those of a woman unafraid, still silently praying. It faded from her body, flowing downward from her shoulders in such a way that Peter half expected to see it form a pool of liquid green on the floor around her. No such pool was to be seen, but the light deserted her and became part of the whirlpool still spinning around her. Then that, too, began to fade and lose momentum.

It disappeared more swiftly than it had attained speed and brightness in the first place. In a matter of seconds the motion had ceased and the room was back to its original glow. Then that, too, began to dim, and from the center of the Eye where the woman still knelt in prayer, a circle of darkness began to spread outward. The glow retreated before it. In a few seconds the chamber must be totally dark.

Linford Grant saw what was happening and screamed a command that echoed from the walls. "Shoot her!" he screamed, lurching forward. "Shoot her! Kill her!" In panic, he jerked himself around to direct his command at Georgie Dakin. "You, Dakin! Quick!"

Bronzie Dakin's son stepped forward. Spinning on one bare foot, he aimed his rifle not at Mother Jarrett but at Grant—and squeezed the trigger.

In the fading green light the burst of fire sent the leader reeling. Taking him horizontally across his open mouth, it all but sliced his head in half. Then it shifted to those others who had guns, and sprayed them, too. In a bloody death ballet they followed Grant to the floor.

Georgie swung to cover those who had no guns. "No

one move!'' he said. ''You move, you dead!'' When
sure they would not challenge him, he glanced at Peter.
''Mr. Peter, you is all right?''

With the last faint glow of green disappearing, the
room was nearly dark. Whatever the light had been,
Mother Jarrett had conquered it in some final, supreme
effort. With a final effort of his own, Peter freed his
wrists and started toward her. ''I'm all right,'' he
said in answer to Georgie's question. ''Thank you,
Georgie.''

''Me no Georgie,'' the boy said. ''Me Gerald.''

Peter turned to stare at him. ''What?''

''Me Gerald, Mr. Peter. Manny Williams have Georgie. We must call them.'' The boy moved toward the
entrance, where he peered into the corridor and called
out, ''Coo-e-e, Manny!''

Peter groped in the darkness and found himself clasp-
ing Mother Jarrett's hands.

''Coo-e-e!'' Georgie Dakin's twin called again.
''Coo-e-e, Manny!''

''Keep calling, Gerald,'' Mother Jarrett said. ''I've
been talking to him. He knows where we are. But unless he has been here before, he may have to follow
your voice to find us.''

''Coo-e-e, Manny!'' Over and over the boy sent out
his summons, while Peter stood next to the naked black
woman in darkness and waited. If no one came with a
light, how would they leave here? The green glow had
altogether vanished now, even in the passage.

''Are you all right, Mother?'' Peter asked.

''Yes, Mr. Sheldon. Just tired.''

''How did you get here?''

''Emmanuel brought us.''

''You and Gerald?''

''Yes. After I let myself be caught, I sent them to
find Georgie so Gerald could take his brother's place.''

"After you *let* yourself be caught?"

"Yes, Mr. Sheldon. It was the only way, don't you see?"

"But how could you talk to them then?"

A tired smile briefly touched Mother Jarrett's lips. "I was able to, Mr. Sheldon. As I was able just now to reach someone more powerful than Lucifer. There are ways."

In the entrance to the chamber Gerald still called for Manny Williams. Now from far down the passage came a faint reply. "Coo-e-e . . . That is you, Gerald?"

"Yes, Manny! You is coming?"

"Me coming, boy. Just had to find some light, is all. Me soon come now!"

In the passage a glimmer of torchlight became visible and grew brighter. After a time it became a flickering yellow glow. Better, Peter thought, than the hated green haze. So much better.

38

FOLLOWING THE OLD PIG HUNTER INTO THE NOW blind Eye of Lucifer came Edith Craig, and at her side walked the man Peter had last seen on a cross: the Englishman, Alton Preble. Behind those two shuffled the handful of Grant's captives too broken by torture to have been brought to the chamber earlier. All carried pinewood torches that smoked and sputtered but gave welcome light.

When Edith had been stripped in the chamber with the bed, her clothes had been tossed to the floor. She wore them again now, but Preble was still naked, as were those others who had been whipped and tortured.

Holding the torch high, Manny glanced at the bullet-riddled bodies on the floor, then at the trainees huddled against the wall. Scowling at the latter, he said, "What we supposed to do with these, Reverend Mother?"

Mother Jarrett said, "It is not too late for them, I think. For most of those with the guns it probably was, but not for these. I can try with them. Where is Georgie?''

"Me leave him tied up in the room where them sleep. Now we know we can get out of here, we must have to go back there for everybody clothes, anyway." Holding his torch higher, Manny moved toward her and looked closely at her face. "You is all right, Mother?"

"Yes, Emmanuel."

"Me have to say me did worry, even though me do exactly as how you instruct. To put Gerald in Georgie's place, that is, then find these others and wait for you call. You know how long me and these others been waiting?"

"A long time. I know." Mother Jarrett looked at those with him. "We won't be leaving anyone behind, Emmanuel?"

"No, ma'am, we not leaving no one." The pig hunter scowled down at her ankle, still chained to the ring in the floor. "Except you, it seem, if we don't free you foot from that thing."

"I believe the key is in their leader's pocket."

"I'll look, Manny," Peter said. He had been talking to Edith and Alton. Fumbling in pockets sticky with the dead man's blood, he discovered a ring of keys, then knelt before Mother Jarrett to find one that would fit her leg iron. She stepped free with a murmur of thanks.

Manny Williams said, "You is finished here, Mother?"

"Quite finished, Emmanuel. Thanks to you."

"Not me, ma'am."

"Well, then—not I, either. You and I—and Gerald, of course—were merely instruments."

Manny solemnly nodded. "All right. So now which way we leaving here?"

"How did you get out before?" Peter asked him.

"Is an exit back of the fall of water at the intake pool, squire. It closer to the Great House, too."

Peter looked at the men against the wall, the dead on the floor, the tortured ones waiting patiently behind Edith and Alton. Without Mother Jarrett, the question of how to get out of this incredible underworld would never have arisen, he thought.

"By the way, squire," Manny said, "some soldiers likely to show up here any minute now."

"Soldiers, Manny?"

"In Look Up, when me coming with Mother and Gerald, me hear say them was going up through Whitfield Hall, with Sergeant Wray to guide them. Them should be near here soon. Should me wait outside to show them the cave and tell them what happen, maybe, whilst Mother and Gerald take you to the fall of water?"

Peter looked at Mother Jarrett. "What do you think, Mother?"

"I think he should do that. But we should leave at once so I can try to help these people."

"Then let's find Georgie—and some clothes for these others—and get started."

Manny Williams discovered his first soldier not a quarter mile from the cavern entrance, standing beside the wrecked helicopter. He had apparently just come upon it and discovered the decapitated body of the forestry man, and was frightened almost into shock when Manny suddenly appeared before him.

He led Manny to his commanding officer, one Captain Laidlaw, and the captain, having been told about the cavern, decided his duty required him to remain there with his men and explore it. They did, and brought out the dead. A week later, after a round of discussions with his superiors and certain high government officials—discussions at which Mother Jarrett was called upon to tell what she knew—the same Captain Laidlaw was sent back there with a team of demolition experts.

First they set off a shattering charge of explosives in the Eye. Then they demolished both entrances, incidentally damaging the Armadale intake when they destroyed the one at the waterfall. For in St. Alban the word of that tall, mysterious woman known as Mother Jarrett was not taken lightly, especially when she calmly bared her upper body to the members of an investigating commission and showed them a most unusual mark on her left breast.

It was a mark not quite an inch and a half long—they measured and photographed it—of a peculiarly iridescent green, and apparently quite deep, as though burned into her body with a branding iron. In shape it resembled more than anything else a vulture's claw in miniature.

It had not been there, Mother Jarrett assured them, before her session in the underworld's Eye.

39

"**H**OW DID YOU LEARN TO USE A GUN THAT WELL, Gerald?" Peter asked.

It was seven o'clock in the evening, the sun gone, twilight sliding down the mountain slopes to the Great House where Peter sat with Edith Craig on the veranda. In the morning Edith and her fiancé would be leaving the island on their way back to London. Mother Jarrett had come calling with Gerald and his brother Georgie.

In answer to Peter's question, Gerald said with a shrug, "Manny Williams carry a gun when him escape from there with Cob Dennis, sir. Me and him study it together."

"You did a good job with it. We owe you our lives."

"You must remember that when me ask you a raise in pay, sir," Gerald said with a grin.

Peter looked at Georgie, leaning silently against the veranda railing. Mother Jarrett had come, he realized, mainly to demonstrate that Gerald's twin was well on the way to being himself again, as were most of the others rescued from Grant's hellhole. Georgie did not remember much of what had been done to him. Perhaps, God willing, he never would. But he would soon be a true son of Bronzie Dakin again—a cheerful lad and a good worker, with a normal life ahead of him. "If you can possibly put him back to work again," Mother had said, "it would hasten his recovery."

Peter had been unable to promise anything. "Miss Craig and Mr. Preble are leaving tomorrow. I haven't been told yet whether I'll still be working here myself."

Mother stood before him now, offering her hand in farewell. "Well, Mr. Sheldon . . ."

He rose and clasped both her hands, recalling how she had knelt in the Eye of the Devil's Pit with them pressed together in prayer. "Thank you," he said.

She turned to Edith. Edith stood up and suddenly, impulsively, embraced her.

Mother departed, with Bronzie Dakin's twin sons trailing her down the darkening walk. Standing at the veranda rail, watching them, Peter and Edith were close enough for their shoulders to be touching. Alton Preble had gone to his room, to pack for departure in the morning.

"Will you ever come back here?" Peter wondered aloud.

Edith turned to look at him. "I want to. But I don't know, Peter."

"Because of Alton?"

"I've promised to marry him."

"And he's a good man." Peter recalled the moment in the cave when he had stood before Preble with a whip, and the man on the cross had said, "Get on with it. You're forgiven."

"But I'm deeding Armadale to you," Edith said.

He looked at her in disbelief. "You what?"

"My father said in his will that if I didn't want to be responsible for it, I should deed it to you. He said it was nothing but a dream when he bought it, and without you it would still be only a dream. So"—she reached for Peter's hand—"I want you to have it."

"But he paid good money for it, Edith."

"If you want to pay it back someday, all right. Or I know a home for children in London that could use the money."

Mother Jarrett and the sons of Bronzie Dakin had disappeared down the track to Look Up. There was a sound in the drawing-room doorway. Peter turned and saw his housekeeper, Miss Coraline, coming with a tray on which were three glasses, an ice bucket, and a bottle of Scotch.

"Mr. Preble tell me to bring this." She set the tray down on a veranda table. "Him soon come."

A farewell drink, Peter thought. Tomorrow they would be gone.

The housekeeper departed. In a moment Alton Preble stepped out onto the veranda and approached the table. "Hello, you two. I took the liberty. . . ." He poured three drinks, handing one to Edith and one to Peter as they joined him. The veranda was almost dark. In a few minutes Coraline would press the button to activate the diesel power plant, disturbing the silence for the sake of light.

"I've something to say to you," Preble announced quietly. "Drink, will you? It may take a little time."

Neither Peter nor Edith spoke. Both sipped their Scotch while waiting.

"Edith and I leave tomorrow," Preble said, gazing at them. "I think you ought to come back here, Edith."

"What?" she said.

"You'll need a little time over there to put your affairs in order. I'll help. Then I think you ought to come back here. You're a first-class nurse. You could be useful here.''

"I don't understand," Edith said.

"From the moment you two met, there was something between you." Preble's voice was that of a calm, self-possessed lawyer pleading a case in court. "I saw it, in spite of being so damned carsick on that godawful road from the airport. I thought at first it was just something that happened because you, Edith, are an incurable romantic and this is a romantic island. But I'm not blind. The two of you have something. I envy you. I don't have it. I don't want to deprive you of it. So do something about it, will you, for God's sake?" He looked at his drink. He lifted it to his lips and drank half of it down. Then he looked at Edith and smiled.

"You and I would never have hit it off, you know, love," he said. "It would have been like mating one of these bright little St. Alban hummingbirds to a—what do you call them, Peter, old boy?—a John Crow. Let's get a little drunk, shall we? This isn't my Scotch, Peter, it's yours."

Stepping to the veranda railing, he gazed down over the roofs of Look Up, where lamps were winking on now in the windows of peasant houses. "It's a pretty place, this Armadale," he said. "I wish I knew why I hate it so bloody much."

Miss Coraline had pressed the button. The power plant clicked on. The veranda lights glowed yellow and began to brighten. Edith Craig reached out to touch Peter's hand while the man she had been going to marry scowled down over the darkening island as though angry with himself for not being able to understand it. Or himself.

40

A Front-Page Editorial
From the *St. Alban Daily Post*:

The *Post* has learned from an unimpeachable source that a hitherto unknown cave in our Morgan Mountains, when discovered recently by our Defence Force, was occupied by a gang of terrorists who were using it as their headquarters and training center.

After a surprise attack which resulted in a number of the gunmen being slain, the soldiers, instructed by certain high government officials, permanently closed the cave by blowing up its two known entrances.

We deplore this hasty and inappropriate move on the part of our officials. The caves of our island are famous for their beauty and are an important tourist attraction. That this one, said to be one of the longest ever found here, was being employed by criminals in no way justifies its being closed to furth exploration and possible exploitation as a lure for our more adventuresome visitors.

Speleologists have come to St. Alban from all over the world to visit such caverns as Glowrie Cave in Dorchester and Riversink Cave in Devon, not to mention others. Several less dangerous underworlds in our tourist areas have been equipped with lights and walkways to attract the ordinary visitor. We believe that this new cave, if as intricate as described to us by our informant, might have become a genuine asset to our island.

Shame on our politicians for closing it so precipitously, without time for a proper investigation!

But who knows? Some other entrance may yet be found by which it can be restored to us as a national treasure. Or in time, with more knowledgeable men in charge of our destiny, those entrances so stupidly destroyed may yet be reopened.

Let us hope.